Aurora's WILDERNESS LOVE

Just a Little Fall Crush

Harmony Noble

TrueLoveWriters

ISBN 978-1-963074-41-3 & ISBN 978-1-963074-42-0

Story creation, cover, and illustrations by Melody Noble & Harmony Curtis

Thank you for choosing this book.
We hope the story
brought you as much joy reading it
as we had in creating it!

We'd love to hear from you! Feel free to reach out via email at TrueLoveWriters@gmail.com, and follow us on Instagram, Facebook, TikTok at @truelovewriters for the latest updates and behind-the-scenes fun.

Get access to exclusive offers, bonus content, new release updates, and recommendations for more great reads.

Sign up for our e-newsletter at HarmonyNoble.com.

To Lucy —

I'm so proud of the strong, fearless woman you're becoming.
You've brought so much joy and love into my life — more than I could ever put into words.

I love you forever,
Mom

Aurora's

WILDERNESS LOVE

Just a Little Fall Crush

Harmony Noble

TrueLoveWriters

Chapter 1

Unpacking My Mess

Oh my god, I just kissed my therapist.

Donna, my new and first therapist ever, is holding a paper plate, a neat wedge of quiche resting on wax paper. She is dazed and stepping back, like she didn't just give me her bedroom eyes and lean in to ask if I wanted a kiss.

"You—" Donna's words are lost, as I process the situation and realize my mistake.

"Oh my god. I'm mortified and so so *so* sorry," I say, running out of her cozy home office's open door.

Outside, Alaska air slams against my face with an honest clap of cold that I deserve. Sunlight glares judging me.

"Quiche," I mutter to the empty sidewalk, stomping toward my Subaru. "She said quiche, not kiss."

Who kisses their therapist?

I have not gone to therapy before but in movies the sessions usually ended with a big clock buzzing. There was no clock in sight, only knick knacks, crocheted blankets, and books in a room that looked more like a tv room than a therapy room.

My brain replays the inappropriate moment in horrifying slow motion as I stumble through the sunlight burning my retinas accusatively, unusual for the start of Autumn in Alaska, as if even nature scorns my social misstep.

"Quiche," I mutter, stomping towards my beat-up Subaru. "Who even offers someone quiche at the end of a therapy session?"

"A super-friendly therapist, trying to make a connection and be nice to the mess of a new patient–that's who." I answer myself before I can get mad at Donna, which only makes me more upset at myself.

"Arrrg! Aurora, why do you hate yourself?" I shake my head, look up, and pull my sunglasses out to cover my burning retinas. *Stupid Alaskan weather!*

A passing elderly couple gives me concerned looks as I continue my self-directed tirade, internally. I force a smile and wave, which probably makes me look deranged. Perfect. Add that to today's list of mortifications.

My phone buzzes. *Darius.* Of course, he has a sixth sense for when I've done something monumentally embarrassing.

"So?" he demands without preamble. "Did your therapy fix your life in ninety minutes?"

"I kissed her."

"You... what now?"

"The therapist," I groaned, slumping against my car. "She offered me a kiss–*oh my god*– I mean 'quiche.' I thought she said 'kiss.' And I—ever the compliant-people-pleasing-person—leaned in and gave my therapist a small peck on the lips, Darius."

His laughter erupts so loudly that I have to pull the phone away from my ear. "Oh. My. God. Aurora. You beautiful disaster. This is why we're friends. Only you could turn therapy into a rom-com meet-cute."

"It wasn't a meet-cute! It was a meet-horrifying! And my real meet-cute date is with *Alexis*..." I realize as I say this, that I don't have time to run home and hide in shame under my covers. I'm meeting Alexis for a late lunch and to discuss my schedule. I can't miss it since Alexis graciously gave me the week off to recover.

"And now, I obviously *need therapy* for my therapy. Donna was totally cool, but you can't continue therapy with someone you sexually harassed, right?"

"I have so *many* follow-up questions. Was there any body contact? What did she look like? Did you snap a pic?"

His stream of questions only makes me turn more crimson. I slide into my car, resting my forehead against the steering wheel.

Luckily, he fills in the silence. "Girl, you didn't attack her. You are way too naive to seduce a therapist. I swear every time you are around a powerful woman you melt. You gotta get your libido under control."

"You're right. There was *no* tongue, and I'm sure Donna understood that I had misheard her. It was an honest mistake," I ramble, hoping to believe what I'm saying, because that's the only way I'm going to live down, attacking my super-nice and hot therapist. Darius is right, I'm apparently attracted to hot women who have it together, probably because I'm a hot mess.

He reassures, still chuckling, "O-kayyyy, then. So, besides your failed attempt to seduce your therapist, Donna, did the session help?"

"Actually, yeah. She basically diagnosed my entire personality in fifteen minutes. Apparently, I'm a 'people pleaser' and a 'peacemaker' who will 'do anything to earn the acceptance and love my mother withheld.' She said it all boils down to being raised by a narcissistic single mom."

"Well... she doesn't sound wrong?"

I sigh. "No. And she said I need to stop trying with Mom unless she apologizes, and that I should 'choose me' first."

"Hmm," Darius hums thoughtfully. "Revolutionary concept, and the *same thing* Lisa and I have been telling you. And what about Alexis? Did you tell her about your workplace dumpster fire."

My stomach clenches at the mention of her name. "She said she doesn't give advice, but she had never seen a dating-your-boss situation that didn't go badly. In fact, she thinks I need to look for a new job."

"Now, she's totally wrong there. You *do* need to date Alexis, or this therapist. Who is going buy you dinner and pay for your university costs? Besides, you can work summers part time, since the agency is paying for your business schooling. There's time for Alexis to warm your bed, right?"

"Maybe I should date her before I sleep with her?"

Darius's advice is starting to sound more like the wham-bam queen, Lisa.

Reading my thoughts again, he laments, "I wish Lisa wasn't getting waxed right now. She is going to die when I tell her your new drama."

"Darius, I'll tell her when I get home. Now I have to somehow control myself to meet Alexis."

"To quit? To break up? Or to admit you love her and move into her mansion and be her plaything?

"Not every lesbian owns a U-Haul!" I look in my mirror and wipe my smeared mascara while grabbing my lip gloss. "And yes. And no to the job questions. Just because I got a full-ride scholarship doesn't mean I'm quitting at the temp agency while I take classes. I still need money, and it's a really great job. Why can't I enjoy starting university, keep doing accounting work that'll look good on my resume, *and* having a freaking awesome girlfriend?"

"Aurora—"

"I know, I know," I cut him off. "I'm dreaming and not making a real plan. The therapist basically said the same thing. That it can't be a real relationship if I need emotional support and I'm still figuring out what love is. God, I'm a mess but seriously, Alexis seems like the only unmessy thing in my life."

"You know Alexis will let you take whatever work schedule you want. And the best decision you made was ending feeding your mom's drama. Richard and I totally support whatever you decide. Go talk with Alexis and give me and Lisa the tea tonight. No matter what, you got us all in your corner babe."

Tears prick at my eyes, and I dab them again and sniffle. "Thanks."

Chapter 2

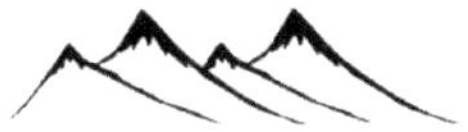

Special SaLmon Kisses

"So thanks again for giving me the week off to process everything," I say as Alexis looks through the Ronnie Sushi weekend specials menu and places her phone on the table.

"Did you use your health benefits to see a professional? Your mom dropping that bombshell about your dad really threw you for a loop." Her brown eyes soften, and I'm starting to think this is a date-date, not a work date.

"I did go to therapy. I still have some self-reflection and work to do. But I'm feeling more... grounded?" I say without conviction.

Alexis doesn't notice and swirls the sake in her tiny ceramic cup. Meanwhile, I'm over here pretending I'm totally fine and wondering if I need to admit to kissing my therapist. Also I'm trying to figure out if this is a date or a work meeting.

She sips and smiles.

I nod and smile, pretending to enjoy sake. Mmm, yes, ancient rice wine, I totally have a refined palate and not the taste buds of someone raised on Costco pizza and Anchorage tap water.

The restaurant mood? Technically romantic. It has low lighting, a lazy jazz playlist, and tiny soy sauce dishes I'm afraid to touch in case I knock one over. But with Alexis' phone on the table and her in a blazer, this has a work lunch vibe.

Alexis checks her phone, so I lift mine as if I'm equally important. What do I get? A highlight reel of how unglamorous my life is:

Oil change overdue—87 days.
Doctor's office nagging me.
Parking ticket waiting to double if not paid asap.
Trash pickup reminder for tomorrow.
Low storage. Delete 500 selfies.

My phone doesn't scream successful adult—it heckles me, more my disappointed electronic friend.

"Do you want to discuss your schedule this week? I really need you for our new client since you are our best accounting temp." She shifts to allow the waitress to place edamame in front of us. Her knee brushes mine under the table, casual, confident, electric. I forgot what language is.

My cheeks flush. I think I'd do anything this woman asks. I am a sucker for a powerful woman, especially one wearing a perfectly tailored suit, who is buying me an expensive lunch.

"This edamame is exquisite," Alexis says, lifting a piece to her mouth with chopsticks as precise as a surgeon's scalpel. "Try it."

I reach for mine, but chopsticks are invented by evil spirits to remind me of my fundamental lack of coordination and sophistication. The slippery bean flies off my chopsticks, splatting on the floor. I try to recover my dignity by giggling and sipping my sake, which tastes of warm regret.

Alexis arches an eyebrow. "You don't like Asian cuisine?"

"No, I wasn't really raised eating foods from other cultures, so my chopstick skills are pretty bad," I explain, wondering if I should pick up the bean, but then my cloth napkin would be dirty. I bite my lip and push the offending chopsticks away.

"You're very brave to try. Here," she waves over the waitress and asks for silverware for me. "There. All taken care of now." Her lips twitch in a smirk that borders on affection. "You're lucky you're pretty."

"Thank you," I whisper, and the vibe is bordering on first-date vibes. "Don't forget I also look good in a ball gown, and you said I'm your best accountant."

She grins, and I'm glowing, winning something important—like an Iditarod trophy or her eternal devotion. Either works.

"I like your confidence."

And I was confident with my fork and sass, until... The caviar was served.

I try to lean forward seductively, but my elbow knocks into the little caviar tower. Black pearls rain down onto my dress, my lap, the pristine white napkin I barely used because I didn't want to mess it up.

I freeze. "Oh no. No, no, no... Sorry!"

Alexis blinks, then her grin turns to a laugh. It's that low, warm sound she doesn't give out easily. "You make everything more exciting."

"I am a walking seafood hazard." I try wiping the caviar from my blouse and lap, leaving dark streaks.

"Hold still," she says. Then she shrugs off her actual designer, probably ridiculously expensive, blazer and drapes it over my shoulders.

"Oh my god," I say, clutching it tightly. "I would have spilled something sooner if I knew you'd let me wear your power blazer. Money and boss energy, that's how I smell wearing this blazer," I blurt.

"It's dry-clean only," she deadpans. "Which is code for 'your problem now.' You can wear it at your new assignment."

Then, before I can classify this as a friendly work date, she leans closer, her breath warm against my ear. "Besides, you look good in my clothes."

And now I'm malfunctioning with heat blossoming at my core and making my breath come out in a gasp.

She doesn't move, studying my eyes, then slowly looks down at my stained chest and her blazer on my body.

"Which sashimi do you prefer today, Miss Anders?" The waitress asks while replacing my napkin with a fresh one.

"The sal-mon," she says with authority despite mispronouncing Alaska's biggest export. The waitress says nothing and nods.

"Um. So," I blurt, desperate to change the subject before I melt into a puddle of sexual distress, "did you mean to say 'SaLmon' with the L or—"

"Sal-mon," Alexis replies, crisp and confident.

I squint. "Wait. You really mean Sammon, right?" I am unsure if this is an inside joke because she can't be serious. How does an Alaskan not know how to say salmon?

"It's pronounced the same as it's spelled."

I lean back, eyeing her, and she is totally serious.

The busser stops to clean up the mess around our table—poor guy. I grab him like a lifeline. "Excuse me, how do you pronounce salmon?"

He blinks, his smile tight. "However Miss Anders prefers it."

My eyes dart between Alexis and the poor guy, and something clicks. "Oh my god. Do you own Ronnie's Sushi?"

"Technically, my family owns the building," she says, casual, sipping her sake again. "But yes, the restaurant leases from us."

I throw my hands up. "Alexis, just how rich are you?"

Before she can reply, a crash rings out across the room—a waiter drops a whole tray of drinks and glass scatters everywhere.

I'm up in a heartbeat. "Oh no."

"Aurora—" Alexis starts, but I'm already kneeling, helping to pick up shards, napkins, and glass stems.

The waiter stammers 'thanks' while Alexis stays seated, arms crossed, watching the scene like it's inconvenient rather than a crisis. When I sit back down, brushing off my hands, she hands me her napkin without a word.

"You didn't need to help."

I sip my now lukewarm sake and shrug. "Alexis, tell me, since you are always saving me and have this secret posh life—are you for real? You seem too perfect."

She leans closer again, brushing a loose curl off my cheek, her hand lingering on my blushing face. "I'm real. Would you date the perfect woman?"

"If he were a lesbian with great taste and stilettos? Absolutely."

And then her lips are on mine. Soft, confident, addictive. One of her hands lands gently on my thigh, her blazer still warming my shoulders. I kiss her back—I've been waiting for this exact level of electric, surprising, world-rearranging affection since we met.

I forget about the spilled caviar. I forget whether this is a work date or a real date. I forget how awkward I felt walking into a place where the menu doesn't list prices and where I had one of the worst dates of my life last month. I forget everything except Alexis, her ridiculous smoothness, and her perfectly lipstick-free kisses.

It's unfair how great she looks without needing makeup.

My heart does gymnastics. How is this incredible, controlled powerhouse of a woman attracted to me? Me, with my discount dress and fake confidence.

Before I can spiral too hard into the imposter syndrome abyss, she pulls back slightly, eyes scanning mine. "What's that look for?"

"I'm just surprised and trying not to have a full anxiety attack at this table."

She smiles, and somehow that calms the tornado in my chest.

"I've been thinking," I say, twisting the sake cup between my fingers. Now that I know that Alexis likes me more than as my mentor, I can ask what I was thinking about. "About my mom and the whole family drama situation."

Her expression sharpens, and she lifts a perfectly plucked brow.

"Yeah. She never told me who my dad is, she just ghosted me after saying I knew him. And I know you want me back to work, but all I can think about is finding my dad—finding out where I come from?"

Alexis's hand slides into mine. "Everyone deserves to know their family. I'm sorry you and your mom aren't talking. But I'm sure you can look for your dad and still work."

"I guess," I shrug, realizing that in my week off, I mostly hid in my bed and had my one disastrous counseling appointment. I could have used that time to research who my father was or even hire a private investigator to find him.

Alexis tilts her head. "Why don't we just get your birth certificate?"

I blink. "What?"

"Your birth certificate. It will list your father."

My mouth falls open. "You... you are brilliant."

"You're welcome."

Suddenly, the family stress that's been strangling me all week melts into the soy-scented air. There's a way forward. A clue. A plan. I have a plan.

She squeezes my fingers. "Simple."

I lean in, catch her lips again, quick and sure. My heart pounds, trying to escape my chest, but in a good way this time. The right way.

She leans closer, her woodsy sweet smell invading my body, her fingers warm against my skin. They linger. Not by accident. Not a casual gesture. She's looking at me as if I'm more delicious than her posh sake.

Every nerve in my body flips on. She's found and slammed on my main breaker. The restaurant disappears—waiters, soft music, fish egg trauma—all of it dissolves. The only sound left is the blood roaring behind my ears and maybe the hum of whatever magnetic pull is tugging our mouths together.

Her voice drops low. "Let's call this our official first date."

Already breathless, I whisper, "absolutely."

Her lips catch mine mid-laugh.

There's nothing tentative about it. Alexis kisses to ruin me in the best way possible. Her mouth is soft but focused, warm, and sure. It is as if she mapped out every nerve ending on mine and decided to make each one light up. One of her hands slides behind my neck, fingers threading into my hair, gently tilting my face to deepen the kiss. The other presses firm on my thigh under the table,firmly pinning me here, steadying me, and branding me as hers.

I make a tiny, embarrassing sound. A whimper. A squeak? Definitely not a cool, sophisticated sound.

Her lips curve into a grin against mine. She heard my squeak and it made her smile. Her tongue teases the seam of my lips. I part them without hesitation. And she's kissing me deeper—slower, but with devastating precision. Her mouth tastes faintly of sake and citrus, and she kisses with this blend of heat and control that's wrecking my ability to function. Every pass of her tongue pulls me further under. My whole body leans into hers, chest buzzing, heart tripping over itself drunk on the kiss and Alexis.

I kiss her back like my life's on the line.

This is the only time, the only place, and the only girl who's ever made me think that kissing might actually be the point of being alive.

I lose track of everything except her.

Her scent becomes more defined, a clean and sharp–bergamot, and something so expensive I'll never afford it.

The silk of her blouse against my fingers as I grip her sleeve, desperate for more.

There is a slight hitch in my breath when she bites gently at my bottom lip after the kiss.

That tiny move sets off fireworks inside my ribcage. Her blazer slips off my shoulder as my boss pulls me closer across the table, both half-aware of the sushi casualties being knocked around. Chopsticks clatter. My soy sauce dish tips. Something squishes under my elbow, but I don't care. Nothing matters but her lips on mine.

By the time we come up for air, I'm flushed, dazed, still clutching her sleeve. Alexis's lipstick—usually perfect—is slightly smudged now. There is even color blooming high on her chiseled cheeks, and her eyes are darker, unreadable.

Holy hell.

I did that.

She brushes her thumb over my bottom lip, gentle but possessive, eyes locked on mine. She memorizes the way her kiss breaks me and winks at me.

"You're trouble."

"So are we—"

Alexis's phone buzzes. She hops up–*I guess her legs aren't jelly like mine after our kiss.*

"I have something important," She throws bills down and doesn't even glance up from her phone to say goodbye.

So are we really officially dating now?

Are we allowed to tell people or is this a sexy secret relationship?

Do you like the way I taste?

These are the questions she ran away from before I could ask.

What call is so important that it ended our first official date?

Chapter 3

Thirsty Tabby Cats

"Wait...You...No!" Lisa wheezes out between laughing fits, which makes her appear to be having an asthma attack.

I cover my face and nod. "I totally kissed my therapist and my boss today."

"And you still have a therapist, and you didn't get fired?" she manages to squeak out, rocking and holding her stomach in pain as I recount my story.

Moving my fingers, I give her my wide-eyed innocent look and shrug.

"Omg. I don't know why I watch TV. You are so much better than any who-dunnit mystery or Kardashian episode. I want to hear more, but I can't. I have my singles mixer I organized for tonight." She slips on her red, shiny wedges and then looks at me over her shoulder. "You can come if you want?"

"I've had enough drama for the day." I laugh, shaking my head. "Staying in is definitely my safest bet."

"I'll get more details later." She winks and giggles. "Anyway, don't get too comfy at my place, babe. You'll be in the dorms soon with all the hot university student stories to tell me."

I wave, and she clucks, rushing out the door, letting in a whoosh of cool wind that makes me hug my boss-slash-almost-girlfriend's oversized wool blazer.

Anchorage in the fall season is weirdly deceptive, so you must layer a tank top with a sweater and bring a rain jacket if you plan to survive. Earlier, it flirted with sun-kissed sidewalks. But now? The air's gone cold, a bitey wind curling under the collar of Alexis's fancy jacket.

I pull the jacket tighter. It smells like Alexis—the sweet bergamot, maybe a sharp note of sandalwood and... sushi. Is sushi a sexy smell?

God, I kissed her. And for longer than acceptable workplace HR standards. My lips are still tingling, and not from wasabi. That kiss...it was a door unlocking. Or maybe a trapdoor. I'm honestly not sure yet.

Alexis rushed out of our lunch for her business call before I asked her to define our kiss, and us. And now I'm wrapped in her scent and drenched in pheromones.

A weird swelling warms and grows larger inside me, a mix of pride and nerves. The *Anchorage U* scholarship award still feels like a prank, and realizing there's an easy way to find my dad makes this the best day ever. I half-laugh, touching my lips and jumping on the couch to veg and enjoy my perfect life.

"I'm staying out late tonight, if you want to invite someone over."

I quickly typed, "I'm trying to stay out of trouble and drama-free."

I stuff my hands deep into the blazer pockets, hoping maybe there's a candy or note tucked in there, and I can learn more about Alexis. But they are empty. Alexis left so fast, it's hard not to feel like I hallucinated her. Was the kiss real?

I reach for the remote, and a rogue chip clip bites my hip. Classic Lisa.

The apartment smells like hairspray, pink wine, and jasmine incense. Her candle collection has taken over the bathroom.

The TV does little to distract me. My mouth remembers the kiss, but my brain rewinds to her face when she checked her phone. The soft crinkle between her brows, the way her fingers twitched before she forced a smile. Corporate emergency? Or a personal issue?

I flop over on the couch. Alexis kissed me like I mattered—like she wanted me. And then she left me like I was an empty sake cup. Kiss coworker. Eat sashimi. Exit stage left.

My phone buzzes.

It's *not* her.

Darius, "Tell me why you're on Lisa's Close Friends story wearing a blazer that costs more than your rust bucket of a car."

"Long story. Sushi. Kissing. Confusion. Cold."

He texts back a laughing emoji. "That's a short story. And here I was, eating leftover spaghetti and waiting for your titillating Alexis update."

I sigh, fingers flying. "We kissed. There was tongue–loads of tongue! Then she got a call. Said she had to go. No real explanation. I'm spiraling, harder than a funnel cake."

He sends a photo of a dramatic sigh with the caption: *Romance is a knife fight in a ballgown.* "Maybe she panicked. Maybe she cares. CEOs are allergic to emotions. You're like... a glitter bomb in her curated professional world."

"You think?"

"I *know*. But she hired me as an office manager so she likes glitter and drama. And even if she doesn't workout. You're slaying, baby. You kissed two hot professional women today–I'd be jealous but my love life is pretty exciting, too."

"Well, are you going to give me details on Richard and you?"

"You can check my socials, like everyone else," he jokes. "Don't derail my Aurora cheerleading. You are on fire-amazing! Your love life is banging. You escaped your mom's toxic vortex. You are slaying! You are the main character, no cameos for you, girl."

God. I love him. "Thx."

I toss the phone on the floor and stare at the ceiling. The smoke detector blinks at me, and I blink back.

Pulling a fuzzy throw blanket over myself that smells like Lisa's perfume and her last Tinder date, I don't care. My mind's back at the restaurant.

The way Alexis leaned in was whisper-smooth and warm. Her hand on me. Her breath against my cheek like gravity shifted.

I didn't imagine it.

But now the silence in this apartment feels too *loud*.

I wish I knew where Alexis went. Or why.

I wish I knew if the kiss meant anything to her.

I wish—

The front door rattles. I sit up, heart racing.

False alarm. The neighbor's cat. Probably trying to break in again. He has boundary issues.

I collapse back, draping Alexis's jacket over me like a pathetic, romantic tortilla. I'm going to smell like Alexis for a week.

It's south of midnight, and I can't sleep. I light my pumpkin spice candle, rearrange the living room throw pillows twice. Then, I make hot cocoa, only to remember that we're out of milk. Using Lisa's oat creamer, I taste it and I am most definitely not a Top Chef competition candidate.

I'm tempted to text Alexis.

I *almost* do.

I should pick up the apartment–It's a disaster and I am staying here for free.

Instead, I pull out my journal and start a list:

Things I Know Are True:

1. I kissed Alexis Anders and survived.

2. I'm going to college.

3. I'm going to find my dad.

4. My mom's opinions do *not* matter.

5. I have the best friends in all of Alaska's frozen tundra.

6. I want more—

I stop writing. What do I want more of?

Not more sushi.

Not more kisses.

More of her.

If she wants me.

I stare at the list. My throat tightens.

Maybe the sushi date wasn't a fairy tale. Perhaps it's chapter one of a messy, real, frustrating story. The kind where the heroine doesn't get rescued, but she *does* get stronger.

Lisa's right. I'm not home in her cramped apartment. Not really. Not yet. But I'm building toward something. A dorm room. A future. A life I picked for myself.

Maybe Alexis shows up in that life.

Maybe not.

Either way?

I'm showing up for myself.

I pull the blazer tighter. Take a breath, saying aloud, to no one, "She's totally gonna text me first."

The neighbor's cat, Mr. Whiskers, pushes at the door again, so I open it and let him pass to jump on my warm spot on the couch, as if he owns the place.

"Okay Kitty, I'm letting you in because you're going to keep me from texting Alexis. I need to play it cool and let her text me first. I can't be *too thirsty* right? No one likes a needy girlfriend."

The tabby cat purrs and meows at me in agreement.

Chapter 4

From Bleary Blazer to Coffee Confidence

The shrill beep of my phone jolts me awake, lighting up from under the throw I'm using as a pillow, and knocking off the couch cushion I was using as a blanket. I groan, reaching for it without dislodging the loaf of fur across my ribs.

It's nice to wake up with a hot, furry creature on me–maybe I need to rethink my stance on cats.

Mr. Whiskers gives me a disdainful look for waking him early, before leaping off and sauntering away.

"Sorry, Mr Whiskers," I whisper to the neighbor's fat orange cat, adding, "but you did use me as a human mattress and you're paying zero rent."

I glance at my phone. There's a picture of Darius and Richard, in matching bowling outfits, grinning like they've just won the lottery. They are a cute couple. I guess after their date last night, they decided to go public with their relationship by posting this cutesy bowling alley picture. Matching bowling shirts. Matching poses. Matching gay confidence. I snort and click the like button.

"So they're done pretending they're *not* dating. Well, I guess I'll be seeing Richard at our karaoke nights. Whadda think, Mr Whiskers, is he going to slay the stage or be a tone deaf backup singer?"

I chuckle softly, even though it feels strange to be happy instead of weighed down with my usual worries. Worried about my job, my finances, my mother, my love life, and trying to be an adult. Everyone's finding their happily-ever-after, including me—and I'm almost afraid to be happy.

Something's bound to happen that'll ruin everything.

Mr. Whisker rubs his head against my hand. "You're right, Mr Whiskers. I should be happy and enjoy it, even if I have to fake it. Everything is yummy cat nip and cozy cuddles for me, too."

Squinting at my cracked phone screen, I'm wearing reindeer pajama pants. Alexis's blazer is buttoned over my shoulders—my cape of successful-smelling, boss vibes.

Knock. Knock.

Knuckles drumming on the door makes me jump. I quickly shuffle to the front door, forgetting my embarrassing outfit.

Mr Whisker growls. Or coughs on a furball. Or maybe he is summoning a demon. I'm not a cat person, so it's unclear. But the ominous sound is definitely not happy.

I peek through the peephole, nearly trip over the cat who somehow snuck under my foot.

"*Oh no.* Oh yes? Oh! What the actual sourdough dessert pizza?"

Mr. Whiskers meows, and I debate if I'm still dreaming.

Pulling open the door, there *she* is. Alexis. Holding two coffees like it's our normal routine for her to look like a Vogue spread at 7:03 in the morning and bring me coffee.

She raises one perfectly arched brow. "Good morning, Aurora."

My body malfunctions. My mouth opens, but my brain chokes. I make a similar noise to the cat demon-summoning sound, which makes the cat meow in delight.

"Cute Cat."

"Uh. Yeah. I mean... wow. Hi. I'm just... getting ready for... I mean... looking like... So. Yeah."

She smirks. "You always look like this before work?"

"Wait!" I hold up my hand. "How exactly did you know where I live?"

"Your employee paperwork," she says with a wave, barging into the chaotic apartment.

I start to smooth my frizzy, long hair and give up. "I wasn't expecting company this early."

"I wanted to see you." She says this frankly, and her brown eyes hypnotize me with their intensity.

I blink. "Are you trying to flirt, or make sure I'm coming to work today?"

"Can't it be both?" She lifts a coffee. "Truce?"

"Only if that has an illegal amount of sugar."

"I got three. One extra-strong for your wake-up. The second extra-sweet for your mood. And the third is for me to cope with you needing two cups of coffee before you're functional."

"Ah, I didn't think you noticed my morning routine." I step back, letting her further inside. The living room-slash-my-bedroom is a war zone of Lisa's various shoes and old takeout containers. Alexis walks in like she's conducting a property inspection.

"You're sleeping on the couch?"

I shrug and giggle. "Ummmm... Technically it's a vintage fold-out, and if it's good enough for Mr. Whiskers—"

"I didn't know you had a cat."

I smile and smooth down her crumpled blazer. "I don't. He's the neighbor's. But I use him as my emotional support pet."

"That doesn't qualify to bring him to work, FYI." Her gaze flicks to the blazer on my shoulders. "Did you sleep in that?"

"Absolutely not! I slept *under* it. I was hoping for some badass CEO dreams," I say with a sleepy, defiant smile.

We sit. Well, she perches gracefully on the only clean chair, wisely deciding not to remove her red sneakers, peaking out from under her pinstripe pants. I collapse back onto the couch, trying not to spill the hot coffee on my best holiday pajama pants.

"You left pretty fast last night," I open with and grab the coffee tray to divert her wandering eyes before she notices my lucky green thong peeking out from under the coffee table. Smiling, I set the coffee cup on old muffin crumbs and quickly use my foot to stuff the underwear under the couch.

She nods, eyes soft. "Work emergency. I'm the CEO. I'm never off, so I have to handle everything."

"Oh," I say, embarrassed that I was worried she was using it as an excuse to leave or that she wasn't as wow'd by the kiss as I was. "You don't have to explain. I mean. I was kissing you, not handcuffing you. You could leave whenever," I blurt, embarrassed that I sounded accusatory and needy after our lunch meeting date.

A pause. She sips. I want to crawl under the couch and live with the dust bunnies and crumbs forever. Why didn't I take the time to pick up the apartment last night?

"I wasn't trying to be rude. But I do owe you an apology for disappearing." She pauses and leans forward, her knees perilously close to touching mine. "Sorry."

I nod, swallowing my worry. "It kinda felt like I got ghosted by my boss on my first real date with her. And that's after I learned you have really soft lips and good taste in sushi."

Her lips twitch, and she lifts a brow, sipping her coffee.

Another pause. "Lisa is letting me stay here until school starts and the dorms open. She won't see me much with how many business classes I'm taking."

Alexis blinks. "You're starting university this semester and taking a full course load?"

"Yeah. Next week is orientation. Which means, statistically, I'll cry in at least two bathrooms before Friday."

She tilts her head, and the line between her brows appears. "I'll need to have Darius adjust your schedule. You didn't mention that you're starting this fall semester."

"Well, we haven't exactly talked about our future plans yet," I mumble. "I mean, I have everything paid for this year. I want to get as many credits as possible and finish my degree early. Most of my classes are evening or the seven am lectures. I won't miss much work," I explain suddenly, nervous that Alexis will get mad or rescind the scholarship.

She sets her coffee down. Checks her phone, all business-like and scrolls a quick note. "Okay. Let's talk before we hit the office." Her phone vibrates, distracting her, and prompting her to scribble another note.

Quickly, I push the crumbs off the table. Then smile brightly when she looks up. "You won't put me on probation if I start school, right? I mean, I'll be learning even more business-y stuff, so I'll be a better corporate office worker for the company."

"True." She sips her coffee and pauses.

I take a deep breath. "Fine. I'll be honest. I am trouble. I'm a walking tornado of chaos. You're the perfect career woman in retro shoes that cost more than my annual tuition. I want to be a career woman and be put-together like you... Getting a degree is part of that. I mean... I'm wearing Rudolph pants and couch surfing right now."

"You're also sharp, and scrappy despite your life resembling a Netflix-worthy drama. I like how you are able to adapt and be spontaneous."

I bite my lip, thinking Lisa said almost the same thing yesterday. I guess there's no denying it with my recent family drama–estranged from my mom and searching for my bio dad—I'm the definition of a reality show disaster.

I look at her. She means it nicely. She's not teasing or judging me.

"Why are you here?" I sigh, unsure if this is all about work because there's no romantic vibe at all and her sitting in this messy apartment is more nightmare than fantasy.

"Because I couldn't stop thinking about how you looked at me last night. And I didn't like disappointing you by walking out."

My cheeks turned a full cherry tomato color as she lit the romantic flame. Her knee is now touching mine. "I don't even know what we are. Or what we're doing."

"We're figuring it out." She places a hand on my thigh, and her finger traces my inner thigh lightly through my pants. "Slowly... or quickly, if you'd like," she says with a wink.

"Slow is okay," I breathe. "As long as there's caffeine and you."

We stare into each other's eyes, and this is definitely a kiss-your-boss-and-make-up sorta situation. The silence buzzes, in a warm way.

Then the front door flies open.

"Why is gravity trying to kill me?" Lisa groans, stumbling in and tripping on her Barbie-pink cowboy boots. She's wearing glitter eye-liner and a man's button-up. Backwards. And I can only assume her singles-mingle date night went well from her morning walk of shame look. Although, I'd guess that most people who work at matchmaking companies, don't also go out dating with clients.

"Is that CEO, SuperStar Alexis, in my dining room?" Lisa shouts, rubbing her eyes and smirking at me.

"Is this the kitchen?"

"It's a studio apartment. You are in the living room, entry way, kitchen, dining room, gameroom, and spare bedroom," I explain, then spread my hands.

"Welcome to our luxurious home," Lisa announces.

"Hello, Lisa," Alexis says politely.

She waves a hand, then dramatically face-plants onto the other couch cushion, one shoe dangling.

"I'm gonna die, and I still have to get ready for work," she mutters. She looks at the extra coffee. "Is that for me?"

"I should go," Alexis says, standing.

"Already?" I blurt.

She steps closer. Brushes my cheek. "I wanted to see you. Make sure we're okay."

My chest squeezes. "But–"

"I'll see you at work." Her phone vibrates and she adds, "I have to go put out these CEO-sized workplace fires."

Then, she leans in and presses a soft kiss to my temple and one of her notes falls from her pocket landing on my lap.

"See you in a few, Trouble."

I don't have time to react, and my hand flies to the warm spot on my head and then to the forgotten note as the door shuts behind her.

"So she did come over," Lisa croaks, drinking the sweet coffee.

I smile, heart pounding, and take a big gulp of my strong coffee, which is way more of a career-woman-focused drink anyway.

Maybe my perfect future includes my usual chaos, black coffee, pajamas, Lisa, and Alexis.

"Meow." Mr. Whiskers rubs his warm body across my shins.

Edit that... My usual chaos, black coffee, pajamas, Lisa, Alexis*, and Mr. Whiskers.*

"Did you see Darius posted about his new boyfriend. How am I, the professional matchmaker, the single one out of all of us?"

I laugh and sip my serious coffee. *Am I not single anymore?* How is it possible that Alexis stopped by to clear the air and I didn't ask her one serious question about our relationship? *Are we officially dating?* That's the simple question I should've asked.

I unfold the note in my lap. The sticky note has a doodled cat + heart.

"Ugh! How did this overgrown rat get in here," Lisa complains, but lifts Mr. Whiskers, setting him between us as we drink our morning coffees.

Chapter 5

Business Casual (Emphasis on Casual)

The rest of my Monday hits like a moose in mating season—loud, awkward, and nobody's fully prepared for the tall, gangly animals' romantic trysts.

After my very strong career-woman coffee, I'm *ready to slay*. My curls puff in a way that looks intentional—thank you, mousse miracle—and my mascara gives me "hot intern" instead of "exhausted raccoon." If my look doesn't catch Alexis's attention, I will slowly bend to pick up an accidentally dropped pen, and Alexis will be unable to resist my charms.

I'm strutting into Alaska Professional Temp Agency in Lisa's borrowed Mary Janes, an oversized belted shirt that technically belongs to one of Lisa's old suitors, and Alexis's blazer. Because I kinda like being trouble to Alexis. She saw me wear it Saturday, didn't demand it back, and possession is nine-tenths of the law, thus it's mine.

My plan is to march into Alaska Professional Temp Agency like it's my runway, with the air of a girl who kissed her boss and got a special morning coffee delivery from her.

I have zero shame and one hundred and ten percent confidence!

My time-to-leave alarm buzzes against my thigh, and I wave to Lisa, who hasn't moved from the couch despite my loud, caffeinated squirrel hurricane of a morning routine.

"Promise you won't look at your birth certificate until Darius and I are with you? You might need us," she calls out.

"Have you seen how slow state offices process paperwork? I probably won't get it for days." I called back. "But I'll wait to open it with you."

Ten minutes later, I'm at my work's glass door, nervously tugging at the blazer lapel.

Inside, Darius radiates power. He's draped in a cobalt-blue double-breasted suit that hugs his frame like it was tailored by competing queer designers on *Project Runway.* Black silk shirt open at the collar, silver cufflinks catching the light. He's running two phones, AirPods in, highlighter in hand—basically orchestrating Monday morning like a glam symphony conductor.

He catches my eye, and mouths, "Girl, don't start with me," before stabbing his highlighter toward Alexis's office.

And oh. My. God.

Alexis. My maybe-almost-girlfriend, definitely-boss, Alaska's sexiest workaholic. She's in a charcoal pinstripe suit, sleeves rolled, hair sleek, phone tucked between shoulder and ear while she slices the air with sharp hand gestures like she's commanding Wall Street from Anchorage.

She spots me.Smiles.Winks.

Oh. My. God.

I bite my lip and straighten the blazer. Her wink ignites every nerve ending I own. My entire frontal lobe melts. My inner thighs have filed a workplace complaint. The blazer I'm wearing? Suddenly too hot. My bra? Useless. This whole "showing up early to impress her" strategy? A failure. I'm not slaying. I'm slayed.

I rush to my desk, but my fingers forget what spreadsheets are. Darius appears next to me, waving a sticky note in my face.

"VIP client folder–It's Grant from Alaskan Cruises and Tours. It's a small family business but they are growing fast. Remember they are an important client for us, you already slayed the interview with them. So slay their assignment like your Monday look, girl," he stage-whispers, tossing it onto my desk. "Also, stop giving Alexis bedroom eyes. HR is already writing you up for making this an R-rated workplace."

"You're not professional either," I mutter, smacking him with the folder.

"Please. I'm professionally irresistible."

Before I can clap back, Alexis's voice slices across the office. "Aurora. My office."

I grab the file as a shield and march in, pretending I'm not seconds away from swooning or combusting.

The door shuts. Blinds snap closed. Lock clicks. And Alexis undresses me with her eyes.

Holy suspense. I haven't even pretended to drop my pen, accidentally and do the sexy bend over I practiced.

Alexis presses me against the door, eyes sharp, mouth curved. "You wore that on purpose."

"What? The blazer you forgot or my new lipgloss? It's cherry cheesecake flavored." My voice is confident but I'm suddenly weak.

Her voice drops, velvet and steel. "You're distracting. You are *trouble.*"

"Oh no," I gasp, fake innocence. "Am I about to get written up?"

"No. I'm conducting your permanent employee performance review."

Then her mouth is on mine, fierce and hungry. My knees wobble, but she holds me steady. I realize that she kisses like she runs meetings: decisive, strategic, dominant.

I melt into her lapels, knocking her pen holder sideways. She slides her hands under the blazer-that's-not-hers, mouth tracing fire down my neck.

I gasp between kisses. "I perform with—amazing—enthusiasm."

"Mmhmm. Exceeds expectations," she whispers against my throat.

The folder falls from my hand as her hands are on my hips, and her mouth is on mine, hot and hungry and way past polite. I put out my hand to steady myself and almost knocked over her fancy crystal pen holder.

And we'd probably keep going if—

BZZT! The intercom crackles.

Darius's voice sings, "Hey Boss. Aurora has a visitor.."

Alexis doesn't move her mouth far from mine. "Tell her to wait, Darius."

"Copy that," he says. But the line stays lit.

Which means as Alexis groans against my collarbone, I giggle breathlessly, and every sound is piping through reception.

"Oh my GOD," Darius cackles faintly through the speaker. "Y'all are feral!"

Before Alexis can hit the phone. There's a pounding on the door. "A-HA! Busted! I have a delivery."

We spring apart like teenagers, me panting, Alexis calmly straightening her blazer like she hasn't been tasting my tonsils.

Lisa bursts in, juggling two coffees and an eyebrow raise sharp enough to cut glass. "Don't mind me. I brought caffeine for the lovebirds. I mean the *hard working professionals.*"

"Lisa," Alexis greets smoothly, buttoning her jacket, "What a surprise to see you so soon." Her voice is *flawless professional CEO* again.

I'm blotchy, breathless, and trying not to choke on my shameful desire.

"I know. It's been forever," she teases with a laugh. Lisa plops a cup in front of me. "Here, babe. And FYI, here's your birth certificate request paperwork you left at home. You're welcome."

"Thanks." She must have gotten dressed at light speed. "But, what do you really want?" I narrow my eyes. "You only coffee-bribe me when you're scheming."

She fake gasps, hand to chest. "Slander! Ear muffs, Alexis."

Alexis cocks her head and starts to open her mouth, not understanding Lisa's meaning. She's probably never been told to cover her ears, and especially not in her own office. I know that this means disaster.

Lisa shrugs and giggles. "Okay fine—you can listen in. Aurora, I need you to go on a date tonight. A client bailed on me. You're cute and her type. And she's definitely your type: hot, professional, butch."

"Did I tell you Lisa works for a professional matchmaker?" I say trying to explain some of her weirdness to Alexis.

Alexis shakes her head and covers her mouth with her hand, trying to look business-professional. Her brown eyes dance, and she steps to the door as if she's ready to escort Lisa out.

Oblivious, Lisa steps further into the office. "Yes. And Aurora saves my butt when I need a last minute fill-in," she says, batting her eyelashes and handing Alexis a coffee. "It's a work thing, you understand?"

I shoot Alexis an apologetic glance. "Sorry."

To Lisa I explain, "I'm not available as your emergency date fill-in anymore."

Still standing by the door and opening it further, Alexis states, "You *can* go out tonight. I have to work late with everything going on."

I blink. "But I'm not available. My date card is full or punched or whatever the saying is. I'm *taken,*" I say, ending my excessive nervous talking.

Alexis lets out a dry chuckle. "I'm not going to stop you. You are young and I'm busy working. Let's keep our thing casual."

Casual? Casual. Casual!

The word slices through me like frostbite on a summer frolic. I nod, slow, unsure.

I lick my lips and try again. "Are you sure?" I ask, my eyes flicking to Alexis. "I'm fine staying home. I need to start organizing for university anyway."

Lisa, unbothered by my relationship crisis, types on her phone. "Great. I'll text you the deets."

Alexis crosses her arms with CEO-perfect posture. "As the youngest CEO in Alaska, who's female and LGBT. I'm doing more than taking over my father's place here. I'm following a detailed career plan that includes a lot of late nights. That's how you succeed."

She says this like my mentor, not like a girl sharing a caring situationship with me.

"I need to be laser-focused on work for the next few years. Then, at thirty, I'll start a family by marrying the right woman, raising kids—she'll do charity work or be a board member at St. Hilary's preschool academy." Alexis lists off.

My brain short-circuits.

Alexis doesn't have a five year plan–she has a detailed *fifteen-year plan.*

When was she going to tell me?

So I'm what, the warm-up act? The seasonal lesbian before her *real* wife's auditions?

Outside, the phones ring. The copier spits out reports. Someone laughs near the break room.

Lisa blinks, then whispers, "Who knew such a modern corporate lesbian would have such a *traditional life plan*? A family and stay-at-home mom?"

I shake my head because her plan doesn't seem to include me.

"Enjoy your Dirty London Fogs!" Lisa says, finally exiting and sashaying out as if everything is settled.

She continues out in a caffeinated tornado. Tossing her head and calls over her shoulder, "Thanks for the help! You guys have the best, casual, relationship, *ever!*"

On her way past reception, she calls, "Darius, you're still backup date material, right? I really need to keep my dating numbers and reviews up this month."

He snatches her coffee like a sea gull stealing fries. "Girl, I'm booked. I got Richard. You handle your own chaos."

Lisa sniffs and rolls her eyes. "Some cousin you are!"

"I'll provide emotional support. And I *will* bring Richard to our karaoke night."

Lisa blows a kiss and disappears into the elevator.

Silence.

Alexis is already on another call, CEO mask firmly in place.

I shuffle out, clutching coffee, stomach hollow, and my legs on autopilot.

At my desk, Darius leans over the divider. "Girl. That was awkward AF."

"No. It's fine. I'm fine," I lie.

"She called you 'casual.'"

I look at him, and shrug then realize his desk isn't close enough to catch that, even if Alexis had the door open.

Reading my mind, he grins. "Girl, the intercom was still on. I heard *everything*. The panting. The 'casual.' Honestly, it was funny, if I didn't know how much you want a serious relationship. But you'll win her over, Excel-sheet sexy Queen. You're only starting your illicit, workplace love affair."

I bury my face in the coffee, cheeks on fire. My dream board at home feels like a joke now—cutout magazine images of campus life, bright colors, words like *believe in yourself*. Alexis has a fifteen-year roadmap. I'm doodling glue-stick collages of positivity for next week.

He nudges me gently. "Don't worry. You still have main character rizz, babe."

But my chest is hollowed out. *Am I even close to being her girlfriend*? I'm not asking to be her wife in her fifteen year plan, but we have a super-strong connection. I thought I was more than casual.

He nudges me, ignoring my frown as random thoughts of not being good enough for Alexis whirl through my mind.

"Do you think Alexis'll let me sneak out early today? I'm planning to take Richard to that experimental jazz bar featuring harmonicas and kazoos."

I can only blink in response. I'm not sure if Alexis would even care if I left early.

Chapter 6

Defining & Defying The Open, Casual Relationship

Lisa pirouettes across the living room in a flurry of florals and citrus perfume, her oversized earrings clinking like windchimes caught in an Arctic gale. She stops dramatically in front of the mirror, striking a pose that is more swagger than poise.

"Someone's gotta show these Alaska neanderthals the dating standard—what women expect and what they deserve on a date," she declares, fluffing her curls with both hands. "I'm just the aggressively sexy lady to do it!"

Mr. Whiskers, our semi-permanent couch dweller, blinks slowly–unimpressed–and buries himself deeper in the throw blanket.

I recheck my phone.

Nothing.

Still nothing.

Cool, cool. Maybe Alexis is buried under a stack of contracts or alphabetizing and color-coding her new client files. We haven't talked since our interrupted morning makeout sesh.

My last text is waiting, unread: "Hey, checking in if you want to chat or grab a drink later tonight. Miss you!"

God, I'm thirsty! Which immediately makes me think of Darius's jokes about U-Haul lesbian relationships.

I shoot off a text to him, "Should I leave a voicemail for our boss? Asking for a thirsty friend."

Two seconds later, my phone lights up with a call.

I answer. "Hey— "

"No," Darius says immediately, with zero preamble. "First, voicemail, who does that anymore? You're hanging out with a cougar. Next you'll want to write her an old-fashion love letter!"

I glanced at the cute stationery I had sprayed my perfume on and had planned to use. I might be channeling too much Victoria-romance-book romance. "Alexis is only eight years older than me. And she loves old-fashioned stuff, like little notes and her retro sneakers. "

"Don't you have a date tonight with Lisa's client? Play hard-to-get, for once. Alpha people, like Alexis, love chasing. Let her have to hunt you a little. Rawr baby."

"Pffff," I say with a shrug and climb onto the couch with my new furry therapist. "Did I tell you she calls salmon, saL-mon? No joke."

"With a hard L?! She was joking around. I've never heard her say that."

"No–she definitely said it. But you know, rich people have different rules. They are allowed to mispronounce things to be sophisticated."

"It makes them sound fancy, foreign, and sophisticated," Dairus agrees.

"Well, what's worse is that no one corrected her or noticed," I explained, adding, "Or maybe it's not a rich thing but her hot, badassery thing. No one argues with beautiful self-assured women. I know because everyone argues with me–and I'm none of those things."

Darius laughs and then Richard's voice chimes in from somewhere too close to Darius. "Alexis is so black and white she tries to pronounce every silent letter. Try to get her to say 'schedule.'"

I sit up straighter. "Wait, why is Richard on the phone with you? Do you ever take a break from each other or...?"

Darius snorts. "Oh please, Richard can give you deeper insight into Alexis, and he makes me happy. Of course, Richard is here–we're a lifestyle brand. You should see our matching beanies."

"First, I can't talk about Alexis in front of her workout partner and friend," I say, trying to remember what I've said and how embarrassing it'll be if it gets back to Alexis.

"And it's a total party foul," I say, shaking my head and rubbing Mr. Whiskers' ears. "You're supposed to tell someone when they're on speaker phone before they spill their guts!"

"Baby, you're so loud, you're always on speaker."

"Rude." But I laugh because it's true.

Richard chuckles in the background. "We love you. And I promise I wouldn't tell Alexis you're playing hard to get."

"Anyway," Darius says, dropping into his supportive bestie voice. "Any updates on the dad saga? The Mysterious Missing Man on your birth certificate?"

I sigh, poking at a suspicious fuzz ball on the couch cushion. "Well, about that... I totally forgot to tell you because of all the workplace drama. I tried to get a copy of my birth certificate. But when I stopped by their office, everyone was either on vacation or called in sick this week to go to the Alaska State Fair in Palmer. I guess giant veggies, carnival rides, deepfriend twinkies and the Benson Boone concert is considered a holiday for the Office of Alaska State Vital Statistics. They said to fax my request, and it'll be ready for pickup next week."

"Does anyone even own a fax machine?" Richard asks.

"You can do it with a fax app," Darisu explains, then says to me, "I'm surprised your mom hasn't just told you. She's been way too quiet. You know how she loves to be the center of attention and cause drama."

"Well, I'm glad she hasn't called or I'm sure I'd end up apologizing to her, somehow. I've been so much less stressed without her ongoing emotional theatrics playing in the background." I can't believe I've had so much going on that I haven't even had the chance to enjoy my freedom from my mom.

I vow to add independence and successful adulting to my "wins" on my dream board.

"Hey, I'm proud of you," Darius says, clapping.

"Thanks, personal cheerleader," I respond.

"Hey, that's what I call him, Mr. Cheeky Cheerleader," Richard adds with another deep rumbling laugh.

"Well, I'll save that pet name for your use."

"You know someone really *really* likes you when they give you a cutsie nickname," Darius purrs and I hear a sound that suspiciously sounds like a kiss.

Trouble. Alexis did give me a nickname. Maybe she is more into me than her career/life plan suggests.

Darius interrupts my internal monologue with a question. "Do you want me to help with your dad thing? You know I've got CIA-level stalking skills."

"Thanks. I might cash in that offer when I figure out my dad's name."

Lisa appears again in the hallway, spritzing herself with something glittery, tropical, and flammable. "Okay! I'm heading out with a cute North Sloper!"

"Sloper? Are you sure a Roughneck oil guy is your type," I say, lifting a brow from the couch.

She twirls. "Rich and casual is always my type." Then she laughs and winks, "I guess that's both our types. Besides with two weeks on, two off, if I don't like him, he'll be gone soon. I don't even have to break up with him."

"Maybe that's your type, but I'm not so good at casual. I was sorta hoping for something more solid, permanent in my life. I really need a solid relationship to anchor me. Alexis seemed like she'd be that."

"Oh, honey. It's not you," Lisa coos, rummaging for her other heel. "Lesbians just don't do casual things. Lesbians get serious on date two and buy a house together by date five. You got a unicorn with Alexis. You should enjoy the freedom."

"Well," I mutter, "I want more. Or at least someone who texts me back."

Lisa chides me, "You're overthinking it. She's into you. You guys were just making out this morning. Talk to me after date five and we'll see where your romance is at."

I sigh. "Well, you are the dating expert. I guess you'd know best."

She grins. "Yup. Now you better get ready for your totally fabulous date set up by your favorite matchmaker. You're doing this for all of Anchorage's single lesbians. And for my client retention rate. Keep my client happy, and she's the bait that'll bring in more clients. Think of yourself as a lesbian saint."

"Great. So this will be a charity date."

"You're a professional decoy. I'll find her someone. I just need extra time. I don't have anyone in my books that is a match for her. You're doing cupid's work. Huge difference."

"Do I still get paid?"

"You get wine, dinner, and a fun date–you won't be bored. Besides I overheard you are planning on playing hard to get. This is the perfect setup for your relationship games." She finishes applying lipstick and smiles.

I groan, dramatically tossing my phone aside. "Fine. If Alexis is too busy to text, I might as well practice my dating. Maybe I'll learn some pickup lines to use on Alexis."

Lisa beams. "That's the spirit!"

She zips her coat, adjusts her cleavage, and tosses a kiss in the air. "Okay, I'm off to work to seduce an oil guy. Wish me luck."

"Break a heel."

"Never!" she calls, disappearing into the cold night.

Mr. Whiskers sighs dramatically. Or it came from me.

I scratch his head. "I'm surrounded by workaholics, Whiskers. Are you working on being the cutest cat tonight?"

From outside, Lisa yells, "And return my neighbor's cat before he calls the police on us for cat-napping!"

Chapter 7

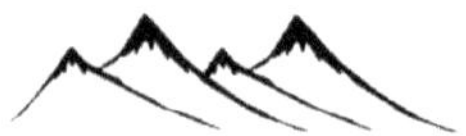

The Dating Game

My phone buzzes as I sit at the bar with water, waiting. I jerk upright so fast the barstool squeaks and my water splashes. My heart does a hopeful little dance—then crashes into a wall when I see it.

"SOS. Answer or perish. FaceTime me."

I hit accept, praying Lisa's calling was about a lip gloss emergency and not new drama.

Her face fills the screen in her chaotic glory—she's wearing thick black fake lashes, a leopard-print sweater, and drinking what I think is an actual martini with two olives.

"Heyyyyyy!" she chirps. "What are you wearing?"

"Lisa, I can't talk."

"Your date texted my coworker at the dating agency. She said that she can't find you."

I blink and pull the phone back to pan my outfit.

"Okay so you look like a librarian on trial."

"Hey this is a nice dress," I say, defending my flowered summer dress under the blazer.

Lisa adjusted her camera angle, as if she were shooting a beauty tutorial, with glossy blonde hair spilling over one shoulder in Hollywood waves. "No. Seriously. What *are* you wearing? Take off that blazer and let your hair down."

I roll my eyes, pull out the bun to let my auburn curls escape, and then remove the jacket. "Better?"

"Are you trying not to get laid tonight? I swear you either dress like you've never left the house or like you are Cinderella rushing to the ball. Next time, I'm telling Darius to dress you!"

"He'd love that. Also, I wasn't planning on getting laid," I whisper-yell, glancing nervously toward the hostess's stand. "I look fine."

"Says the woman who wore mismatched shoes to a job interview with a shoe-obsessed Alexis," she responds.

"And I got hired!" I hiss, slightly proud. "I'm more of a personality date than a fashionista date."

"You can be both. Hey, FYI, my Hook and Reel dating assistant booked the reservation under your fake name, Summer. Now, go find your date. You will flirt. You will *not* wear that un-sexy blazer or talk about... well anything. Try not to be you. Just ask her about herself and listen, okay."

"I can be charming."

Lisa rolled her eyes so hard that I could hear it. "You need to focus. You are doing this for me, the friend who's letting you stay on her couch for free. I need to prove to our client list that we can deliver quality queer. Don't let me down, *Summer.*"

I open my mouth to sass back, but the phone buzzes again—this time it's Darius asking me to save him from the terrible jazz bar. I ignore him–he's being overdramatic.

Lisa's voice cuts through my fog. "Earth to Summer. Please tell me you are going to have a fabulous, hot date."

I exhale through my nose. "Define hot. Like, Alaska hot or LA hot?"

"First stop at the bathroom, tighten your bra or stuff it because your boobs are not your best feature. Make your eyeliner bigger, like you're about to steal someone's girlfriend."

"I *am* someone's *almost*-girlfriend," I mutter, low and half-hearted.

"Not tonight, babe. Tonight you're single looking to mingle. You are the flirty bait to sink my new client. Break hearts. Order wine like you know what tannins are. And for me, do *not* bring up your taxidermy trauma again."

"That was one time," I say.

"That was *last week.* She literally said, 'Tell me about yourself,' and you opened with 'I once carried around a dead porcupine dressed like Taylor Swift.'"

"It was a conversation starter and formative experience!"

Lisa hangs up with a war cry of "Go get her, Summer." I'm left staring at my screen, debating whether to cram in a miracle-level transformation or bolt out the back door.

A throat clears behind me.

"Summer?"

I spin so fast my curls whip me in the face. A tall brunette stands there, with a black leather jacket, a confident stance, and eyes sharper than a glacier ridge at dawn. She raises one perfectly arched brow, and I immediately forget my name—both my real one and my fake one.

"Uh—hi," I manage, voice cracking like a middle school clarinet. "That's me. Summer. Sunshine. Um, salmon season."

She blinks. "Salmon season?"

Kill me.

Lisa would be cringing if she were still on the line.

"What I meant," I scramble, tugging at my suddenly choking dress neckline, "is, uh, yes! I'm Summer. You must be..."

"Harper." She gives a little tight smile. "Your friend Lisa told me you'd be hard to miss. Tall. Quirky. Chaos written on your forehead."

I point at my actual forehead. "Does it show? I tried a new concealer."

Her laugh rings out warm, not mocking, and I relax for a split second. Maybe Lisa's date setup won't be as horrible as I expected. She looks friendly, and I'm always up for making friends.

"Shall we?" she says, gesturing toward the hostess.

"Sure," I reply, too quickly. My legs don't seem to coordinate with each other as I follow her. I nearly trip over a chair and mumble something about floor hazards. The hostess smiles like she's filing me under her too drunk to drive patrons list.

We sit at a corner booth—candle flickering, menus glossy, waiters zipping by with plates of king crab legs and artistic-looking seafood plates. I tuck myself in, knees knocking the table which starts a small earthquake.

Harper slides off her jacket, revealing a slinky maroon top that looks painted on. My brain does a backflip as I wonder what Alexis would look like in that shirt.

Focus, Aurora. *Summer*. Whoever I'm supposed to be.

"So," she starts, leaning her chin on one hand, "how's a cutie like you still single?"

Lisa's lecture scrolls through my head like neon subtitles: *Ask about her. Listen. Do not mention taxidermy.*

I plaster on my brightest grin. "The question is how you're still single? You are super hot!"

Her eyes sparkle. "Deflecting already. Clever."

"Well, I call it my first-date strategy. That way you do all the talking, and I just have to nod. It makes me look mysterious."

"Hmm," she muses, "I'm not sure you do *mysterious*."

Ouch.

Correct. But still ouch.

She launches into a story about moving from Fairbanks, her law degree, and how she's "ready for something exciting." Her voice is smooth, confident, practiced—like she's pitched herself a hundred times in court. Meanwhile, I'm bobbleheading her, wondering how long this date will last, and if Alexis will text me back for late-night drinks.

"That's amazing," I chirp, pretending I didn't drift off. Harper is funny and attractive–the type that would usually melt me. But I'm dry ice, and itching to leave.

"You?" she asks suddenly. "Tell me all about you, Summer."

Crap. I knew this part was coming.

"What do you do?" She prods.

"I'm... between things."

"Things?"

"Jobs, schools, you know. I'm like—like still working out what my talents are. I'm kind of mysterious. Wait, you said I'm not mysterious, but I swear I—"

Her laughter interrupts my ramble, thank God. "You're cute."

Heat shoots up my neck. Cute? Me? What if she is really falling for my silent, nodding act? I'm in no place to go on a second date with her, and I'm definitely not going home with her. She shifts her leg, and it rubs against mine. I choke on my water.

"Oh! Well. I mean. Thanks. You too. Not—you're not cute, you're drop-dead. Not that you're not cute! You're—um—"

"Relax," she says, sipping her wine like she's immune to embarrassment. "I like an awkward date. It's refreshing."

Awkward. Refreshing. Great. I'll have to remember to put that on my Bumble profile. "Okay, full disclosure, but don't quit the Hook and Reel Dating Agency's thing. Your real date, who was perfect for you, cancelled at the last minute. I'm the cute fill-in date."

Instead of looking upset, she laughed. "That's okay. I figured I'd be going on quite a few dates before I found my soulmate."

"Your next date will be amazing. And I will pay half the bill and be a very polite date tonight. I promise."

After my admission, we joke around and compare lesbians we both might know in the community, which is a surprising amount. Halfway through the appetizer—tempura shrimp that crunch too loudly—my phone buzzes again.

Alexis.

My stomach lurches. I flip the screen down on the table before Harper notices, but my chest is already burning.

"Important?" she asks, her lips curving.

"Nope," I squeak. "Work but nothing important. I do accounting work at a temp agency for now. I mean who's ever heard of an afterhours accounting emergency?"

Harper grins, and dips another shrimp into the red sweet pepper sauce.

If I could have, I'd run away to the bathroom and check my phone immediately.

I wish I hadn't promised to be a polite date because the truth is that I want to be rude, reading my text messages at the table. I want to lie about having a work emergency, so I can escape. I want to hear Alexis's voice more than I want to share dessert with this nice lawyer.

And dessert is mochi ice cream, so that's saying something.

I finish the meal and dessert, somehow resisting my phone's alerts. Alexis can wait thirty minutes–I'm playing hard to get.

Later, as we leave the restaurant, the Anchorage night is filled with stars and a sharp odor of seaweed and car exhaust. Harper steps close under the neon sign, and I swear the universe holds its breath because with the darkness and the neon lights outlining us, this is a romantic backdrop.

"This was fun, Summer," she whispers, forcing me to lean closer to hear.

"It was?" My voice squeaks up an octave.

"Yes." She smooths an escaping curl behind my ear, bold and charming. "I'll walk you to your car."

"Oh, you don't have to do that. I should walk *you* to your car," I say quickly, trying to end the date on a good note. "I'm your polite fill-in date."

Also, my car is a wreck, and my school paperwork with my real name is in plain sight sitting on the passenger seat. Harper doesn't seem like a stalker, but better safe than sorry.

Harper's face is getting dangerously close, as if she plans to end the date with a kiss.

I stammer, "Uh—I walked!"

Her brows rise. "In heels?"

"I'm athletic."

"You tripped over a chair."

"I'm... *selectively* athletic."

She laughs again, softer this time, like she almost believes me. And she definitely is finding me cute and charming. Then she leans in, lips brushing the air between us.

I freeze, my lungs short-circuit.

"AURORA THOMPSON, STEP AWAY FROM THE STUNNING LESBIAN!"

The loud and familiar voice cuts through the night, and I unfreeze to stumble back before her lips collide with mine.

I whip around. Darius and Richard are swaying on the curb. Richard is holding two neon oversized kazoos, and Darius is waving his free hand like he's directing airport traffic.

"What the Fuck?" Harper mutters, baffled.

"Sorry," I croak, "my... friends."

"Friends?" She looks at the drunken gays and back to me.

"I TEXTED!" Darius yells.

"Sorry, I'm pretty sure I'm their DD tonight."

Harper's lips twitch like she's deciding whether this is endearingly cute or a setup to end our date. "Okay, Summer. Call me." She presses a card into my hand and saunters off, hips swaying like she knows I'll watch. Which—I definitely *don't*.

Darius swoops in before she's out of sight. "Girl. GIRL. Who is that? Wait, is that the Lisa client you got booked to do? I love Alexis, but you need to get some biker chick taco tonight. She's a smoke show!"

"I don't *love* Alexis–she massacred me this afternoon on the pickleball court. But, I agree with Darius. Hit that fierce woman, asap," Richard slurs.

I groan, shaking my head. At least I'll be able to look through my phone now and see where Alexis wants to meet. Maybe my place?

"She's none of your business," I mumble, shoving the card in my purse and processing that Alexis had time to play pickleball, but didn't text me until after dinner.

I quickly scroll and all she texted me was, "See you at work tomorrow. Nite."

"Shesa Nunobizzes is a weird name, but I'm digging it," Richard's low laugh rumbles. Darius's laugh follows. He starts hiccuping between chuckles as I stuff them into my car.

"Thanks for saving us, girl," Darius says, hugging me as he falls into my backseat.

I wasn't wrong–they did need a Designated Driver tonight.

Chapter 8

CEO Lockdown

It's one of those moody Anchorage mornings where the sky looks like it lost a bar fight with the sun and is morose and bruised with a storm. Heavy clouds squat over every building, gray on grayer with a side of passive-aggressive drizzle. The sunny season? She's toast–she lost the fight. The fireweed is surrendered and blooming to cotton whisps, an obvious indicator that the golden months of sun are over. Even the trees outside the agency have ditched the pretense—they're dropping their last rust colored leaves with resignation.

I'm wasting the better part of the morning watching raindrops slide down the corner of the window. Hypnotized as they slowly ruin the morning–kind of like my boss. Casual-almost-girlfriend who hasn't stopped by to chat or wink at me today.

I mean, I would've thought she'd ask about my date or bring me a coffee–but there's been *nada* from her.

Alexis is in full "please book an appointment with my assistant, Darius, before you breathe in my direction" mode—blazer off, sleeves rolled, her sexy librarian glasses on, and her jaw set sharp enough to slice a bagel.

I texted her, "Good Morning." But she hasn't smiled at me or responded with *anything*. Not even a cryptic thumbs-up text. My phone sits face-up on my desk, just in case she sends me a note, or even looks up to see if I'm waiting for her text.

Nothing.

Zero new notifications. Not even a spam call or disgruntled creditor. Those calls have, thankfully, significantly decreased since my regular paychecks have started.

So much for my game of playing hard to get. She still doesn't want me. I poke the screen with my finger. "Do something."

From the next desk, Darius hums. "Tough morning, babe? I'm super hungover, so I don't mind at all Alexis being in meetings all day."

"She hasn't even *looked* at me today." I flop my forehead onto the desk with a dull thunk. "Two hours. That's, like, an entire Hallmark movie. I could be starting a family Christmas tree farm with her by now."

"Who watches Christmas romances in September? Girl, you should be finishing up your accounting work here before you start your new assignment," he quips.

"I came in early and did it. I thought maybe I'd catch Alexis and impress her."

Darius starts filing his nails and looking through emails. "She's in CEO Boss mode lockdown. She's working so there's no interrupting her. You're spiraling. And needy."

"I'm not needy, I'm attentive."

"You're serving gift-wrapped and ready," he corrects, looking at my cute blue sweater set and bow tied in my hair. "Simmer down, girl."

"She didn't call or see me last night. What am I doing wrong?"

Darius blows on his nails. "Is that how you play hard to get? Let her chase you. Let her win you, girl. We talked about this–just simmer down."

Before I can argue, my phone buzzes. I sit up straight, spine snapping and shoulders back, ready. Alexis's blinds are closed, and there's no movement from her office.

"Hey, Lisa!"

"I guess my pep talk worked, because Harper thought you were ah-may-zing! Good job! And gold star to me, for being the best queer matchmaker in Alaska," she says, in a way that makes me think she's shimmying and high-fiving herself. "I'm totally going to take over the LGBT singles matchmaking scene."

I blink. "Yeah. It went fine. She's nice, but not Alexis."

"Sure, of course not. No one needs multiple sultry bad ass bitches in their lives. I mean that in a flattering way. Are you ready for another set-up?" She asks.

"With Harper?"

"No! This is a university girlie. And nothing serious–this one is just for fun, making friends. I told you about it this morning. You were obviously spacing out."

I pause. "Sorry," I say, biting my bottom lip. "I was hypnotized by the rain. My brain is emotional soup. Tell me again about her?"

"Her name is Zara. You *promised* to meet her for drinks. She's a fun Alaskan girl. And you need to get your groove back anyway. Also, Alexis needs a push to commit, The best way to get a serious commitment is competition."

"You and Darius are following the same dating playbook."

She ignores me and asks, "Nothing's changed with Alexis—you're still casual and open for dating, right?"

"Ugh. I guess I am, but I'm kinda dated out and what if Alexis wants to go out tonight?" I whisper-yell, shooting a nervous glance toward Alexis' closed blinds.

"I texted Darius, and she is there late with meetings," she says, triumphantly killing my excuses.

I shoot Darius a look, and he pretends to look in another direction. "Really?" I hiss.

"Tonight. Summer is meeting her at six. I'll text you all the details," Lisa says.

"Fine. But I'm just doing drinks, and I'm only doing this because I'll be exclusive with Alexis soon, so you better beef up your lesbian singles roster. I'm not going to be on it anymore."

"Okay dokey. If you aren't exclusive by next week, I might have one more date. I want you to screen someone for Harper. Please?" Lisa pleads.

I open my mouth for the inevitable "tell me more"—because apparently my people-pleasing streak is alive and thriving—when my phone buzzes. Alexis's name flashes, and my heart lurches while my fingers do an involuntary jazz-hands celebration.

"Sorry for the silence. Back-to-back meetings. Dinner tomorrow?" Alexis typed.

I'm so ecstatic for any morsel of attention from her that I immediately type back, "Sure."

My smiley face with hearts feels like too much, and I wish I had just added a thumbs-up emoji. I stare at the bubble, hoping she'll type something more. It appears, then disappears. Nothing else comes.

Lisa's voice cuts through my heartbreak fog. "I'll ask Darius to put together a casual cocktail hour outfit for you. You don't have to do anything but check your text and enjoy drinks. Thanks alot! I super-appreciate you, and I promise I'll stop asking you to cover dates."

I exhale through my nose. "No prob. I'm going to try and connect with Alexis today–become exclusive! I'll give you an update on our casual status later."

"Hey, don't move too fast. I *am* a matchmaker. Maybe I'll find you a better match than your frosty CEO." She laughs. "Someone who doesn't have to schedule you in between client calls and for seven am coffee dates."

I wince. "Hey, Alexis just took over her family business. And it's only been a few days since we started dating."

"Okay. I won't poke the hot-for-her-boss bear anymore. But you have to try to have fun. Gotta run! Love and hugs!"

Before I can say goodbye, there's a loud crack of an office door suddenly opening.

Not our outside door.

It's *Alexis's* office door.

Chapter 9

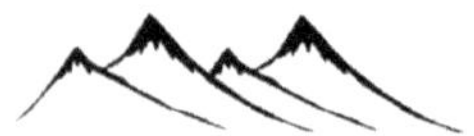

Drizzling, Despair, Disaster & Dad Drama

Every person's head, in the office, turns in a synchronized swivel at the sound. The air hums with that electric "someone's about to get fired or promoted" energy.

Alexis's door cracks open and—*oh boy*—her silhouette is pure CEO-butch perfection. Black slacks that make her look way too intimidating. She's wearing a crisp white button-down that announces her authority over a loudspeaker.

But she's not alone.

There's a man behind her. He must have been there for the last two hours, which is unusual. Definitely not a new hire unless the agency suddenly recruited silver-fox models, instead of corporate and government office workers. He has charcoal slacks, and a navy wool coat that shows he's prepared for the weather. Hair thick, silver with a ghost of reddish brown–the last remnants of his youthful color. The distinguished older man belongs in an expensive scotch commercial.

Something in my ribs shifts. Recognition? Dread? Heartburn?—Note to self: maybe don't eat leftover reindeer hot dogs for breakfast.

"Miss Thompson," Alexis calls across the bullpen. Her voice is smooth and unbothered, like she didn't kiss me yesterday and make a date for tomorrow. "You are needed here."

The entire office suddenly remembers how to *pretend* to work, but watches.

Darius sips his oat-milk latte with the glee of a drag queen watching bad contour. "Not your usual morning meeting," he whispers behind his mug, eyes glittering.

I push back my chair, heart starting a slow drum solo against my ribs. "Thanks for the heads up, Darius."

"Anytime, sweetheart," he stage-whispers. "Break a leg—or a corporate policy."

I march past the rubber plants and the buzzing printer. Alexis holds the door for me. No smile. No secret wink. Just that clean, unreadable CEO mask. It's colder than the drizzle spitting against the windows.

Inside, I barely look at the man, offering a polite smile. What's going on with Alexis and with us? My brain finally coughs up a memory, and my eyes snap back on him. I blush at recalling how I called him a sexist pig at my interview with him.

"Hello. I'm Grant Fairbanks. We met last week."

"Oh," I say, because words are hard when your boss' expensive floral scent is making you dizzy and you are suddenly stuck with a new boss, who you've created an even more awkward workplace situation than here.

I hear Darius walking slowly outside the office, trying to eavesdrop.

Of course, I remember Grant from my interview at Alaska Cruise & Tours. I was just hoping to forget the whole disaster and bury myself into the accounting work.

Alexis clears her throat, all business. "Grant has signed our contract to use the agency exclusively. He's ready for you to start over there next week."

My stomach plummets like a salmon over a waterfall. Wait, is Alexis trying to ship me off because I've been too clingy as an almost-girlfriend?

Grant extends a hand. "Nice to see you again, Aurora."

My voice decides to take a personal day. "Right."

Alexis adds, "There's an unexpected development we should discuss before we finalize your schedule. Grant, I'll let you lead."

"I didn't realize… until the gala… seeing Sandra… and I thought you would've known…" his words trail off. Grant shifts, eyes flickering like he's about to confess to hunting a moose outside of hunting season. He pulls out his wallet. "Maybe this will help."

He opens it, and my knees do that fun jellyfish thing. Tucked behind a credit card is my seven-year-old school photo: gap-toothed grin, pink corduroy overalls, blunt bangs I thought were fashionable, and I now know only enhance my weird forehead.

I blink. "Uh. Why do you have a picture of me in your wallet?"

Alexis leans back, poker-faced. Half curiosity, half unreadable, as she turns away to stare out the window.

Grant's voice softens. "Aurora?"

My skin prickles. "Yes?"

"I'm positive I'm your father."

I laugh. It bursts out of me like a startled raven—short, sharp, defensive. "No you're not."

He nods, tired eyes steady. "I am."

"No." My voice snaps like frozen seaweed. "My dad left when I was a baby. He doesn't live in Alaska and is probably dead. You're not him."

Alexis's gaze flicks to her laptop as if she'd rather be scheduling a dental cleaning than watching another dramatic episode of my life.

"I tried to be there," Grant says quickly, holding a paper bag like a peace flag. "I have a file—letters, birthday cards—"

"See. My dad never sent me anything. He didn't call. He didn't remember my birthday."

Grant continues, patiently, "The cards and gifts were all returned. I was blocked. I couldn't do anything. Your mother, Sandra, wouldn't let me contact you."

The air goes thin, like someone opened the office windows to the September wind. My ears almost pop with the sudden change of pressure.

"That—" My throat tightens. "That can't be right."

But it could. Sandra, queen of social climbing and emotional booby traps. We haven't spoken in days, and this sounds exactly like her toxic MO.

Grant pulls out a creased card, purple dinosaurs dancing across the front. My eighth birthday.

I know that card. I found it on the porch the night before my party. There were photos and a crisp twenty inside until Mom snatched it, calling it "junk mail." By morning, it had vanished—pictures and all.

I thought I'd dreamed of the smiling people and my name on the card.

"Wait." My voice is barely a whisper. "You sent that?"

He nods. "I barely knew your mom. Didn't even know about you until after. I tried to stay in touch. All I could do was send child support."

My mind scrambles. Sandra always said my father was a ghost story: gone before the credits, never left a trace.

Grant keeps going, words spilling like the rain outside. "...I connected the dots after our interview, but I could tell you didn't know."

"Oh my God."

"She told me you didn't want contact. That you were better off, especially after your—well, I could have reacted better to the news. And I—" He swallows hard. "I believed her. I regret that every day."

I press my fingers to my temples. The room tilts, fluorescent lights swimming.

"When did you know?" I ask, though my voice sounds like someone else's.

"It's okay," Grant says quickly. "I asked Alexis not to say anything until I could talk to you."

My gaze snaps to Alexis. *She knew?* She knew and didn't tell me? The betrayal bites sharper than the drizzle against the glass.

Grant raises both hands. "This is my fault. I—"

"Nope." I push to my feet, heart ricocheting harder than a startled ptarmigan. "I need air."

I shove past them, out into the hallway.

The rain turns the windows into watercolor smudges. Grey light drips through like an old film reel. I walk fast, not caring where, until the bathroom door is under my palm. I lock it and lean against the cool metal, chest heaving.

The fluorescent light buzzes. My reflection in the mirror is all wide eyes and windblown curls, like I've just wrestled a bear and lost.

A knock. Soft.

"Aurora?" Alexis's voice. Smooth, low.

I squeeze my eyes shut. Of course, she followed me.

"Go away." My voice cracks, betraying me.

Silence. Then, a voice says, "I can't."

I twist the lock, and the door clicks open a sliver. Alexis slips inside, bringing a whiff of cedar cologne and rain-chilled air. She shuts the door, leans against it, and the CEO mask is gone for once.

"I'm sorry," she says quietly. "I should have told you."

My throat tightens. "You knew. And you let me... just sit there thinking my dad was—" I swallow, the mirror fogging from our combined breath. "Do you have any idea how many Father's Day crafts I made for a man I thought was imaginary?"

Her lips twitch—almost a smile, then not. She is silent. Her eyes catch the fluorescent light, soft amber with the steel reflecting underneath.

"Why are you here? Why do you care?" I ask before I can stop myself. "You're only my boss and casual... *something*. You can leave and let my friends comfort me."

Her brow arches. "Do you really think I don't care?"

Something in my chest flickers.

The rain outside drums harder. Alexis steps closer, slow enough that I could back away. I don't.

For a breath, we just stand there—rain thrumming, fluorescent light buzzing, the whole world a wash of grey outside.

Her thumb grazes my jaw, gently. "Aurora."

"Yes?" It comes out as a squeak.

"Breathe."

I do. Finally, tears flow as I grip the edge of the sink until my knuckles match the clouds outside. The fluorescent light hums like it's about to blow. My reflection is a storm: red cheeks, wide eyes, mascara smudged enough to terrify a raccoon.

I shake my head at my reflection and at her. She should have told me. "No. I don't accept your apology."

She steps back and stays by the door, posture straight as the spine of a legal pad. "Grant asked me to give him time. I respected that. This morning's meeting—he needed to tell you himself."

I bark out a laugh that tastes like salt. "Respected *him*? You knew for how long? Minutes? Hours? Days? And you let me sit there— clueless and stressed out?"

Her jaw tightens. "It wasn't my story to tell."

"It was *my* story," I shot back. My voice wobbles, but it doesn't break. "My life. My dad. You should have told me the second you found out. Or at least warned me before I walked into an ambush."

"Aurora—"

"No." I slice the air with my hand. "You chose Grant's timeline. Your contract. Your job. And you decided I could wait."

She steps closer, then stops, her eyes flicking to the buzzing ceiling light. For a fraction of a second, I see regret. But it's buried under the steel of someone who built her life on schedules and signed deals.

"I have responsibilities," she says quietly. "This agency—"

"It's always work, *the agency*," I whisper. The words burn, but they're true. "That's what I am to you too, isn't it? A responsibility. A temp you have to manage."

Her silence is louder than any excuse.

Something inside me that's been bending toward other people's storms finally snaps straight.

"I'm done trying to be the perfect employee and your casual relationship," I say. "My mother. My dad. You."

Alexis flinches, just barely.

I grab a paper towel, swipe at my mascara streaks, and toss it into the bin. "I'll talk to Grant. On my terms. Not yours. Not my mom's. Mine. Send me my schedule, or just have Darius give it to me. I don't want to see you."

"Aurora—" Her voice cracks, the first fracture in her perfect composure.

She then stops, nods as if she's made a decision. She steps back and walks out, leaving me alone in the cold bathroom.

Chapter 10

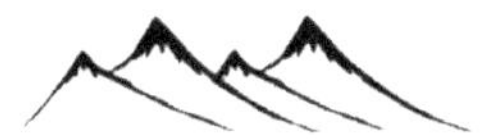

Harmony of Heartbreak & Hiding

Locked in the bathroom door with the same energy as a skunk trapped in an outhouse, I cry until my mascara is off my eyelashes and staining my cheeks.

"Okay," I whisper, aiming my phone at the ceiling in a desperate search for a signal. Darius must have left early—otherwise he'd already be kicking in the door with an oat-milk latte and a rescue plan.

"Lisa. I need Lisa. She'll know what to do." I tap her contact.

One ring. Two. Voicemail.

"Lisa, pick up. I'm hiding in the bathroom at work. There is major *drama*. I need an immediate rescue because I cannot walk through the office right now."

Before I can try again, my phone buzzes.

Unknown number.

I squint. "Ugh. Telemarketer roulette?" Maybe Lisa lost her phone and is calling from a stranger's. Or maybe I've won the lottery. Neither could make this day weirder.

My thumb hovers. My stomach flops. I answer, because apparently I'm clinging to the illusion of being a functioning adult.

"Hello?" I try sounding normal, not the mascara-raccoon-in-the-middle-of-an-identity-crisis mess I really am.

"Hi, this is Linda calling from Dr. Winters' office. I'm reaching out to schedule your follow-up appointment regarding recent labs and screening results."

I don't breathe. My tongue's too dry, and my heart rate increases.

"Uh—sure." My voice cracks. "Let's schedule that." *Before I lose my insurance.*

I drag myself upright, leaning against the sink. Lemon bleach and regret scent the air. My stomach fists into a tight ball.

"How's this Thursday?" Linda chirps. "You'll meet with Dr. Winters to go over your test results in person."

"Super," I manage, even though my brain is still juggling my surprise-dad revelation and the boss who gave me frostbite instead of the emotional support I needed.

'Test results.' I roll the ominous phrase around in my brain. *What could they have found?* Flesh-eating gonorrhea? I think I saw pictures of that in my high school biology class.

"Eleven o'clock on Thursday. See you then," she says. Click.

I slump against the cool wall, eyes on the speckled ceiling tiles as if they might hold divine instructions for my future. Alexis might fire me. My dad has been living in the same city my whole life. The universe is drunk and hates me.

Opening my phone and calendar, I add the appointment since I'm pretending to be an adult.

A knock rattles the door. Lisa? Grant? Darius? Alexis?

"Occupied!" I squeak, scrambling to wipe my face.

"Janitorial," a muffled voice answers. "Just checking."

Of course. Even the janitor gets to witness my meltdown.

"Totally fine!" I call back. "Just... uh... doing important emotional maintenance!"

Silence, then an annoyed sigh. Footsteps retreat.

Great. Somewhere out there, a stranger now knows that there's an emotionally unstable woman hiding out in the bathroom.

"Pull it together, girl," I tell myself.

My phone buzzes. Salvation?

Lisa—finally. Thank God.

Except... not a call. A text.

> MATCH CONFIRMED!
> Meet your date: Zara
> Age: 19
> Pronouns: She/Her
> Major: Biology at Anchorage University
> Interests: Dogs, hiking, obscure memes, reading thrillers, experimental muffin baking
> Fun fact: She once performed an impromptu puppet show about yeast. You'll love her geeky & cheeky vibes!

I groan. *Muffins?* Maybe she's an expert on obscure sexually transmitted diseases–that could be a bonus.

A picture loads. And—*Wow!*

Zara's got a leather jacket slung over one shoulder, a purple streak in her dark curls, and a grin that says I absolutely know where the spare handcuff keys are hidden. She's a university student hot enough to short-circuit my phone and make my stomach loosen with butterflies shaking out.

Maybe Lisa's right—I need a date and to run away from my workplace tornado.

Two weeks. That's when I start at Anchorage University. Two. Weeks. You'd think a soon-to-be freshman would know her start date and already be ready. But here I am, having a mental breakdown that's totally un-school-related.

Textbooks. I should buy them before the bookstore sells out. My scholarship does not cover therapy for "ran out of used and have to pay full-priced for textbooks drama." And with my work—and my health insurance—in limbo, I can hear my mom's laugh echoing at how disastrous my life is.

A purple-streaked university wing-woman would totally be perfect right now.

The phone pings again.

"Heard Lisa set us up. Drinks tonight still good? Or do we cancel and start a black-market university muffin ring instead? I'm game for some university shenanigans."

A laugh bubbles up—unexpected and real. Lisa matched me with a fun date---I'm totally into Zara.

My fingers fly. "Tempting. But I'm more of a cupcake-crime kind of girl. Drinks are safer... mostly. I can't start my university career off with a criminal enterprise."

"Define 'safer.' Planning our university mafia takeover is a tame first date."

"I do know a few good places to hide... cupcakes. Let's plan!"

Three dots flash. My chest warms for the first time all day.

"Okay," I whisper to the mirror. "I deserve a carefree date. Zara, here I come!"

Because what else am I going to do—cry over a CEO who couldn't pause her power schedule long enough to ensure I was okay after my life changing event of meeting my father?

Not tonight, Satan. Nope. No. There will be no emotional doom spiraling for me. I'm faking like I have a normal university student life. I will be drinking trendy cocktails and discussing university stuff, if we don't decide to be mafia-bad and make muffins together.

Tonight, I will meet an edgy science major who might be weird enough to match my chaotic energy. Plus, Lisa worked hard to set this up. She promised me the perfect setup and threatened my spot on her couch if I didn't go.

I grab my makeup bag and dig for my boldest red lipstick. In my haste, it slips, smearing a crimson streak across my cheek.

"Perfect," I mutter, blotting the mistake with a paper towel. The smear leaves a rosy smudge—so I roll with it and smudge the other cheek. Nothing is stopping me from finding fun tonight.

Another buzz.

"I'll be at the bar wearing mafia black. Lisa said you'll be in a green dress, right?"

My green dress is killer-level seduction. I text back a thumbs up. Taking one last look at the accidental blush, I decide it works.

When I open the door, the hallway is quiet. No trace of Alexis. No ghost of judgment. Just me, my phone, and a plan to ignore my personal dumpster fire and play at being a normal, happy, university student.

"Okay, world," I whisper. "Let's go flirt and ignore everything else."

Because if I've learned anything?

Heartbreak can wait–it'll wait for me behind the next corner of happiness.

Chapter 11

Crab Dip and Accidental Catfishing

What is my first rule for psyching myself up for a date? Blast Lizzo until my eardrums ring. The second rule? Pretend the rogue Enya track that sneaks onto your "You Got This, Girl" playlist is there on purpose—like a mystical hype-woman.

I sit in the car outside Glacier Brewhouse, fingers tapping the steering wheel like I'm auditioning for a nervous-drummer competition. My hair is a red, frizzy halo, which I've labeled "intentionally chaotic." I'm wearing the baby-pink bomber jacket I thrifted for six dollars on the way here, because my green dress was a little too formal. I look chic and quirky— I'm going for the Alaskan university student vibe.

This is the opposite of Alexis's steel-gray CEO blazer that still haunts my closet and what I've been wearing all week.

Alexis. Even thinking her name is pressing a bruise. I'd wear the blazer if I had a fifteen-year life plan—which I don't, because that requires grown-up things like savings and a defined career path. I'd *be* the blazer. Instead, I'm a girl in a bubble-gum jacket who sweats through it like a Costco rotisserie chicken.

"Fun," I mutter, wiping my palms on my dress. Tonight is supposed to be about fun. Not about the blazer-wearing woman who broke my heart. Maybe I was too harsh on Alexis. My mom really screwed up normal relationships for me, so I could be pushing away the best chance at a healthy relationship by giving up on Alexis.

The cold air hits like a peppermint slap when I finally step out. Across the parking lot, a moose lumbers through a strip of frozen shrub—because Alaska is Alaska even in the city. The beast, utterly unimpressed, flicks an ear at me, then disappears behind a pickup. Good omen? Bad omen? Ambiguous moose omen.

Zara stands by the Brewhouse doors, scrolling her phone. She's tall, with a black blazer draped over a dark black-green top, making her olive skin glow like a Northern Lights ad. Tiny gold clips pin back short curls. She looks like a sexy academic who moonlights as a jazz pianist. I'm relieved she's wearing a blazer since I hoped blazers would still fit my university-student vibe.

I promptly catch my toe on an invisible crack and flail. "Oh, hey! You must be... Zara?"

She looks up to see me stumble towards her. And her dimples appear. *Lord help me.*

"I am," she says, smiling like I'm as harmless as the lumbering moose. "And you must be Summer?"

"Yup!" My voice leaps an octave. "Well—technically Aurora. Summer's just my nickname. You can call me Aurora. Or Summer. But not Winter, obviously, that would be confusing."

Smooth.

Her dimple deepens. "Aurora fits you. I like it."

Cue blushing.

Inside, the hostess leads us to a corner booth near the stone fireplace. Not close enough to roast my bomber-jacketed armpits, but the glow warms the room in that cozy, tourist-trap way.

Zara scans the menu. "So, Aurora, is it your policy to impress dates with aggressively Alaskan entrees? I see at least three species of salmon competing for our starter."

"Only the best ones," I shoot back. "If it smells like salmon, you're in the right place."

She grins. "The fishy motto I base all major life decisions on."

I laugh. We've skipped the awkward small talk and jumped straight to the "I already get your weird " stage.

"I have to ask," I say, leaning in conspiratorially. "Did you drive your U-Haul to this date?"

"You know me." She winks. "Three cats and a sourdough starter are waiting in the parking lot."

I snort. "How did you know what my favorite after dinner activity is?"

"Lesbian Romance 101. I'm a third year university student," she fires back, batting her eyelashes.

Conversation flows like we've been doing this for years. She listens with a calm, anchored energy while I babble about when twelve-year-old me tried to sell lemonade but only had Jell-O mix. Customers paid out of pity. I bought a bumblebee-werewolf-tooth-fairy costume and wore it to school. She counters with a story about asking the tooth fairy for marbles instead of cash until she had a collection big enough to start a small black market.

We trade thrift-store secrets. She shows me her prom photo—rocking her mom's old wedding dress like a queer Disney heroine—and I snort water through my nose. Twice.

"Careful," she says dryly, passing me a napkin. "I'm not premed. I can't save you from dry drowning."

"Too late," I say, dabbing my chin. "I've survived the near-drowning... but I'm not sure if your marble fever is contagious?"

"That's incurable," she deadpans. "Might mutate into a case of sourdough muffin mania."

"A muffin mania," I repeat, grinning. "Sounds delicious and very contagious."

Her eyes sparkle. "It's airborne... but only if you exhale near me."

I nearly choke again. She just smirks.

The waitress arrives with coconut prawns and a deliciously cheesy crab dip. As she sets the platter down, she catches a fragment of the conversation and politely asks if we'd like some disposable masks, to which we both laugh and shake our heads.

"So are you using a matchmaker because online dating is brutal?" I ask as we share the coconut prawn starter.

"No," she says, pulling out her phone. "There's nothing like a family wedding to force you to find a date."

She turns the screen to me and—

BOOM.

My heart drops. The photo is a nuclear bomb disguised as a marriage announcement.

Jaime.

Jaime Gunderson, the intern whose copy-room kisses cost me my last job. Jaime, the woman I thought was a butch lesbian, is in a tiara perched at a tipsy angle, holding a glittery "Team Bride" sign. She's next to a man I recognize, Mark, from the wedding announcement I doom-read after our fling imploded.

"Oh!" The word erupts as a strangled cough.

Zara beams, misinterpreting my horror. "Yeah, that's my little sister. Total high-maintenance princess. Changed her wedding date three times to get her perfect ice-castle Disney Frozen wedding."

I nod so hard my brain rattles. "Totally. She's... disturbingly symmetrical."

Zara swipes to another photo: Jaime dressed as Elsa, her prince at her side.

"She finally settled on October," Zara says. "Girdwood. She wants actual ice sculptures of Olaf and Sven. I wish I were joking."

A snowball of dread smacks me right between the eyes. Jaime is her sister.

"...She's all frilly and blonde. We're total opposites, right?" Zara keeps chatting, not noticing my frozen face.

"Oh," I managed. "Your sister... is not queer."

"She's as straight as I am lesbian. I've never even kissed a boy," Zara murmurs with a wink. "My sister works some boring office gig." She tilts her head, noticing my silence. "You work temp jobs in offices. Ever run into her?"

Every nerve in my body searches for the nearest exit sign. "Um. Maybe? She looks kind of familiar."

"Probably the wedding announcements," Zara says. "Anchorage is basically a small town."

I laugh, high-pitched and haunted.

So much for "honesty is my new dating policy." Outing Jaime would be a betrayal. Admitting I did get fired for a copy-room make-out with her... Also not casual, fun first-date material.

Zara sips her lager, unfazed. "I've been braving the dating pool mostly because her wedding's coming up. I need a date. My ex bailed—moved to Juneau to raise pygmy goats with her ex."

"That's... aggressively Alaskan," I say, trying not to hyperventilate.

"I'm not looking to get married to compete with her," Zara adds, amused. "I was hoping to have a fun date. I want to meet someone who could be my date for her wedding next month. It could actually be really hilarious and fun."

My pulse thuds. Lisa set me up on this date knowing... *what, exactly?* Does she know who Zara's sister is?

"I'm not asking you to go... Yet," Zara says. "Lisa promised you are chill. I'm just warning you of my nefarious intentions that this is a rehearsal for a potential posh wedding date." Then she leans forward and with a sparkle in her eyes ass, "That and the cats waiting in my Uhaul in the parking lot."

She clinks her glass against mine.

"That sounds... fun. *Funny.* I mean fun times. An Alaska, very posh Disney wedding," I say, my tight around the rambling words.

"You're weird," she says warmly. "I like it."

My *be myself* and *be honest* plan has left the building. I'm halfway through the crab dip and no closer to an escape route.

"You okay?" Zara asks. "You look like you've seen a ghost."

"I always look like this," I say, scrambling. "Auburn hair. Genetic condition. I need a tan to look less... haunted."

She laughs.

Kill me now.

I sip, stall, wonder if there's a hotline for "Help, I accidentally dated my ex-fling's sister."

Zara leans in, voice soft. "If you're not terrified, want to go out again? We could hit some university orientation events."

Her dimples tempt every reckless cell in my body. My heart screams 'Yes.' My guilt screams, 'Run.' My brain screams, 'Tell her.'

"I... think I'd like that," I whisper. "But it's... complicated."

Her smile falters, but she nods. "Recent breakup?"

I bite my lip and nod at the easy out she's given me.

"That's too bad," she says gently. "I was looking forward to our goodnight kiss."

Oh no. What if she kisses like Jaime—too hot, too much, too everything. And then there's Alexis, whose kisses are a whole different kind of wildfire.

My spine locks like an emotional taser hit.

Abort mission.

"Wow, look at the time," I blurt, springing up like a startled cat. "I just remembered I have a... taxidermy emergency."

Zara blinks. "Really?"

"My aunt's ferret is getting stuffed. I promised I'd help pick the pose. Very emotional. Lots of grief." Words tumble, nonsensical from my lips.

Across the room, the waitress glides past again. "Pick the sleeping pose," she advises, deadpan. "Trust me." Then she disappears, carrying a tray of halibut.

Zara bites her lip, eyes glittering. "Text me whenever," she says, amusement spilling into a dimpled grin.

Outside, snow begins to fall—slow, lazy flakes spinning in the glow of the parking-lot lights. The moose from earlier stands in the distance like a silent chaperone.

I hug my bomber jacket tighter, heart a mess of guilt and what-ifs.

Zara isn't the problem. Zara's amazing—smart, funny, flirty enough to make my pulse misbehave. But what I want from her is starting to feel less like fireworks and more like the warm glow of a best friend I don't deserve yet.

The problem is me. I'm the constant in creating my hot messes.

Chapter 12

Emo Wingwoman Wanted

Lisa sits cross-legged on her kitchen counter, a pretty blonde gargoyle in high-waisted jeans. She is shoveling handfuls of caramel popcorn into her mouth while I pace the tile floor and chew on my nails.

"Okay, back up," she says around a mouthful, pointing at me with the bag like it's a wand. "You went on the date I set up. It was going well. She was hot. You were wearing the green dress, chatting her up. And then?"

I pivot on the tile, chew a fingernail, pivot again. "And then," I say, voice climbing into a whine, "I realized I already knew her sister. Well—knew her. Biblically."

Lisa chokes so hard that popcorn sprays across the stove. "There's a threesome with the sister?!" she shrieks. "Please tell me you mean Zara—motorcycle dyke vibes Zara—and not boring-lawyer Harper."

"No!" I flop into a chair with a tragic flourish. "This was before. Her sister is Jaime—the intern I was... You know. Office-closet situation. The engaged intern."

Lisa's jaw drops, then she fans herself with a pizza-stained paper plate. "Jaime. Really?"

"Jaime was a mistake," I groan. "And Zara has the same modelesque face, same humor, same—ugh—vibes. I need to stay far, far away."

She throws her head back and cackles so loud Mr. Whiskers yowls from the porch. "You have the worst luck. I'm never splitting a lottery ticket with you."

"We were vibing," I insist. "I told her my real name. We even planned to hit some university events. But I can't now. She doesn't even know her sister is... well... at least a little bi."

"Dramatic! Your dating life is like those snow caves we built when we were on the playground. Remember, they collapsed and almost killed us!" she laughs, then gasps. "What happened next?"

She gasps. "Wait—did you kiss her?"

"No!" I clutch my heart in mock offense. "And the cherry on top? Zara invited me to Jaime's wedding."

Lisa almost slides off the counter. "Yasss! You have to go. Can I come?"

"No." I shoot her a death glare. "So I panicked and ran."

Lisa folds over in silent laughter, shoulders shaking. "Tell me you at least left, claiming a dramatic workplace emergency."

"Worse." I cover my face. "I claimed a taxidermy emergency. Aunt's ferret. Emotional grieving. And then I bolted."

Her slow, pitying nod is the kind normally reserved for reality-show eliminations. "So... you're an emotional mess. And you can't keep bringing up taxidermy, like it's normal. That's so bizarre. Anything else?"

I groan into my palms. "Oh, just a casual morning surprise–not the good kind!"

Lisa stops mid-crunch. "Did Alexis break up with you?"

My mouth falls open. "No! Why would—" I swallow. "I might've sort of broken up with her? I'm not sure."

"Knew it," she says with a shrug.

"She chose work over me," I blurted. "The surprise was that my long-lost father showed up at work. I'm at the office, and my new boss strolls in. Turns out *Grant is my dad. And* Alexis knew."

Lisa's popcorn bag freezes mid-air. "Wow. Brutal." Then, more cheerfully, "When I saw him at the Gala I thought he was totally a Zaddy! He's tall like you. Total wholesome-dad energy."

I press my fingertips into my eyes. "Maybe. He shook my hand, said it was great to meet me, and—get this—had a picture of me in his wallet. I panicked and ran again. Two for two."

"Drama magnet," she declares. "What does Darius think?"

"He left early. Missed the whole thing."

Lisa flings both arms up like she's summoning thunder. "Only *I know* this? SHUT. UP."

"I wish I could."

She grins, wicked and delighted. "This proves I'm your best friend. Also, if your long-lost dad is as rich as he looks, can he adopt me? Oh wait, he could date me!"

I sigh. "Anyway, I bolted. Then I went on the date with Zara and bolted again." I cover my red face.

"And you ran away from talking to Alexis, too," she added, "It's a triathlon event!"

"Lisa. My hot mess is spreading to every part of my life. I'm seriously more of a disaster than I was when I thought I'd have to give up on university and move back in with my mom."

Lisa shakes her head. Darius and I would never let that happen to you."

I grab some of her sticky popcorn and chew.

Mr. Whiskers chooses our conversational pause to saunter in and meow loudly with his tail flicking. He hops onto the counter, sniffs the popcorn, and deliberately knocks a kernel to the floor.

"See? Even the cat agrees," Lisa says. "You are a big hot mess."

I swipe the rogue kernel from under my sneaker. "He's just being playful."

Mr. Whiskers yowls again, which definitely sounds like "He's agreeing with the hot mess sentiment."

Lisa laughs so hard she nearly falls. "Your cat-therapist is totally telling you to stop running and eat the messy popcorn."

"He's not," I protest, though Mr. Whiskers immediately starts eating a popcorn kernel.

Lisa cocks her head and grabs another caramel handful. "So, what now? Are you going to actually talk to Grant?"

I shrug. "Eventually? Maybe? My avoidance skills are Olympic-level at this point."

"You have to," she says, pacing. "What did Alexis say?"

My chest tightens like it's caught under a snowplow. "She apologized, kind of. But we haven't had a real conversation. She's been... distant. Busy. CEO-butch in full work mode."

"Her first duty is to *you*," Lisa declares. "Not telling you? *Unacceptable.*"

"She tried to explain," I mumble. "I didn't exactly give her a chance."

Lisa softens. "You'll talk to Grant and Alexis–it's inevitable. And Darius—if he weren't in a love coma with Richard—would already be here with a sweet therapy latte."

"I have my schedule in my email inbox from Darius so I'm not fired," I mutter, stroking the purring cat, and realizing my mistake when the hair is stuck to my caramel fingers. "I should *call* Darius."

"Nope." She bats the phone from my hand. "Let me keep the secret a little longer. It gives me power."

"Evil," I say, laughing.

"You'll miss me when you move to the dorms," she singsongs.

"I won't miss your bad dates."

"That's on you, babe. Zara was a solid choice—you just turned your chaos magnet up to eleven."

I rub my fingers through the soft fur of the caramel kitty pushing against me begging for more attention, and sigh. "Tomorrow, I'm going to talk to Grant."

"Very mature." She salutes me with the popcorn bag. "I'll come as your emotional wingwoman."

"Darius is there. I can handle it. I think."

Lisa hops off the counter, sets the bag down, and slips beside me. Her warm hand squeezes mine. "Still. If you need backup, I'm in."

"Maybe I'll talk to Alexis too," I say quietly. "If she's worth it—"

"You're worth it," she cuts in, firm and quick.

My eyes sting. I blink hard.

"Talk to her before this turns into one of those tragic workplace romances where everyone ends up emotionally scorched," Lisa says.

I groan, leaning on her shoulder. "I'm having PTSD from my so-called fun date. Maybe I should call my therapist."

Lisa nodded and pressed her cheek to my hair. "Sounds like you're already figuring it out."

Mr. Whiskers purrs his approving little therapist engine, and looks outside the kitchen window. The birch trees drip golden leaves onto grass crusted with the season's first frost.

Chapter 13

From Cat-astrophe to Coffee

Rawrh!

Mr. Whiskers jumps at me, his tail catching in the door for a second as it slams shut. I huff, looking down at the warm bundle of cat in my arms. We are now, officially, locked out of the apartment.

"Not great," I mutter, standing barefoot in a towel, holding a tabby. This was the absolutely wrong day to call in late and take an extra-long, blissful shower.

I can't knock because my roommate, emotional wingwoman, and best friend Lisa snuck out earlier. In her sweet, soothing voice, she'd reminded me, "I will be ready to rescue you and get a mani/pedi with you, if needed. And even if *not* needed, Girl."

I *actually* do need her. *Now!* With my stressful new assignment this morning and anxiety-inducing to-do list looming over me, I wasn't paying attention. An early morning knock disrupted my verbal rehearsal of what I'll say to Grant this morning. And after tackling that–the worst daily task–I can finally focus on my university book list, then try to clear things up with Alexis.

But today's dumpster-fire triage plan is lost, turning into an uncontrolled wildfire. Because in one second, disaster has already struck. Now I'm here, barefoot, shivering, towel-clad, cradling a warm loaf of cat fluff, and jiggling a locked doorknob that isn't budging. My thin towel is soaking wet. The only thing worse than being locked out is being locked out in freezing weather with only a dripping towel.

"Are you locked out, or starting a morning clothing-optional running club?" a deep voice calls out.

I freeze. Literally, my toes are tingling from the cold ground. I turn around slowly, trying to keep the towel in place.

Our hot next-door neighbor is standing ten feet away, in his full navy fire department uniform, biceps stretching the sleeves in a way that should be illegal. Lisa calls him "Hot Ember Daddy," which I've fought her on, since fire people deserve respect. However, the nickname... fits.

"Uh," I say, because all brain function has temporarily abandoned me. "Wow! You have the fastest response time in history. I haven't even dialed for help yet."

He grins, which makes his serious face light up with a cute, mischievous sparkle. He's attractive, for sure. But there are no butterflies or weak knees for me—just a calm reassurance that I'm one hundred percent team lesbian.

"I respond quickly to cat-related emergencies. They can easily get out of hand," he says with a sparkle in his eyes.

Mr. Whiskers meows at him. *The traitor.*

My arms tighten instinctively around the cat. He purrs louder, the sound rumbling against my chest.

"Yep," I mumble, shifting my weight and praying the towel doesn't move too. With the morning chill, I'm too cold to be embarrassed.

He chuckles and walks closer, hands raised like I'm the skittish cat. "I'm your neighbor. Liam. I've seen you and your partner before. It's nice to meet you."

"Oh, no, Liam. I'm Aurora," I say, my words tumbling over each other. "And Lisa's not my partner. She's my... I mean she's my partner in late-night ice-cream crimes and questionable life choices but... We are just roommates. I mean, *I'm gay.* She's straight. *Not that it matters.* I just... I don't want you to think... anyway. It's nice to meet you, too." I finish in a breathless rush, my cheeks flushing crimson.

He laughs, a warm and genuine chuckle that instantly melts away the awkwardness of the encounter.

He blinks, then snorts cutely.

Suddenly, I'm acutely aware that my towel is way too thin. He nods at the purring traitor. "I can't help but notice your pussy."

"Uhhh," I exhale, holding my town tighter around myself. "Excuse me?"

My mind races. Did he just... did he *really?* My cheeks burn even hotter. I check my towel. It's still covering my important bits. Thank God!

He points. "My cat. Mr. Whiskers. He cheats on me constantly and thinks I don't notice that he's sneaking off."

I groan into the cat's fur, burying my face in the soft fluff. "Oh, you're Mr. Whiskers' owner. I thought I'd be arrested for public indecency."

"No charges yet," he teases, the playful glint back in his eyes. "Also, I'm not a cop. But can I help you get back inside?"

I nod, my teeth chattering. "Thanks."

"No worries." Liam sets down a large bag, his fire department jacket crinkling. Then, he reaches behind it and magically pulls out a long crowbar.

The door swings open with a satisfying thud.

"You," I exhale, "Are a hero. A cat-saving, door-opening hero of half-naked damsels in distress."

"Always happy to rescue a damsel in... a towel," he responds, his boyish grin appearing again.

"Well, I promise that I'll write you a glowing Yelp review. Five stars. Would recommend being rescued by Liam."

He laughs. "Do you have time to discuss Mr. Whiskers' custody arrangement? He could use the extra love this week since I work one week on and one week off."

Ding! *An idea.*

Before he can escape me to rest after what was probably a long shift, I blurt out, “Liam, are you single?”

He blinks. “Uh, yes?”

“Perfect. My friend is allergic to commitment but not hot firefighters. She’s blonde, with good vibes, and likes cats.”

“Only if I can set you up with my hot firefighting friend, Brenda*,” he says with a charming sparkle in his eyes. “Brenda is looking for a fiery redhead, just like you. I think she’d find you adorable.”

His laugh echoes in the hallway. Then tilts his head and adds, “But I can tell you’re not exactly single.”

I furrow my brow, confused. “What do you mean? I just said I’m gay.”

Liam’s grin widens as he points to my doorway. “You might want to grab that before it freezes, Aurora.”

I glance at the doormat, “Welcome-ish–depending on if you brought tacos!” Something large and absurdly beautiful sits beside it—*how did I miss that?*

A cookie the size of a steering wheel, frosted in pale pink swirls and edible glitter. In the middle, the looping cursive spells out:

> Aurora, I’m sorry. You’re it. You’re my #1!
> —Alexis

My breath trips over my tongue, and I choke on spit. The morning chill disappears in a rush of heat that has nothing to do with the rush of warmth radiating from the open door.

Alexis.

The world narrows to two things: the sound of my pounding heart and the name printed on the card.

Liam follows my stare, eyebrows lifting. “Whoa. That’s... one hell of an apology cookie. Somebody’s trying to win you back.”

Enjoy Brenda's misadventures in the bestselling Lesbian Disaster Romance set in the small town of Cooper Landing, Alaska in *Wilderness Rescue: Flooded Hearts.*

CHECK IT OUT HERE or at HarmonyNoble.com.

Chapter 14

A Workplace Family Reunion

The scent of fresh-brewed coffee and wet spruce follows me into Alaska Cruise & Tours. Grant's laugh echoes from down the hallway, deep and too warm for the tirade of righteous, eighteen-year-old guilt I'd prepared this morning. My inner script had me delivering a withering monologue about abandonment, but his chuckle derails me.

Kathleen, the sweet receptionist—or is she my step-mom now—waves from behind a towering stack of brochures. "Morning, Aurora! Coffee's fresh. You're here early and not soon enough, dear," she says, her smile radiating that specific, calming energy only found in people who genuinely love spreadsheets. "We have a mess of summer accounting files that need your magic touch, dear."

"Thanks," I croak, my voice not cooperating with my confident blazered look. "I wanted to catch Grant... about, you know, everything. Before I start my assignment."

Her eyes soften. "He'll be right with you," Kathleen sings, leading me to his office to wait. "He's been nervously looking forward to today, actually," she says, leaning in conspiratorially. "The man has been here since seven am."

Nervous? Good. He should be. He's the guy who lit the match yesterday and has taken a rain check on me for my entire childhood.

My phone pings with an email.

> From: Alexis Anders
> Subject: Meet after lunch?
> Body: You free at 1 pm? I'd like to check in.
> ~A

Alexis. It's hard to stay mad at someone who bought me an oversized, gourmet chocolate chip cookie as a peace offering. My internal dialogue is a mess, but my fingers are surprisingly cooperative. I type back, "Sounds good. Thanks again for the sugar bribe. Hugs, Aurora."

Hugs. I instantly second-guess it. Is *Hugs* too much? Too fast? Too... not-professional-but-needy-girlfriend? But she *did* send me a pastry the size of a frisbee this morning. And having a proper, adult talk with her is the next item on my to-do list.

I lick my lips, thinking of her. I picture her clearing her calendar for a scheduled make-out session with me in her sleek, glass-walled office, making me bite back a smile. At least with her apology and meeting, that's one thing I don't have to worry about today.

I text Darius, "I'm at Alaska Tours and Cruise. About to face the man who says he's my dad. I'll be stopping by your office after lunch. And hopefully, I'll be reporting that there's much less drama in my life."

He responds instantly, "Less drama? This is Aurora, right? You're adorable. Never change."

I'm sweating sitting at Grant's pristine, mahogany-topped desk. Not a cute glow. I'm talking about my full-on nervous hands-shaking level. "You've got this," I whisper to myself, trying to project confidence. "Channel your inner Alaskan wolverine. Make eye contact. Assert dominance. And tell Grant how you feel."

How do I feel?

Happy? Confused? Angry? Like I need to scream into a pillow and eat another ginormous cookie.

A sudden, aggressive need to bolt out of this office hits me. I don't move, refusing to give in to the impulse. My all-weather, cute office boots stay glued to the polished floor. I glance at the door. *I could escape.*

But then I see it.

The photo frame is on the credenza behind Grant's desk. It's a double wooden frame.

One side: Me. Laughing during a fifth-grade school picture, where I decided wearing fairy wings was totally appropriate. And the other side is a crowded, blurry picture.

What is that doing here?

Kathleen notices my attention and moves the picture to face me. "He keeps it right on his desk," she explains.

I can't breathe. I pick up the photo, unable to talk, possessed by the sudden, brutal weight of my father's unseen love.

Grant walks in and stops dead, looking at me holding the double frame. He offers a warm, hesitant smile. I look at the other side of the frame—a far-off, blurry picture of me on stage for my high school graduation. It's zoomed in, grainy, but unmistakably me in my itchy cap and gown with slicked back hair and very red lipstick, thanks to Darius's styling.

"Your mom told me not to go," he says, nodding at the graduation shot on the other side. "But I *had* to see you graduate. With honors, no less. Great job."

He's grinning like a proud dad, making me shake my head in confusion.

I glance back at him, and I grip the frame. "Hi... Grant."

He's tanned like he's the client of the cruise business, not the head of it. And he's wearing one of those rugged, outdoorsy Alaskan fleece zip-ups instead of a corporate suit. His eyes—they're the same arresting green as mine.

"Hi, Aurora."

My perfectly articulated rage speech is now shredded confetti in my brain.

The silence has weight, like a blanket woven from missed moments. My stomach's rebelling, and my mouth is dry. I open my mouth to shout—to rage—to ask where the hell he's been for eighteen years of science fairs, scraped knees, and prom nights with no one to threaten my dates.

But the photos anchor me. I look back down, trying to make sense of them, this, him, us.

"I know it's not the best pic,," he says quietly, gesturing to the blurry graduation shot. "It was from the very back of the auditorium, and I couldn't really see much."

"I don't understand," I whisper, the words feeling too fragile for the cold Alaskan air. "Why didn't you—why now?"

He steps around the desk, stopping at a polite distance away. "I was trying to find an easy, non-threatening way to reconnect since you're an adult now. I had made a promise to your mom—a painful promise, but one I kept—that I wouldn't contact you and I'd let *you* reach out if you wanted to contact me. After you turned eighteen, I was finally free to try. I didn't expect to see you at a job interview for my company, and it felt like a sign that you were ready."

"I didn't... I didn't know who you were then," I finish, lamely. Heat floods my cheeks, anger and wonder all tangled. "She told you to stay away?"

Grant sighs and runs a hand over his face. The businessman's facade cracks. "Your mom, Sandra... she told me it'd be better if I stayed away. She said you were happy, thriving. She said any contact from me would complicate things, that your life was challenging enough. I would confuse you. Every year, she'd send me a photo, a report card, and proof that you were doing well. She always said you didn't want contact. I believed her and thought I was doing the right thing for *you*."

Sharper than glacial wind, betrayal slices through my frozen emotional confusion. "Well, she lied."

"I should've guessed." He nods, his gaze heavy with regret. "I don't know you, but I did know her. I should have tried harder to break through the wall she built around you. I'm sorry, Aurora. That's on me. I regret every day that I didn't try harder to get to know you."

"I wanted... I wondered so many times... I never knew what happened," I say, my words jumbled as my hand clutching the picture shakes violently.

"I wanted to be in your life, Aurora. I did tried when you were little, but Sandra made sure you never heard from me. She insisted I'd confuse and upset you," he says, adding, "She said that you didn't need the extra chaos."

I blink fast, a humorless laugh escaping. "I got plenty of chaos anyway."

A slow, genuine grin tugs at his mouth. "Maybe that's from the Fairbanks family side. We tend to bring chaos and be the spirited type. I hope you'll get to see that side of the family."

And just like that, my emotional volcano of eighteen years of built-up anger sputters. It doesn't die—that would be impossible—but it melts into grief. My sad confusion tastes like missed birthdays and Christmases with no dad jokes and school dances where I made up some fake 'cool dad' who lived in Oregon and was a professional ice sculptor.

I wipe under my eyes with the sleeve of my absorbent wool blazer. Dignified? No. But functional? Absolutely.

"I wanted to hate you," I mumble, looking at the pictures. "But I didn't know enough about you to feel anything. Now I'm not sure."

The glowing Alaskan sun, a rare treat in this cloudy weather, peeks out from the morning clouds and hits my face in the photo. My face lights up even more, the smile mocking my current state.

"I know anything I say is too little, too late. I'm just hoping to be a part of your life now, if you'll let me." Grant's voice is soft and warm.

"Well, I did sign a contract to work here," I say with a shrug and smile.

He steps closer, voice low. "Maybe we can start a relationship now. *If you want.*"

Something in my chest unclenches. "Yeah," I whisper. "I'd like that."

He gently takes the frame from my hands and pulls me into a hug. His hug is warm, steady. He smells of the outdoors and office paper—everything I didn't know I missed. It's the kind of hug I've never had, the kind a dad gives—firm, unconditional, and utterly grounding.

Kathleen peeks in, all smiles and sparkling eyes. "Tissues? I brought tissues. And also, your sister."

I blink, pulling back from Grant. My internal monologue screeches to a halt. "My what?"

A girl, slightly younger than me, walks in. Tall, slender, and beautifully sweetly gawky. She has a brown braid down to her waist and holds a thick, worn notebook like a shield. She's wearing an oversized hoodie that says "Otters Rule" with an otter playing a lute. She looks beautiful and shy.

Grant beams, his eyes shining. "Aurora, meet Indie. Your half-sister."

Indie waves awkwardly, a quick flick of the wrist. "Hi. I like your boots."

I blink. "I… have a sister?"

"You do," Grant says.

Kathleen nods and places a hand on Indie's shoulder. "Grant and I met shortly after he and Sandra broke up. We didn't even know about you until we were married and pregnant with Indie. When we found out, we told her as soon as she was old enough to understand. She's been begging to meet you since she was little."

I'm a big sister. My heart does a cartwheel.

Indie inches forward. "Will you come to Friday pasta night?"

"I—" My vocabulary has been reduced to single-syllable exclamations.

Kathleen explains, touching my shoulder gently. "We have a family dinner night at our place every Friday. You have a big family in Anchorage," she says, pointing at other pictures lining the desk. "There are cousins, aunts, and more who live nearby and come to the city for family dinners." Then she laughs and adds, "They really come to the city for Costco shopping trips, but they come to dinner, too. They'd all love to meet you."

My throat chokes up again, like someone shoved a whale-sized lump of emotion in there. "I'd love that," I whisper. "I mean, pasta. And family. I'm in."

Her face lights up. "You can listen to my music."

"She's in a band," Kathleen says, beaming. "They practice in the garage, usually to the confusion of the neighbors."

I crack a grin, finding my awkward footing. "Of course."

Kathleen laughs, the sound like wind chimes. "Welcome to the family, Aurora."

Grant clears his throat, shifting back into the CEO role with a new, softer edge. "And whenever you're ready, you can start your temp accounting work here. There's no rush, you can take your time."

"Alexis just approved my schedule and I'm supposed to be here this week," I explained.

"We'll work around your university schedule. Data entry doesn't need to be during office hours, especially during the slow season," he says with a shrug, ready to accommodate me.

I nod, still wonderfully dazed. "Well, Alexis said I'd be working here for a few months. Since she's writing the paychecks, I'll make sure she's okay with the hours."

"Great," Kathleen says.

"Alexis is more than my boss," I say, then, "She's my mentor, and she took a big chance hiring me." I decide to not mention the oversized cookie or the possibility of her becoming my girlfriend. That can wait until after I talk with her. Maybe I'll even bring her to Friday's dinner and she can meet my family with me.

I turn to Indie, who nervously flips through her notebook filled with handwritten notes. "Guess the awkward tall-girl gene runs strong. I'm thrilled to have a sister. It's great to meet you, Indie."

"I'm so so happy that I'm not taller than my big sister," she says with mock drama standing on her tiptoes to try to be taller than me.

I laugh. "Well you are still an impressively tall, little sister. You're perfect."

"You're perfect too—better than your pictures!" she blurts, causing us all to laugh.

The laughter relieves the lingering tension, and the office suddenly feels less like a corporate landscape and more like a home.

Kathleen squeezes my shoulder. "I'll email you our address."

"Fridays," Grant confirms, his hand resting on my shoulder momentarily. "Or really, you can stop by the house anytime." A simple, easy, familial gesture.

I excuse myself, slipping away to the dimly lit employee restroom, seeking refuge from the relentless buzz of the office. The office's loud atmosphere replaces the nervous pulse thrumming in my head—phones jangle insistently, and the excited chatter of tourists entering as they eagerly plan their adventures.

Standing before the mirror, I confront my reflection: eyes swollen and puffy, cheeks a chaotic patchwork of color.

Yet, in this disheveled state, I feel so much more alive... so much more... me.

Gone is the polished professional facade I planned to be in this office, the one I wear for Alexis. It's the put-together persona that masks my insecurities, and hides under her expensive blazer.

I'm not the confused, insecure girl who didn't know if I could make it or even fake making it.

Instead, here I stand, a beautiful contradiction: a happy sister, a welcomed daughter, an industrious office worker, and a dedicated university student all rolled into a messy bundle. In my unguarded honesty, I realize I have never looked more like my authentic self. I'm a radiant embodiment of joy and raw truth.

Chapter 15

After-work Karaoke Madness

O'Malley's pulses with reckless energy that can only come from cheap Ice Hole IPA, karaoke night, and locals with zero shame about belting out Celine Dion like they're headlining the Grammys. The air's thick with sweat, laughter, and the salty scent of stale bar nuts.

I'm still buzzing, a combination of my successful day with my newfound family and the promise of seeing Alexis again. She did make time for an afternoon meeting with me and repeated her apology in person. She assured me she will prioritizing me and not her work. Which is probably the most romantic thing a new CEO has ever said to their employee, almost-gf situationship.

O'Malley's is *my* domain. My turf. Not like the apartment that still needs to be cleaned or Alexis's polished, glass-tower universe. Here, I'm in my element.

"Tonight," I shout over a group rendition of "Bohemian Rhapsody," "we're testing our group chemistry. I'm hoping adding Richard and Alexis to our karaoke nights is way better than you trying to sing Britney Spears."

"It wasn't that bad," Darius says, raising his vodka cranberry. "And let the chaos begin."

Lisa is already halfway to dancing on the bar, shimmying in her sequin crop top. Her glitter eyeshadow could be seen from space, let alone through an Alaskan snowstorm. "I give it twenty minutes before I inspire someone to start stripping for us!" she yells, grinning like a blonde banshee.

"Please let it not be me," I mutter, tugging at the hem of my thrifted local band tee. I paired it with ripped jeans, a load of jangly bracelets, and a wide leather belt for a chaotic look. I can't show up to karaoke looking like a responsible, career-focused adult, because I'm leaning into artistic university student vibes tonight.

I click 'Yes' on my phone's pop-up reminder for tomorrow's doctor's appointment.

Alexis saunters like a Vogue cover come to life, all sleek lines and quiet Boss power. She's in a leather jacket that is too sleek to not have been made for her, and her black leather boots that click with the confidence of someone who has *never* tripped over a curb. I feel a weird little surge of pride seeing her here, in my world, out of place in this dive bar.

My heart does a tiny, frantic somersault.

"You came," I beam, pushing through a throng of rowdy fishermen.

She gives a soft smile, her eyes crinkling at the corners. "I told you and Richard I would. He made it sound like I'd miss the social event of the season with his plan to storm Anchorage's karaoke scene."

"Well, Lisa's already threatening public nudity, so Richard's got competition for who's going to be the most memorable tonight," I say, laughing.

"And how many drinks have you had?" she asks, her voice low and laced with amusement.

I grin innocently at Alexis. "One Ice Hole IPA, but Lisa's ordered us tequila shots and a Mystery Fish Bowl. It's a pink, cotton-candy-flavored nightmare. You'll love it."

Alexis scans the room, amusement flickering in her eyes. She stands slightly apart, arms crossed, like she's observing a new species.

Richard swoops in, dragging Darius toward the signup sheet. "Dibs on Shakira," he announces. "I know my hips."

"They lie," Darius retorts, but he's smiling. Always smiling distractedly when Richard's around. Love looks good on him.

I turn back to Alexis, trying to get her to myself before the karaoke madness ensues. "Tonight is about fun. Loosening up. No work, just play. My world, not yours."

She tilts her head, her dark eyes a steady, captivating contrast to the disco lights shining around us. "And what does your world look like? Besides glitter and neon?"

"Do you have a song picked out?" I deflect, pulling out my phone. "Because you can't just stand there looking super-sultry and cool. We've got an entire setlist I made. Tons of options."

Before I push Alexis to pick a song, Lisa claps her hands and shouts, "Okay, everyone! Let's get a booth!"

I'm sandwiched between Darius and Lisa in our usual booth, the vinyl seats sticking to my thighs in that charming way only dive bars can manage. Darius carries a tray for the tequila shots, a blue glittery mixing bowl with straws, and Lisa has a pitcher of the cheap IPA, her eyes sparkling with mischief.

"Okay, okay," Lisa says, slamming the pitcher down. "Remember last week when Aurora almost had a threesome with sisters? I promise you all that tonight's gonna be even better!"

I groan, burying my face in my hands. "Lisa, no."

"A threesome. Really?" Alexis asks, perched on the edge of the booth, looking ready for a gritty modeling shoot. She's staring directly at me, her gaze unwavering. My cheeks are already on fire.

"Oh, yes," Lisa grins, turning to Alexis. "She ran into an old flame's sister with the blind date I set up. Her luck is ah-maze-ing. Crazy sauce, right?"

Alexis raises an eyebrow, a smirk playing on her lips. "Impressive."

Darius cackles and takes the fish bowl from in front of me. "Girl, you have the best stories. I can't even imagine better soap opera dramas than the chaos you cause."

"It wasn't like that!" I protest, cheeks flaming hotter than a campfire. My stomach clenches, a familiar, sick feeling.

Lisa waves me off. "Then there's the BBQ you brought a date and a six-pack to that was actually an AA meeting."

Alexis chuckles, but there's a flicker of something in her eyes—amusement? Disapproval? Pity? My stomach twists.

"Lisa," I say, attempting to nudge the conversation in a different direction. "How about we keep those cringe-worthy tales under wraps until you're giving my wedding toast, huh?"

"Oh, come on," she pouts, her lower lip jutting out in her dramatic way. "I'm just highlighting your irresistible charm."

"Wait, you're really going to unearth my most cringeworthy moments while we're all chilling together for the very first time?" I protest, my heart racing like a runaway train.

"Remember that time Aurora thought she could snag the crown for prom queen?" Lisa chimes in, her eyes dancing with mischief.

A cold shiver races down my spine, and my stomach is on a rollercoaster. Oh no, not high school stories! I have a treasure trove of mortifying teenage angst tales that Alexis definitely doesn't need to be privy to tonight.

Darius freezes mid-sip of his drink, his eyes wide with horror. "Oh no," he whispers, as if he can sense the impending doom.

"Lisa," I hiss, my voice dropping to a frantic whisper, "Please don't."

But she just beams at me, a wicked grin on her face. "Too late!"

Alexis shifts beside me, posture still relaxed, but her eyes focus on my face.

"Picture this! Aurora, wearing a pink thrifted quinceañera dress that was way too big."

"Because it was free and a statement piece!" I shout, my ears burning. At the time, I thought it was a hilarious idea.

"She was trying to prove that you didn't need to be popular to be Prom Queen—you just needed to go big–real fluffy huge big—for the day of the vote," Darius explains to Alexis, trying to add context, but it just makes it worse. "She wore a dress that couldn't fit through the classroom doors for a whole school day."

I bury my face in my hands, wishing the vinyl booth would swallow me whole.

"Her mom, the school secretary, found out about it and removed her name from the ballot, so she did all that for nothing."

"I thought it was hilarious and a real performance art masterpiece, girl," Darius adds, attempting a rescue mission.

People at the next booth are cracking up. Lisa's cackling. I'm hiding my shame, attempting to drink the cotton-candy-flavored abomination in the fishbowl.

And Alexis? She's unreadable. She's not laughing. She's not frowning. Her expression is blank, somewhere between serious and amused, with her lips giving away her feelings by twitching.

My voice comes out tight, small. "Lisa, that's enough history for now."

"Oh come on! It was a funny moment!"

"*To you.*"

There's a silence, not long, but long enough for the weight of my humiliation to feel unbearable. My blood rushes so fast it's a hot tsunami crashing through me.

Alexis meets my gaze. There's a vibe in her expression I can't name. Not judgment. Not amusement. It's a deep, quiet look that cuts right through my defenses, right to the eighteen-year-old girl who was crushed by her own mom.

Lisa blinks. "What? What'd I—"

Darius cuts in fast, without hesitation, before Lisa can tell more of my embarrassing stories. "Time to settle a bet. Richard says he and Alexis will crush karaoke. I say Aurora and I are gonna smoke them like last year's peppered smoked salmon."

Richard grins. "Alexis promised to sing if I won pickleball this morning. Spoiler: I crushed it."

Alexis lifts an eyebrow at him. "I said I *might* sing."

Darius waves a hand. "Alexis, honey, even I know you're not gonna back down from a challenge."

"Fine. Let's settle this karaoke-style. Loser buys the next round," Alexis says, standing, her gaze still locked on mine. The offer is to me, not the group. It's a lifeline.

The tension thaws. We crowd the stage. Darius launches into a Spice Girls anthem with backup from me, complete with an alcohol-fueled interpretive dance. Richard and Alexis answer with an unexpectedly intense "Don't Go Breaking My Heart" duet that makes the bar erupt in laughter and sing-alongs. Their voices together are pure magic—Richard's intense and theatrical, Alexis's smooth and soulful. I watch them, a lump in my throat, half from the shame, half from the sheer, effortless chemistry they have.

Darius leans in, stage-whispering to me, "I was fifty-fifty on whether Alexis would show up tonight or cancel for her late afternoon meetings. But Richard assured me she'd be here."

My heart does a painful somersault. "She scheduled work meetings tonight?"

Darius shrugs but nods at the same time.

Lisa somehow grabs us all and drags us onstage as the music starts—"Don't Stop Believin'." Classic.

Darius grabs the mic, belting out the lyrics with theatrical flair. I join in, our voices harmonizing in a surprisingly decent duet.

Then it's Alexis and Richard's turn. Alexis's voice is smooth, sultry, and utterly captivating. Richard complements her perfectly, and I wonder if they really think they can steal the spotlight and win from Darius and me.

After the performance, we regroup at our booth, breathless and laughing.

"Okay, okay," Lisa says, wiping tears. "That was epic."

Alexis turns to me, her expression soft, quiet. "You were amazing up there."

I shrug, trying to play it cool. "I had a great group of singers with me."

She leans in, her voice barely above a whisper. "I think I can let you have the win."

My breath catches. The promise in her eyes is more than just about a karaoke contest. It's about a relationship, about her letting me in. And letting her see who I really am.

Arms thrown wide, hair a chaotic golden halo, Lisa is hitting her stride. Ever the chaos gremlin, she jumps onto the billiards table, shouting, "Dance party! Let's break your karaoke tie!"

Before anyone can stop her, she starts dancing on the pool table, pulling us up with her. The table groans under her weight. And the people around us are laughing and hooting as I shimmy at Alexis, who nods her head to the music. Richard spins Darius and dips him dangerously low.

The table cracks.

"Oh my god," I squeak.

Lisa topples backward into Richard's arms, laughing. "I was channeling Jennifer Lopez!"

Alexis walks up to the furious manager, pulls out her card like she's ordering room service. "Add it to my tab. And a round for the bar."

Cheers erupt. My heart stutters.

She turns to me, smirking. "You did win afterall, and you are my favorite, wonderful, cute chaos magnet."

"I'm just glad you came and are enjoying a fun night. A night off work," I say, leaning closer, my heart thumping.

Her smile falters, softens. "Yeah. I am too. I needed this more than you know."

I want to kiss her. I want to pull her away from the loud bar and just be in a silent moment with her, to thank her for not making me feel small or crazy or weird. But the tempo increases, and the crowd on the dance floor pushes us in opposite directions.

Later, as I'm catching my breath at the bar, Darius leans in. "You okay?"

"I think so."

He watches Alexis laugh with Richard. "She's got her own shields, babe. Don't take her office poker face too personally."

"Yeah. But what if she sees me—my messy, chaotic self—and decides it's too much?"

"Then she's a fool. And you still are winning at karaoke night, girl," he says, throwing his arms around me.

"Gee, thanks." He kisses my cheek and flounces off.

My phone buzzes. A message from Kathleen.

Hi sweetheart! Dinner Friday details, if you're still free? I made a cheat sheet for you. Warning: Indie sings off-key when she's anxious. Also, I included a pic of Grant in the 80s since I heard you were going to karaoke tonight. Prepare yourself.

Attached is a cheat sheet of family members with photos and hilarious descriptions: Uncle Joe—talks too much, loves fishing. Aunt Marge—brings weird casseroles. Cousin Tim—thinks he's a stand-up comedian. The picture of Grant with spiked long hair and a neon oversized jacket causes me to laugh aloud.

Alexis looks over and chuckles along. "You're getting along at your new assignment, I see," she says. "Remember, you still belong to my agency, though." She lifts a brow and grips my arm protectively.

"It's only the Fairbanks family initiation," I say. "Maybe we could have a dinner date and discuss my family and what's going on more?" The words are impossibly big, a leap of faith to share my feelings with her.

She smiles, her gaze softening. "I'd love to."

"Really?"

"Really. I want to hear all about it and hopefully, learn more about you." Alexis puts her arm around me, and I melt into her.

My heart swells.

I smile. Then full-on laugh. Maybe I'm not polished. Or look like a Vogue cover model. But I'm me. I shimmy to Abba.

And tonight, I'm winning as the dancing queen!

Chapter 16

CEO Flames, Gay PDA, & WebMD Panic

I burst through the doors of the Alaska Professional Temp Agency, slowing my momentum to a gentle, graceful glide—or what I hope is a glide. It's probably more of a hobble, given the coffee cradling like a newborn.

Darius greets me with a dramatic flourish. He's perched on the edge of his desk, a vision in his usual business-casual ensemble, but with one key, delightful difference: sequined suspenders that catch the light and practically scream, "Thursdays are for sparkle, baby." He dramatically checks his nonexistent watch, tapping a patent-leather loafer against the floor.

"You're late," he says, his voice a perfectly calibrated mix of sternness and playful judgment. "You were supposed to be turning in your timesheets from Grant's office and reviewing your upcoming schedule for errors, Aurora. My girl, where have you been?!"

"I brought you a latte," I say, holding out the cup like a peace offering.

His eyes widened in a dramatic gasp that could rival a Broadway starlet. "You're not late! You are right on time!" He snatches the latte, a look of pure reverence on his face, before gesturing for me to sit.

Before I can relax, the door to Alexis's office opens. And out walks Richard. I swear, the man's timing is impeccable. He's wearing gym shorts and a sleeveless top that looks ripped from a powerlifter's body, his expression a mixture of smitten adoration and sheer muscle. He saunters up to Darius, a slow smile spreading on his face.

"Darius," he purrs, a deep, rumbling sound that makes a shiver run down my spine. "Run away with me?"

Darius gives him an amused, long-suffering look. "Your friend, my boss, would be pissed to have to answer her own calls." He grabs Richard's face, pulling him in for a kiss that belongs in a movie, all slow-motion and dramatic flair. It's like *Gay Moulin Rouge: Office Edition.* They're gross and adorable. I love them.

"Oh my god," I say, covering my eyes with one hand. "Get a room."

Richard pulls back, a mischievous wink aimed directly at me. "We will."

"Disgusting," I mutter, a smile fighting its way onto my face. In my head, I'm frantically taking notes. I want what they have. The effortless affection, the inside jokes, the way they can turn a professional office into their own little rom-com.

Speaking of professionals, my gaze drifts to Alexis's office. Glass walls, sleek and unapologetic. Her hair is pulled into a tight bun, her blazer is impossibly crisp, and her lipstick is a lethal shade of crimson. She's a work of art and a force of nature. She doesn't look up when I walk in. She doesn't have to. She knows I'm here.

I knock on her doorframe, and the sound is a soft tap against the glass.

"Hello, Trouble," she says, her voice like freshly brewed coffee—calm, rich, and immediately stimulating. She doesn't look up from her screen, but I can feel her attention on me, an almost-physical weight.

"Boss lady," I reply, dropping into the chair across from her desk, the worn leather a familiar comfort. I slouch immediately, a silent challenge to her perfect posture. I can't help but grin at her seriousness, her complete immersion in her work.

Her eyes flick up—sharp, and amused with a toughness, like she's just found a puzzle she wants to solve. Her lip quirks up, a slow, tiny smile playing at the corner of her mouth. "I see you've chosen glittery gloss again."

"I see you've chosen murdering-contracts-red lipstick," I shoot back.

Her perfect business face breaks, and we share a quiet, unguarded grin.

Boom.

There it is. That spark–our spark, again. Hot enough to melt an iceberg in the Alaskan winter. It's the kind of heat that promises danger, excitement, and everything in between. She's so composed and brilliant and maddeningly in control. I'm all over the place, loud and accidentally feral. And yet, somehow, this thing between us just works.

I shift in her chair, trying not to squirm under her gaze. The longer she looks at me, the more my heart dances nervously against my ribs.

Her smile curves slowly, a lazy, confident thing. "You're impossible, Aurora."

"And yet here I am."

Twenty minutes later, I reapply my lip gloss and float from her office in a cloud of happy delirium. My timesheets were submitted, and my schedule was reviewed–among other things. I find Darius hand-feeding Richard a single, plump grape.

"You two need a chaperone," I mutter, plopping down in my swivel chair and spinning in a slow circle.

Darius winks, the sequins on his suspenders flashing. "Jealous?"

"A little," I admit, catching my reflection in the window and fluffing my hair. It's a mess, but a happy one.

Richard holds out a grape to me. "For your troubles."

I pop it in my mouth without a second thought, starting to chew. Then my mouth puckers.

"It's... frozen?" I sputter, staring at the perfectly frosty orb I spit into my hand.

Darius looks at me like I've just discovered fire. "We freeze them now. It's a whole new texture experience."

I shake my head, a laugh bubbling up. "You two are too cute."

He leans over my desk, his voice dropping to a conspiratorial whisper. "When are you and the Boss Queen gonna DTR? Define the relationship?"

"I know what that means."

"Because this," he says, gesturing toward Alexis's glass-walled office, "is still giving a secret office affair vibe. And I am tired of all the romantic tension. It's not fair to me as a spectator."

I sigh, the high of our earlier banter fading into a familiar ache of complicated feelings. "She's... busy. And I'm working over at Grant's office now, you know? It's complicated and I don't want to distract her from her goals right now. She's a CEO. I'm a glorified temp."

Darius softens, his sassy mask dropping to reveal the genuinely kind friend beneath. He pats my hair like I'm an underfed puppy. "You're not a distraction, boo. You're my girl, and you're the best karaoke date ever."

As if on cue, my phone alarm goes off. A shrill, insistent buzz cuts through our conversation.

Dr. Winters' appt.

Right. The appointment. I immediately start sweating. A cold, clammy sheen that makes my shirt stick to me. The pit of my stomach twists into a tight, anxious knot. My hands tremble, as I bite my lip.

Darius notices instantly, his eyebrows furrowing with genuine concern. "Hey, don't worry. I saw your text asking for the time off, and I already wrote you out early. Just go and get your results—it's not like you have an STD or something."

My face goes nuclear. I can feel the hot and furious blush spreading across my cheeks. "Why would you even say that?!"

"I'm saying you're fine," he says, holding up his hands in surrender. "Probably. I mean, pretty much every STD is cured with antibiotics. Easy peasy."

His words, meant to be comforting, have the opposite effect. A wave of full-blown panic washes over me. I clutch my phone, my fingers flying across the screen. I type, "can you have an STD with no symptoms."

Google, as usual, is no comfort. The first search result glares back at me: "Most STDs have no symptoms at all."

I've had no symptoms. Not a single one. Just... this vague, persistent exhaustion I've been chalking up to my relentless schedule. My breathing hitches. Panic sets in, a cold, icy tide threatening to drown me. What if that's a symptom?

I might have something. Something serious. Something incurable. I might be oozing internally. I spin my chair toward Darius, my voice a frantic whisper. "What if I have something serious and I gave it to Alexis? What if she fires me for giving her clamitditeris?! And then she gets a rash on her face and it's all my fault?!"

Richard, bless his sweet, muscular heart, corrects me patiently. "Chlamydia?"

I groan and drop my forehead to my desk with a loud *thunk*. "Worse!"

"Girl," Darius says, his voice a mix of exasperation and concern. "Get outta here. Your anxiety vibe is too much, and for the love of all things holy, please, grab me some free flavored condoms while you're there. You know, for my and Richard's adventures."

A sudden thought, reckless and impulsive, sparks in my anxiety-addled brain. Alexis. She's calm. She's collected. She's a CEO, for crying out loud. She handles crises for a living. She probably has a crisis management plan for a minor global pandemic. She would be honored to come to the doctor with me to be a supportive friend.

I stand up so abruptly my chair screeches against the linoleum. Darius gives me a worried glance.

"I'm going to ask her," I announce, my voice trembling slightly, but with a new determination I didn't know I had.

"Ask her what?" Darius calls after me, his voice trailing off in confusion.

I don't answer. I just power-walk toward Alexis's glass-walled office, my heart pounding frantically against my ribs. I don't even bother to knock this time, just stop in the doorway, a human question mark of anxiety and hope.

Alexis looks up from her screen, her expression softening almost imperceptibly when she sees it's me. "Everything alright, Thompson?"

"Um, not really," I blurt out, my palms suddenly sweaty, my carefully constructed cool-girl persona crumbling to dust. "I have this... medical appointment." I gesture vaguely in the direction of the whiteboard. "And I was wondering if... if you wanted to come with me?"

Her perfectly sculpted eyebrows arch, a beautiful, sharp angle that could cut glass. "Come with you? To your doctor's appointment?" Her voice is calm, but there's a flicker of something in her eyes, a bewildered amusement.

"Yeah," I say, trying to sound casual and failing miserably. "Moral support? You know, in case they tell me I have, like, three legs or something. Or... a flesh-eating disease. It's a very real possibility."

A small smile plays on her lips. "You're being dramatic. I think you'll be fine."

"It's a possibility I'm dying!" I insist, my voice cracking. "And you're really calm in a crisis. Plus..." I lean in conspiratorially, lowering my voice as if we're sharing a top-secret plan. "Think of the potential for proving... erm... *growing* our relationship."

Her eyes glint with amusement, a dark, rich brown that makes my stomach flip. "Are you suggesting I accompany you to this middle-of-the-work-day medical appointment to test our relationship?"

"Not solely," I amend, quickly, my brain scrambling to catch up to my impulsive mouth. "There's also the potential for... post-appointment celebratory ice cream? Or commiseration wine, depending on the diagnosis. We could deep-dive into some serious conversations."

She considers this for a long, agonizing moment, tapping a pen against her tablet, the sound only breaking the silence. I can't tell what she's thinking, and it's killing me. My nerves are buzzing like a live wire.

"And what exactly is this appointment for?" she asks, her gaze a little too sharp and knowing.

I hesitate. How do I explain this without sounding like a walking disaster, a one-woman public health crisis? "Just... a routine follow-up," I say vaguely, hoping she'll just let it go.

Her brow raises just a fraction. She doesn't agree to go.

"I will be so much less stressed," I say with a nervous, desperate grin, "if I have a cool CEO by my side. Think of it as doing a one-on-one team-building exercise. With potential medical drama."

She sighs, a hint of exasperation in the sound, but her little smirk doesn't quite fade. "You are truly something else, Trouble."

My heart does a weird little flutter-kick. "So, is that a yes?" I press, my voice barely a whisper.

She shakes her head, but her voice has a definite softness, a warmth that seeps into my soul. "Alright. Let me just reschedule this meeting." She glances at her watch, her movements quick and efficient.

My relief is so palpable I almost sag against her doorframe. "Seriously? You're the best. I'll tell the boss to give you a raise."

She gathers her things—her phone, keys, and lethal lipstick. "My name is on the front of the building, Aurora. I am my own boss."

As we head toward the elevators, Darius and Richard watch us, their expressions of curiosity and confusion. I feel a surge of warmth and calm wash over me. Maybe having Alexis by my side will be my good luck charm. Or perhaps I just really like having a person who will choose me first, even if it's for a boring, *maybe* disastrous medical appointment.

"You know," I say as we approach the elevator, the doors sliding open to reveal a deserted car. "Since we have a few minutes in potential close quarters..." I raise an eyebrow suggestively, my courage buoyed by the prospect of a quiet moment alone with her. "Maybe we could, you know, optimize the elevator ride?"

Alexis stops just inside the car, a wry smile curving her lips. "Optimize?"

"Yeah," I say, stepping closer. The air between us is thick and humming with a quiet electricity. Her presence is a gravitational pull, and I can't help but be drawn into her orbit. I want to close the distance between us, to lean in and test the boundaries of this fragile, budding thing between us.

Her eyes darken slightly, a spark of warmth and intriguing flickers within them. She says, her voice a low murmur, "You are trouble with a capital T."

The doors begin to close, a quiet whirring sound filling the small space. My heart is in my throat. This is it. This is the moment.

"Sorry, Alexis. You have a meeting with that oil exec," Darius says, suddenly putting his hand on the doors, not sounding sorry. "You said not to let you miss it."

Alexis's perfect red lips press into a thin, annoyed line. The amorous mood is broken. The air deflates. She turns to me, her steely composure back in place, her CEO mask perfectly fitted over her smile. "That's right. I'm sure everything will be fine at your appointment. I'll call you later."

And just like that, she steps out, leaving me alone. Darius mouths "sor-ry" as the elevator doors close.

Chapter 17

Internal Affairs

I'm ninety-eight percent sure I'm pregnant with a ghost baby. *Or dying.* Maybe both. *Probably both.* My uterus is haunted. I've got bad news vibes.

I shift in the world's least comfy chair. There's a new poster of a kitten riding a moose, which I like. Dr. Winters is mixing her cute kitten aesthetics with Alaskan vibes.

Unfortunately, my stress is growing. I'm less worried about realistic reasons for a follow-up, and my mind is conjuring up absurd ideas of what problem in my bloodwork triggered this follow-up appointment.

Nobody gets summoned for a follow-up to tell them they're the healthiest girl in the Alaskan bush or have the healthiest bush. What if she wants to do another exam? I did not prepare, so she had better not need to check my bush.

Should I go to the bathroom and do a quick wash? Wait, what if she needs another urine sample?

"Simmer down, Aurora. You're fine!" I pep-talk myself while the kitten watches in agreement.

I pick at a rogue scab on my knee. I don't even remember what it's from. I probably fell on my face trying to hold a Frappuccino and breathe simultaneously.

"Multitasking is not your thing," Lisa tells me frequently as she applies mascara, drinks coffee, and drives with her knee on the wheel while I'm hyperventilating. She's actually a better driver when she's only doing it half-heartedly, though.

While Darius called me Peach Princess at softball practice because I "bruised like a peach."

As if he can read my worries, my phone buzzes. "We are running an informal vote. I'm voting for Syphilus. Richard votes for gonorrhea, and Lisa thinks you'll kiss Dr. Winters. Text me after who wins, Girly!"

"At least there's no chance I'm pregnant," I text back quickly.

"You'll probably have nothing," he texts. "Seriously, they just want to bill our insurance for an extra visit. Enjoy the relaxing break from work."

My heart and sweaty armpits don't agree with him.

One more text comes through from him, "Flavored condoms!"

The door clicks. Dr. Winters walks in with a tight smile and a tablet clutched like it's carrying all my secrets. Spoiler alert: *it is.*

She is a tall, broad-shouldered woman with a kind voice and an authoritative air of a woman who's calmed an infinite number of STD-induced panic attacks. Today, she's rocking a golden braid and a sweater with wolves on it, because nothing says "medical authority" like apex predators in knitwear.

"Aurora," she says in a soft but not reassuring voice. Soft means there's a lethal cancer or no easy way to say I've got seconds to live. *Bad news is coming!*

"Hi," I squeak. Then louder. "Hey, Dr. Winters. Good to see you. I mean, glad to. So, I don't exactly remember all the tests. What's—" I stop abruptly, realizing the longer I ramble, the longer it'll take her to give me my test results.

She looks up and nods, "You were pretty high on your last visit. So I understand you might not recall the tests. You are sober, right?" she asks, flipping to another screen on her iPad to take notes.

I giggle with nerves, "Yes. Of course.There's no drug use here. That was a total random accident."

She makes a mark.

I fill the silence with, "You're not asking because I'm pregnant, right?"

I'm pretty sure I haven't had sex with a man in years. But there's also a drinking and karaoke night once a week that makes my recollection a little fuzzy. "I should probably stop drinking."

She looks up, and I realize I said that last thought aloud. *Omg, kill me now!*

She doesn't laugh. And her reaction makes me nervously giggle until I bite my bottom lip to stop.

"I'm not?" I ask again.

"You're not. I see you have been on depo-provera hormone shots since puberty, and your appointment last week was to refill your prescription. Missing a dose by a week would make it unlikely for another person to get pregnant."

"Whew. Well, that's one off my list of worries." Then I process her words. "Another person?"

She nods, tablet glowing in her hand as she scrolls to the next screen.

"Your labs came back. They had unexpected results. I want to walk you through them carefully." She slides onto her stool, clicks a button, and prepares to review the results with me.

My mind races through which STD is the best to have: syphilis, gonorrhea, or some weird bacterial thing from hot tubbing? Wait, I bet it's a crazy parasite–*that'd be my luck.*

She launches into Medical talk with a capital M. "Your hormone levels—specifically testosterone and AMH—are outside expected ranges for someone with a typical female reproductive system. Your blood was then sent for chromosomal screening which indicated an XY karyotype."

Okay. Words. She's using them. But this is what my nervous word salad must sound like to other people.

Which STD do I have? The good one? The bad one? It must be the bad one because of her long pause as she waits for my response.

"Is that the clamitditeris or emphysema?" I ask to prove that she's not the only one who knows long medical words.

She shakes her head. "No. Let me try again," she says slowly, as if I'm a child. "You are negative for all STDs."

"It's negative! It's that bad! OMG- I *have everything!*" I blurt, and my heart leaps in my throat. I'm going to puke.

She sighs, takes my hands, and sits to look in my eyes. "Aurora, you don't have *any* infections. You do *not* have any disease. You are *not* pregnant. Negative results are *good*. Positive indicates you have what we are testing for. You *don't want* positive results."

"That's super confusing," I say, relaxing my shoulders. I don't have anything.

"Do you have a friend or your partner here that might want to listen to your results with you?"

"No. My negative-positive results," I laugh. "No. Just me." I *wish* Alexis were here to hear the good news and have an ice cream celebration with me.

"I like the new kitten poster," I say, then giggle uncontrollably with nerves. "Sorry, I was super stressed out. Great. Can I get some flavored condoms then? Anything with a mocha coffee or fireball-type taste."

"Wait," she says, and opens a drawer to throw vanilla flavored condoms and dental dams at me. She then picks up the phone, and says, "Linda, tell my next appointment that I'm running late, and do not book any walk-ins."

She turns back to me. "I'm going to restart. Do you want some water?" she asks, in her soft voice with an annoyed edge.

"Uh, no," I say with a shrug. "I'm good."

"You are healthy. There's nothing immediately, acutely wrong with your reproductive health," she says, pulling up the chart again.

I nod.

"I understand that you marked female, and you present as a female. But sometimes what we look like and what our body's DNA, the genetic map, your body's instruction manual, can differ," she starts.

"Oh yeah. I know," I laugh. "I marked sex with females on my chart. I'm a lesbian. It's been recently confirmed by a hot male fireman, so I'm all hunky dory with that." I wink and give her finger guns, then wonder if she's going to write "suspicious of drug use" in my chart.

"Did your parents tell you about any test results from when you were born? A blood test called a birth panel is run on every child to check for any genetic differences or concerns. I checked and the test results confirmed the test that was done at your birth."

I frown and shake my head. What is she talking about? *Genetic problems?*

"There's a natural variate that some babies are born with that isn't visible but that their genetics shows. In this case I'm referring to your sex characteristics matching your sex expectations. So I mean anatomy, chromosomes, or hormones don't fit typical binary definitions," she says slowly.

"Okay," I responded, waiting. Because this is all medical speak, and I already told her that I'm a lesbian.

"This isn't a disease, this requires no treatment, and it does not define your sexual orientation. Such as you being straight or a lesbian," she continues.

I nod along while I'm holding my breath.

"Your external anatomy is female. That's how you present and how you identify yourself. But internally—" She glances at the tablet again, hoping it's changed since she last read it. "There's evidence of internal gonads. Male traits. Specifically, you have undescended testes."

My mouth falls open, and my racing mind errors out, leaving my brain blank and requiring me to reboot it to respond.

She waits.

Testes.

Testes.

TESTICLES?

She's quiet.

"That's... what? I didn't... No. I don't have balls!" I shout, offended as my brain stumbles over what she's telling me. She has the wrong chart. This whole appointment is ridiculous and offensive.

My brain flashes to a sixth-grade health poster. That stupid cartoon body diagram with a little hairless nut sacks where boys' sex is, right under the little penis.

"I don't have a penis!"

She nods and continues, calmly, "Everyone starts out as a girl and then changes to have boy features, if that's what their genetic instructions say. Sometimes, for a myriad of reasons that process is interrupted or for a rare reason, the body ignores its building instructions," she responds, not even arguing or correcting my no penis statement.

I touch my crotch to assure no penis has grown since I last checked. There's nothing and no testicles. What's inside of me?

I laugh. It bursts out like a hiccup. Like a balloon squeak. "Testicles? Inside me? Like—a hidden surprise?"

She doesn't laugh. Bad sign. *Super* bad sign.

"Male testicals, not ovaries, and not hidden. They are not visible without the right equipment. You probably would have never known this until you were older. When you were having problems conceiving, special tests would've been done to diagnose this," she says gently.

"I know," I croak. "But, like—How? Do I turn into a man? On full moons does my body hair come out and I attack innocents? Am I going to start watching Joe Rogan and buy kettlebells?"

She takes a long breath. "You should have been told, or at least your parents should have been told when you were born."

"They weren't told I was a boy."

"Your gender identity is valid, you are a girl or a boy, whatever you most identify with, and I'm only talking about your body's specific DNA instructions," she cuts in. "This doesn't change who you are, what you like, or your health."

Sure. Tell that to my internal hidden man balls, Dr. Winters.

I scratch behind my ear because my hands don't know where to go. "So... I'm a trans-person? Or a hermaphrodite?"

She shakes her head. "No. *Intersex* is the correct term. One to two people out of a hundred are intersexed. It's not as uncommon as you'd think. You probably even know someone who is intersexed. I'm going to give you information and a referral. You don't need to do anything. Right now, you can read more about it and process this new information."

"But... I mean..." I'm shaking. "I'm not a guy. I'm not. I'm me."

"And you still are." She slides a pamphlet toward me. *Understanding Intersex: A Guide to Your Body, Identity, and Options.* It's got a cartoon rainbow frog on the front. I hate it, immediately.

"There are in person support groups and online communities... " she continues as I stare at the ugly pamphlet.

I know many different people and have been a part of the LGBTQ2IA+ community since high school. I should know this information, but I've never heard the word intersexed. She blindsided me, first with all my negative results, and now with this nonsensical medical jargon.

"I want you to meet with a genetic counselor," she continues. "We can run additional imaging and hormone panels. I know this seems overwhelming."

"Uh-huh," I whisper, nodding as if my body isn't actively trying to crawl out of my skin.

"Is your partner-," she glances at the iPad, "Alexis, available to drive you home?" she asks kindly. She glances toward the door like maybe Alexis is about to materialize in a tailored pantsuit and solve my internal testicle dilemma.

I shake my head. "She's in a business meeting. An important one. She's... not."

Dr. Winters blinks. "Is there a parent or guardian—?"

"No. No parents." I swallow. "I just met my father this week. My mom... we don't talk."

Another blink. "Would you like me to call her anyway? Or Alexis?"

Her name again, and my heart pounds. My vision starts to black at the edges, and I remember to unclench my lungs for air. "No."

The word comes out flat and too fast.

I don't add that I'm afraid she'd treat me differently since this definitely doesn't fit into her life plan. Maybe she'd file me under work weirdo instead of girlfriend-potential-wife material. I feel like we just started our relationship, and I don't want to give her any more surprises. I want to be me. But now, I'm me plus... testes.

What the hell.

"I'm not sick. I don't want to freak anyone out," I reply. "Can I still drive? Am I okay to drive?"

Mouth opening, Doctor Winters appears speechless. "You can drive. Yes, you're fine. Just go to the follow-ups and read the information. Call me with any questions." She nods and leaves the room.

The second the door closes, I fish my phone out of my jacket.

"Wanna get a drink tonight?" I text Darius.

Darius sends me, "OMG what happened. Please tell me you're getting antibiotics for syphilis. I need this win! FYI, Richard is really competitive."

"No one won. Everything - tests are fine."

Hey, text back, "Is Alexis coming? I want to go to that rodeo bar with the bull riding for free drinks."

Can I ride bulls with testes? Wait, all bull riding cowboys are guys, so it must be a testes-approved activity. "That sounds like a blast," I text back, deciding not to ruin Darius's night.

He texts back a thumbs up with the link to the Rodeo Bar, the Buck You Anchorage Saloon.

Chapter 18

Buck You Very Much

"This isn't ignoring my problems or running away. I'll tell my friends over a pitcher of beer and country music," I promise the moose sticker.

The rainbow moose Pride decal on my dashboard stares at me like it's seen things.

"I'm pro-trans, I'm a queer cheerleader, labels don't own me," I tell him. "And yet the words *intersex* and *undescended testes* make me want to scream into my pillow."

The moose does not disagree. Inanimate objects rarely do and make good listeners.

I breathe fog onto the windshield. It's early fall in Anchorage, that time of year when the air is already crisp enough to bite and every spruce needle smells sharper than my anxiety. Campus lights halo the parking lot. Across the street, the Buck You, Anchorage Saloon blinks neon—pink, blue, a bucking silhouette that winks at my life choices.

"How do I run away from something inside me?" I ask.

I laugh because it's either that or crying. Laughing is cheaper and doesn't ruin my mascara.

"Okay, let's try a lighter tone. Hey, guys, turns out I'm a man on the inside. My balls are hide-and-seek champions, an eighteen-year streak."

Nope. That lands stinkier than a moose turd. I press my palms to my cheeks. They're cold. My stomach isn't. It's a fist. And thinking about telling Darius, Lisa, Richard, and Alexis–*OMG, Alexis!*–stresses me more than the revelation.

The pamphlet is facedown on my passenger seat, and I'm scrolling through WebMD. The words *Androgen Insensitivity Syndrome* weigh me down. AIS. Yet another acronym to add to my collection: right under *WTF*, *FML*, and *BRB—Crying.*

I take a breath to loosen my clenched stomach and pounding heart. *Calm down,* the Moose says. *You're a proud Alaskan lesbian. You're a member of the community. You're supposed to advocate for not letting the world categorize you.*

But the world isn't categorizing me. My body is. The words from Dr. Winters echo in my head: "This isn't a disease, this requires no treatment, and it does not define your sexual orientation."

I grip the steering wheel until my knuckles ache. Is this the reason that Mom insisted on those "hormone shots for my health" starting when I was twelve? A hot, stinging anger percolates inside me, pushing out the fear and confusion.

She knew. My mom knew. The same woman who was so against me coming out, who'd constantly say I was "too young to know," was the same one who'd been secretly managing my hormones since I was a kid.

I'm going to kill her. I'm going to drive to her house, and—

My phone buzzes.

The Buck You, Anchorage Saloon's neon lights flash. I realize that I've been talking to myself for twenty minutes.

"Girl, where are you? I saved you a prime spot at the bar with a direct line of sight to ALL the hot cowgirls. And they have a mechanical moose instead of a bull. *A MOOSE,* Aurora.That's your spirit animal!" Darius texts.

"A moose is YOUR spirit animal. Mine was wolverine," I text back, accepting the distraction and mentally turning my emotions off. I'm pretty good at that—I'll stuff my feelings and process them later. I need friends. I need more than a Moose sticker to talk to.

"Coming. Just needed a minute."

My screen lights up instantly. "Girl, I see your location. How much longer are you planning to sit in the parking lot for?"

"COMING!" I responded. A fresh wave of warmth goes through me, as Darius knows I need him, and right now, I need to talk to him more than I need to be spiraling out here, talking to myself.

I glance at myself in the rearview mirror. Same red hair. Same freckles. I saw the same eyes in my sister, Indie, a hazel with greens with swirls of autumn colors. Thinking of her makes me swallow hard. She's desperate to really know me. Nothing about my reflection has changed, yet everything about me has.

"What will Indie think?" I whisper. "What will Grant think? What will Alexis—"

Nope. Do not crack yourself open in the car. Choose fun. Choose friends. I inhale the cold air, inhaling courage, grab my bag, and step out. The parking lot smells like wet pine and cigarette smoke. Country music thumps from the open door and vibrates my sternum. The neon moose flickers, winks: *Buck you very much*.

Inside is heat and noise and wood and sawdust, the kind of bar that looks like it used to be a barn and still remembers. The floor is scuffed. The laughter is loud, real, and a perfect distraction.

"Aurora! Over here!" Darius waves frantically from a high-top table near the mechanical moose. He's wearing what can only be described as "urban cowboy chic"—a black button-up shirt with pearl snaps, tight jeans, and a bolo tie with a turquoise clasp that probably cost more than my monthly rent.

"I thought you'd stand me up for your fancy CEO girlfriend," he says, laughing, and pulling me into a hug.

I sink into it, holding on one second too long.

Darius pulls back, hands on my shoulders to search my eyes for clues. "Okay, spill. What happened at the doctor's? Please tell me it's not crabs. I can't deal with that, Girl."

"I never even thought of crabs. Is that still a thing?" I blurt.

He laughs and says, "Unfortunately, pouring Fireball on your crotch doesn't kill them. If only I could go back in time and tell that to a fourteen year old me."

"Darius! That's awful. You never told me about that," I say, sliding onto the barstool beside him. "I'm healthy. No STDs. No one wins the bet, thank you very much."

"What gives then?" he prods, his eyes narrowing. He knows me too well.

I take a long, shaky breath. "You and I definitely need a drink before I spill the tea."

"Mysterious," he says, and waves at the bartender, a woman with sleeve tattoos and a cowboy hat. "Two Midnight Sun IPAs and two shots of Fireball, please!"

"Make mine a double," I add, and the bartender gives me a dry smile before she starts pouring.

"Whoa, Girl." Darius raises an eyebrow. "That bad?"

I don't answer, just watch the bartender. She slides our beers and shots across the counter, and I immediately down my first shot, welcoming the cinnamon burn. I took my second one from Darius and went down that one, too. The warmth spreads through my chest, chasing away the chill from the night and the knot in my stomach.

"I'm good now," I say, wiping my mouth with the back of my hand.

He waits, swirling his beer in his glass. "So?"

"Remember when we were sixteen and we found that box of old National Geographics in your grandma's attic?" I ask, the memory bubbling up.

"And I spent the whole weekend looking at their naked pictures while you were busy trying to map out indigenous tribes' migration routes across the Andes?" He nods, a grin playing on his lips. "Hard to forget. Your commitment to anthropology was both admirable and deeply weird."

"Hey, everyone should know about Amazonian tribes– you're welcome very much," I tease. "No, I mean the article featuring hermaphrodite tribal people, and how they were considered holy, more spiritually developed people."

He tilts his head. "Vaguely? You read parts of it to me while I was trying to figure out the average size of men's parts, minus the piercing which we all know makes them bigger, gravity and all."

I laugh, a little hysterically. "Well," I say, "turns out I'm a spiritual one."

He blinks, his drink half-lifted. "What?" He sets his beer down with a loud clank and grabs my arm, his voice dropping to a whisper. "Wait, you're...?" He pauses, then waves me to stop and pulls me off the barstool, dragging me to a quieter, darker booth in the back. "Spill. Now."

I slide into the booth and take a long pull of my beer, gathering my thoughts. "I'm intersexed. I have AIS. Androgen Insensitivity Syndrome. I'm actually a guy inside and a girl on the outside–undescended testes. Surprise!" I jazz-hand so aggressively that I almost knock over my beer.

His mouth drops open. "Wait, you're—"

"He-She. Yep." I take another long pull of my beer, watching his face.

"I've seen you naked, Aurora, and you're a girl... He downs his shot and starts his beer.

"Holy—" He slides the shot over.

I chase the holy with burning cinnamon heat. "My male bits are deep inside, like where my feelings are hiding," I utter, a half-joke to ease the tension.

"Holy Shit!"

"My exact words," I say. "Well, mine involved more avoidance, panic, rage, and hysteria."

"Are you okay?" His eyes search my face with genuine concern that makes me tear up. He reaches out and squeezes my hand.

"I don't know," I admit, the stoney emotional wall I'd built is crumbling a little. "I mean, I'm still me, right? But also, who am I? I thought I was figuring out how to be an adult, and now this weirdness... this secret part of me that I didn't even know about. It feels... big."

"You're Aurora," Darius says firmly, his grip on my hand tightening. "My best friend, who sneaks extra toppings onto my frozen yogurt when the cashier isn't looking. The lesbian who spent two years pining after the captain of the softball team and trying to win prom queen to catch her attention."

"Hey, I'm still not over Stacy. I wonder what she's doing now," I say, lifting my glass and chuckling.

"No more dating drama, Girl. You have Alexis!" Darius says, then cocks his head. "Wait. What are you going to do about Alexis?"

My stomach turns stone at the thought of talking to Alexis about this. "I don't know. She's really work-focused, even when she promises to put me first. We're not even official yet. She said we would talk tonight, but she's ghosting me. What if this freaks her out? What if she's only into... You know. Standard-issue, normal girls?"

"She's a big girl," he says, taking a gulp and waving off my worries. "She likes you so we already know she isn't *into* normal. I don't think she'll be shook. As long as you are still a lesbian and you don't show up late to work."

I laugh a little and chew my bottom lip, tasting the cheesecake gloss. Reminding me: "These are for you." I toss the vanilla condoms on the table and pocket the dental dams.

"Yay! Ohhh, vanilla!"

"I'm still a lesbian. And I still love Alexis," I blush at saying this out loud. "Well, maybe I'm not a lesbian, if I'm a guy inside. I'm just normal. What does that make me?" The question tumbles out before I can stop it.

"Girl, please." Darius rolls his eyes so hard I'm worried they might get stuck. "You've been swooning over women since you knew what swooning was. And you love wearing dresses and being treated like a princess. You are a lesbian queen."

I laugh despite myself. "Thanks. I think telling you is enough for now."

"Hey, I'm glad you don't have crabs. You've always been special and unique to me," he laughs. He clinks his beer against mine. "Aurora, I've known you forever. This doesn't change who you are."

"That's what Dr. Winters said too. But it feels... big."

He squeezes my fingers. "What about your mom?"

"Not tonight," I say, the match-head anger flickering again. "Not before I've had time to process and make questionable choices."

He arches an eyebrow. "Speaking of questionable—looks like it's going to be just us tonight." He looks at his phone, explaining, "Richard isn't feeling well and Lisa's working late. We get to have so much fun they'll regret not coming. Girl, we are going to post epic pics. You in?"

I laugh and tilt my beer back.

The bar roars—the mechanical moose snaps to life with a hydraulic huff. A woman in a loose flannel and black jeans swings on, tips her hat, and the crowd hollers. The LEDs paint her in jewel-tones. She laughs, head tipped back, a quicksilver sound that finds me like a magnet.

Darius follows my stare, grins slowly. "OMG, you still got it!"

My blush spreads, and the cowgirl is much more than a distraction. "That's Zara," I say, the name a whisper on my lips. My heart races and I lick my lips, watching her jiggle and whoop, riding the bucking moose.

She lasts a glorious five seconds on the moose before flying off and landing with surprising grace on the padded floor, a perfect somersault that ends in a bow. The crowd goes feral. She bows. I clap and whistle like I'm single. Maybe I am, at least for tonight.

"Next rider!" calls the announcer: tall woman, platinum mullet, suspenders that are a blinding neon rainbow. A lesbian beacon, daring the crowd. "Who's brave enough to buck the Buck?"

Darius gives me a look. *The* look. The one from school that usually ends in a principal's office and his mom picking us up.

"No," I say.

"Yes," he grins.

"Absolutely not."

"Absolutely yes. You need this, Aurora. Zara needs this," he adds with a laugh, pointing at Zara, who is already pointing at me to ride next.

"And who am I? A rodeo princess," I challenge. "I've never ridden a horse or a moose!"

"You are the baddest bitch in Anchorage who's about to ride a mechanical moose and set a new bar record. Stay on for eight seconds and win the T-shirt. After that go ride Zara. Alexis hasn't locked you down and Alexis needs some competition," he says. He stands up, waving at the announcer. "My friend wants to ride!"

The announcer asks, "What's your name, honey?"

"Aurora," I say, suddenly sober despite the Fireball and beer chaser.

"Let's hear it for Alaskan Bull Rider Aurora!" she calls into the microphone. The bar erupts in cheers and whoops.

As I approach the moose, I remove my jacket and pull my hair into a messy bun.

"Hey!"

I look up to Zara's grin. "Are you going to beat my five seconds? I'll buy you a drink if you do."

"I'm getting the shirt," I say confidently, "You got any tips?"

"Don't let go, and hang on tight until you hear the buzzer." She slaps my butt, flirting back as I pass.

I glance around, wondering if Alexis or Lisa is here. I only see Darius, which makes me realize that I was so caught up in myself that I didn't even ask him where Richard was.

"Everyone give a round of applause for Buckin' Aurora!"

I awkwardly pull myself into the uncomfortable saddle perched on the moose. I notice it's not just any moose—it's bedazzled. Its antlers are wrapped in multicolored LED lights with a saddle embroidered with glitter.

"Eight seconds to win," the announcer tells me. "Ready?"

"I'm not ready for any of it," I say, and swing my leg over anyway. The leather is warm from other bodies. The machine huffs beneath me, animal and not. "But I'm going to do it anyway!"

The announcer doesn't hear me but sees my determined smile.

"Three, two, one… RIDE!"

The moose lurches forward, and I'm a ball of pure adrenaline and flailing limbs. The world blurs into a kaleidoscope of neon lights, cheering faces, and thumping country music. I hold on, my thighs burning, my core screaming, every muscle in my body straining to stay put.

The moose bucks hard, twisting left, then right, and I feel myself slipping. I look up, and there's Zara, on the barstool, laughing, her hands in the air, a beer in one hand. She catches my eye and gives me a wink that says she's in on the joke, and it gives me just enough focus to re-center myself, to plant my feet and hold on.

The crowd roars behind me. I taste cinnamon and sawdust.

"Hold on!" Darius screams.

I am holding on. Not just to the rope.

The buzzer blares. The moose stops with a gentle jolt.

"We have a winner! Eight seconds! Aurora!"

Someone stuffs a T-shirt into my hands: *I GOT BUCKED IN ANCHORAGE.*

"I love you!" Darius shrieks, running at me. He slams into me, and we steady each other in a wheezing hug. Both of us are laughing.

"You are unstoppable!" he says into my hair. "You unbelievable! You are—oh my God—you're so sweaty."

"I'm a winner," I pant. "Winners sweat."

As I decide to end the night a winner, I confidently finger gun people who slap my shoulder and hoot at me. I look at my phone and see no new messages. I wish Alexis would at least send me an excuse for missing tonight.

I send her a pic of me with a huge grin, riding the moose, with the clock at the six-second mark in the background. This will be my new profile pic on everything, even LinkedIn!

"Hey, I'll see you later, cowgirl," Zara says as I skip by her with Darius.

"That's my girl!" he laughs, pulling me into a sloppy hug. "You really are unstoppable!"

And for a moment, I feel it. Unstoppable. Maybe whatever's inside me—balls or the fireball confidence—doesn't matter, because I'm an unstoppable force.

My legs ache from moose. My heart aches from the whiplash of longing for Alexis and the guilt of glancing around to see Zara again.

Darius, sensing my rising emotions, threads his fingers in mine. "I love you, weirdo."

"I love you more, weirdo."

We sweaty hug and it turns into a crazy shimmy dance to the music thudding from inside. My breath fogs. The neon moose hums in the dark, tireless.

Chapter 19

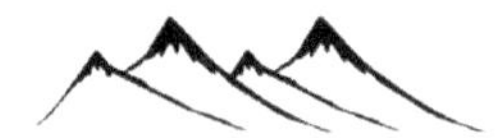

Static on the Line, Girlfriend

A groan escapes me. My head pounds like a drum circle of drunks. I'm not even sure what time it is, but the coppery taste in my mouth and the general feeling of having been run over by a team of sled dogs say it's well past time to get up. Wrapped in a cocoon of my softest blanket, I stretch a hand out, fumbling for my phone on the floor beside the couch. The screen burns my eyes as it flashes to life, a supernova of missed notifications.

My group chat with Darius and Lisa is a testament to the night's carnage. Filled with more emojis and GIFs than words.

I stifle a laugh, which is a mistake. My head protests with a fresh wave of throbbing. The memories of last night—the honky-tonk music, the scent of stale beer and sawdust, the crowd cheering as I wobbled on that mechanical moose, clinging on for dear life—but winning a shirt and Zara's attention. It all comes rushing back. It was a stupid, chaotic, glorious idea.

My thumb hovers over a new message. It's not from Darius or Lisa. It's from Alexis. My stomach does a nervous little flip that has nothing to do with my hangover.

"Hydration station, girl!"

"Holy, fucknuts!" I say, dropping my phone and almost wetting myself.

"Did you forget I stayed over, Princess?" Darius clinks around in Lisa's kitchenette like it's cocktail hour. Banging two mugs of coffee onto the table, he says, "I made tea, also, because I care."

"Thank you," I croak, attempting to sit up and making an old-lady noise. "I think I have a bruise shaped like the state of Texas on my butt."

"Tex-ass," he says, laughing at himself. "Also, you do. It's the mark of a winner, Girl."

I grab my phone from the floor.

Darius watches me watch my phone. "She's a Bossy CEO Queen," he says gently, dropping onto the couch with the theatrical groan of a man twice his age. He drapes the fleece blanket over both our legs. "I'm sure she got caught up with work. It's not like there's someone else. She's a workaholic."

"I know," I say, staring at the little crack on my screen like a metaphor. "I just... yesterday's test results for—it was a big day." I swallow around the word *intersex.* It feels too foreign to use with my head this foggy.

He leans his shoulder into mine. "You told me. Step one. And I told Lisa. So step two is done."

My phone vibrates. My soul levitates two inches.

"Are you awake?" pops up on my messages, under her, earlier text of "Aurora?"

I inhale a tiny gasp and show Darius. He lifts both brows, mouthing, *Call her.* My thumb hovers. The familiar mix of want and wariness fizzes up my spine.

I hit call.

It rings twice. Then Alexis' voice, cool water over hot stones. "Morning, Aurora."

"Hey." My voice does a small, embarrassing cartwheel. "Hi."

"I'm sorry." She exhales. I can hear her swivel chair creak and picture the clean lines of her office, the glass, and the night skyline making a mirror of her. "I got buried. The Westmark account lit itself on fire, and needed a complete overhaul of the contract, and—excuses, excuses. I'm sorry I missed the Buck You thing."

"It's okay," I say, automatically. I twist the blanket between my fingers. "We... I had fun. Darius made me ride a moose."

There's the smallest smile in her voice. "He sent me the video."

"He *what*?"

He whispers next to me, "I posted it, too."

"He's very proud of you," she says. "I am too."

My heart does a stupid jig. "Really?"

"Aurora." Alexis softens, vocal timbre dropping into the private register she uses to make the world fall away, and it becomes only us. "You looked fearless."

"I was mostly terrified," I admit. "And sticky."

"Fearless can be sticky," she says. "How are you feeling now?"

"Like I bench-pressed a car with my thighs," I say. "Like a cinnamon eating powerlifter. Like I might've broken my butt."

"Not your butt! I better book you a butt massage stat!" She adds, "And I am sorry for missing the butt-breaking fun."

"You also missed me telling you something important." The words are out before I can shape them. Darius's head swivels toward me. He raises his brows.

I mouth, *I've got it.*

He presses his lips together and nods.

Her response is almost immediate, as I hear her close her laptop. "You have my full attention, Trouble."

My heart jumps into my throat. Suddenly my voice is a little hoarse.

"Hey," I say, trying to sound casual.

"I think I know your important request. You want to ask me if you can come in late today?" Her voice is a low, warm rumble, laced with a hint of amusement. The sound of it alone is enough to make my brain cells start partying again, hangover be damned.

"No! I'm working on my university skills, so going to work after partying is an important skill to learn. How long have you been there?" I ask, as I drink my coffee and wonder what clean clothes I have left to wear today. I want to wear the, *I GOT BUCKED IN ANCHORAGE* trophy, but I'm pretty sure even being Alexis' lover won't give me a pass to wear that into the office.

A genuine laugh, a bright, clear sound I haven't heard in a long time, fills my ear. "I never left the office. That's why I have a comfortable couch here," she explains.

I can almost picture her, leaning back in her office chair, a sleek, tailored blazer over a crisp t-shirt, a subtle smile playing on her lips. She's always so put together, so effortless. The charismatic person who could ride a mechanical moose and come away without a single hair out of place.

"Well," she says, amused, "I'm glad you had fun. I'm sorry I missed it. Things have been hitting the fan here. This new client is proving to be a lot."

"Oh," I say, my voice going flat. The new client. Right. I should have known this was coming. Her work is the third wheel in our not-yet-official relationship, constantly demanding her attention and leaving me feeling like I'm the last line item on her to-do list.

"I know what you're thinking," she says, suddenly serious. "And you're right. I've been absent. And I'm sorry. I shouldn't have let work consume me like this. You deserve better than a text from me the morning after."

My chest tightens. This is the apology I've been craving. Not seeing her last night was a huge disappointment but her acknowledging it–It's a peace offering, a bridge between us.

"It's okay," I say, though it's not entirely true. "I get it. Building a business is hard. But... I miss you. It feels like we're coworkers more than dating, lately."

"I know," she says quietly. "And I miss you, too. More than you know."

A comfortable silence settles between us, no longer awkward, but full of unspoken things. The air in my apartment is lighter. Alexis is finally, truly present and acknowledging me, my feelings, and our relationship.

"How about I make it up to you?" she asks, her tone turning from apologetic to persuasive, as it does when she's about to close a deal. "No work talk. No distractions. Just us. What are you doing tonight?"

My heart gives another hopeful thrum. "Recovering from my near-death experience. But I could probably be convinced to go out."

"Good. Because I was thinking we could go to that new Italian place downtown. The one with the truffle pasta and wine cellar."

"Oh my God, yes," I say, a genuine smile spreading across my face. "A thousand times, yes. Pasta is my love language. I'll even put on a dress and heels."

"Promises, promises," she teases. "I'll book us for seven. And Aurora?"

"Yeah?"

"This is me asking you to be my girlfriend. Officially."

The words hang in the air, a soft, beautiful little bomb. My breath hitches. I don't say anything for a long moment, my mind blank. *Girlfriend*. My girlfriend. The idea is both terrifying and exhilarating. It's a real title, a real commitment, and not some vague, undefined thing.

"Are you still there?" she asks, a flicker of concern in her voice.

"Yes. Sorry. Just... processing. You're asking me to be your girlfriend?"

"I am," she says, her voice full of that easy confidence I love. "Only if you want to be, of course. No pressure."

But there is pressure. The kind of delicious, terrifying pressure that comes with finally getting what you've been dreaming of.

"I want to," I say, the words tumbling out in a rush. "I really, really want to. But there's something we need to discuss first."

Alexis goes quiet thoughtfully, meaning she's listening with all her CEO-caring energy.

I open my mouth.

My phone *pings* with a text. Then another. Then my screen lights up with a notification banner that reads *INDIE*, followed by thirty musical note emojis and a moose.

I swallow a laugh. "Sorry, my new little sister is... being a little sister–annoying." I angle the phone away and thumb open the text thread with my free hand.

"WE WROTE YOU A SONG!!!" She continues typing, "Alaskan Moose Rider."

Before I can thumbs up, she adds, "Dropping the demo now—pls cry and tell me I'm a genius! *[AUDIO: Alaskan_Moose_Rider_demo.m4a]*"

I hit play. Twangy guitar and a drum kit that sounds like someone taught a glacier to tap dance spring from my phone speaker. Indie's voice—straightforward, earnest, a little wild—rides the melody: *eight seconds on the back of a star / she held on like a born-and-raised northern bar / when the lights go green and the heart says stay / that's my moose rider finding her way...*

"Oh my God," I whisper, a hot prickle behind my eyes. Darius beams and nods his head along to the beat. She wrote me a song?

"Aurora?" Alexis asks. "What is that? It's... catchy?"

"Indie wrote me a song," I say, laughing wetly. "She saw my video. She's ridiculous. She's—" My throat closes for a second. "She's my family."

Alexis hums, a businesslike sound that isn't approval but isn't the enjoyment I'm swimming in. "Speaking of," she says lightly. "Grant called."

My lungs tighten. "He—he did?"

"He wanted to talk about the integration of you into his company as more than a temp employee," she says. "Did you discuss this with him?"

Her question is a sharp accusation. I blink, reeling back to the couch. The cozy fog evaporates. I sit up, dizzy. "No. We talked about my work schedule around school and about family stuff."

"He's a VIP," Alexis says, tone crisp in a way that makes my brain brace. "Which means we treat him as such. I wanted to give you a heads-up so you could prepare for a more business appropriate relationship."

"He's—" My mouth is dry. "He's my dad."

A beat. "He's also a client," she says softly but firmly. "A important one. I need to trust you'll keep those lanes clean."

Lanes. I stare at the stitching on the blanket. Darius goes very still beside me, eyes on my face. Outside, a gull shrieks at the grey sky.

"I will be a professional and do good work," I say, trying to keep my voice light. "You know that."

"I do." Alexis' sigh shivers the line. "And I trust you." A pause. "I also know... families can be consuming. I need to be sure that it won't impact deliverables."

My chest hot-fizzes with a cocktail of shame and anger. "Like I'm going to blow contracts and deadlines because I found my father?"

"That's not what I'm saying," she says, quickly. "I'm saying that I've seen people get swallowed by personal issues. Our business is at an inflection point. We are on the precipice of huge growth and I can't have surprises."

I look at Darius. He lifts an eyebrow in slow disbelief as he shakes his head at her. I press my lips together.

"I don't want surprises either," I say, then a reminder pops onto the screen. "I want you to come to the family dinner. Meet Grant as—" I swallow. "—as my dad. Meet Indie. Meet the whole new family with me and help me not be too weird. If you meet them, you'll change your mind about keeping them at a professional distance."

Alexis is quiet. I can hear the slight rattle of her office forced air heat blowing. "That's... a lot," she says finally.

"It's a casual dinner," I say. "It's Kathleen's casserole and cookies, and Indie is playing her terrible/wonderful songs for us. It's me saying: this is important. You're important. I don't want to hide you. Or them. Or me." I now realize I forgot to tell her the crucial medical thing and why she's on the phone. But the mood is tense, so I let go of revealing that secret.

Her inhale is audible, controlled. "I want to support you," she says, carefully. "You are... God, you are bright, Aurora. You remind me of you–a go-getter, creative, adaptive. You make *me* better."

My heart pitches toward her voice.

"But I also have to consider optics and the business," she continues. "If I start attending clients' personal functions, even informally, that sets a precedent. If the client is also your father—"

"He's my father first to me," I say, sharper than I mean to. "He wasn't in my life, and now he is. I don't want... I've been dreaming of meeting him my whole life. This is important to me."

Darius mutters, "Obviously *not to her*," into his tea, not quietly.

"I hear you," Alexis says to me. "I'm asking for time. To think. To make sure I can show up in a way that doesn't compromise business or our relationship."

The room tilts. It's not a no. It's a... *hold.* I rub the heel of my hand over my sternum where an ache blooms.

"Okay," I say after a second. "I can give you time."

"Thank you." Her voice gentles again. "And I do want to see you. Let's compare schedules later today."

I nibble my lip, warmth spreading through me as her voice softens to me. "Okay. Cool." I immediately want to set myself on fire for saying *cool*–so unprofessional.

She laughs, softly.

My phone *pings* again—Indie, unstoppable.

"Grant says to bring your moose riding energy to dinner! We'll chill and I'll finish your song. Also, I rhymed "antlers" with "banter." Your sister is a genius."

I snort. A laugh sneaks out of me, wild and helpless at her innocent enthusiasm.

Alexis inhales. "Sounds like you're busy," she says, not icy, but there's frost on her words. "I'll see you at work."

"Right," I say quickly. "See you soon, girlf—"

The line clicks softly. My phone is suddenly heavy. I set it gently on the old pizza box, balancing on my dirty laundry.

Darius is doing his Concerned Gay Face. "Scale one to 'we need to set her planner on fire', how are you feeling?"

"Three?" I say, wobbling a hand. "She apologized. She wants us to officially date."

"And?"

"And she wants to treat Grant like a client. Which he is," I add, because fair is fair in the court of my couch. "But also... he's my dad. And she's not committing to coming to meet my new family."

Darius sucks air between his teeth.

Chapter 20

Bye, Mom! Hello, Family!

I smell the extra-fragrant roses and immediately think of Alexis—her hair when she leans close. Closing my eyes, I can almost feel her. She was too busy for anything more than a quick kiss at work, but her kiss was everything! Especially when she whispered 'girlfriend' on my lips.

My face heats up like everyone in the store knows I'm thinking about kissing my boss.

Okay. *Focus.*

"Focus, Aurora," I mutter, making a grandma-looking lady jumps a little beside me.

I nod politely and return to the flower display, fingers brushing over soft rose petals. My fingertips remember everything—her lips, her silky hair tangled in my hands, and her cashmere sweater pinning me against the wall!

I stop fondling the pink roses and grab a family-dinner appropriate bouquet of red and sunset orange mixed flowers—warm and dramatic. Very me.

Then, impulsively, I snatch up a second one with soft whites and blush pinks, because Alexis deserves flowers too. Even if she's not coming to dinner. Even if she is still thinking about it.

My phone buzzes with a FaceTime from Darius.

"Are you buying flowers for your new family or to impress your girlfriend, aka our boss?"

I laugh and answer, "Both. Also don't be rude. I'm adulting. I've never bought flowers for a dinner party before."

Darius says, "Great. Now that you've popped that cherry, you can start bringing them to my dinners too."

"Taco Tuesdays seem a little too casual for flowers," I say with a laugh.

"Tell Grant I said hi. And enjoy your carb overload and meeting more of your family."

"I wish you could come with me," I say with a pleading voice, making a last effort to recruit him as my wing man.

"I thought you were going to convince Alexis to be your plus one?"

"She was unmoved by my persuasive argument," I say with a huff. Really, she stopped the discussion by kissing me and running to a meeting.

"That's horrible. I would totally drop everything but Richard is in the Rocky Horror Picture Show tonight."

I nod and swallow, "I know it's not an emergency. It's just meeting my family. I'll survive." I say, lifting my chin and walking the flowers to the checkout.

"They already love you and who couldn't love you? You are the best!" he says.

I shoot back, "No you're the best!"

"It's true!" he says with a laugh, then waves.

I shove my phone away as I scan the flowers with a line forming behind me.

But out of the corner of my eye, something yanks the air out of my lungs.

My mom.

She's across the store, acting like the carnations are the center of the universe. Like I'm not ten feet away. Like she didn't ignore my call a few days ago when I was falling apart, parked in a medical clinic parking lot, holding a pamphlet about how I have testicles inside my body and my chromosomes are screwed up.

My stomach drops to my toes. I freeze, holding the flower bouquets like auditioning for a romantic tragedy.

She glances up. Meets my eyes.

And then turns away. *Smooth.* As if I'm an old high school boyfriend she's avoiding.

Okay then. I'll need to be the adult.

I inhale sharply, blink back heat behind my eyes, and pivot so fast I smack into an endcap of cards and knick-knacks. One plastic penguin rolls free and takes off like it's trying to join a parade.

"Sorry, sorry," I mumble, grimacing at the people waiting behind me, and I start picking up the random rolling items.

I do not cry. I will not cry. Not here.

I whispered to myself. "Not the time for an emotional spiral."

I quickly start checking out,

"Aurora? Aurora Thompson?"

The voice sounds faux-surprised. I don't need to turn around to know who it is.

"Hi, Mom," I grip the flowers and insert my card before turning.

"I thought that was you." She glances at my outfit—jeans and a forest green sweater Darius had declared "actually cute." I watched her mental calculator tally up the cost.

Her hand reflexively touches her hair. "I was going to call you back."

Lie. But whatever. I had bigger issues than her ghosting me—like the fact that she'd hidden my father's existence for eighteen years, but accepted his child support checks. Or that when I'd called her, sobbing after Dr. Winter told me I had internal testes and chromosomal differences that explained so much about my body, she'd let it go to voicemail.

"It's fine. I figured it out." I lift my chin, channeling Alexis's boardroom confidence. "Actually, I'm headed to dinner with Dad and his family. You know, Grant? The guy who you somehow forgot to tell me about for the last nineteen years?"

Mom paled slightly. *Gotcha.*

"Aurora, you don't understand—"

"You're right, I don't. And honestly? I don't need to anymore," I say, turning to leave as she stops me by placing her manicured hand on my arm.

Something flickers across her face—regret, maybe, or just annoyance at being dismissed. "Are you still working at that temp place? I heard you're... involved with your boss now."

Of course, she'd heard that. Anchorage, despite being a city, is really closer to a small town filled with gossip and family.

"Yep. Living the dream." I force a smile. "Gotta go, family's waiting."

As I push past her, she says, "Aurora, about your... messages... your *condition*. I didn't know how to tell you. And no would know anyway—"

I froze. "So you did know? You kept another secret from me."

Her silence is damning.

"You *knew* I had a special diagnosis? All those times I asked why I was different..." My voice cracks. "And you just let me find out when I'm an adult?"

"You're broken and knowing it wouldn't have helped anyone," she sputters.

You mean *you*. *You* didn't want anyone to know about me. But I remain quiet because yelling at her in a flower shop is a pointless waste of energy.

"You're just... Well... There's some things that should stay a secret." she says dismissively, like genetics aren't important.

"Don't." My chest feels tight. "Don't pretend this isn't a big deal, and that what you did was out of motherly concern."

I yank my arm free and walk out, flowers clutched against my chest.

I will not cry, not over her. I've got new people now. A new family. One that has family night dinners, tells stories around the dinner table, and actually accepts me.

Chapter 21

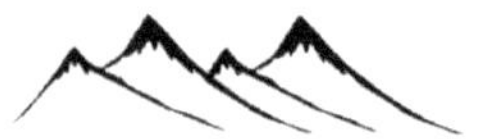

Dinner, Alaskan Style

By the time I pull up to Grant and Kathleen's sprawling lakeside home, my mascara is mostly salvaged and my game face firmly back in place.

The door opens, and the house smells waft out: garlic, heaven, and something slightly burnt, which is how a family home filled with love should smell like.

Kathleen greets me at the door in her cute lemon-printed apron, flour on her cheek like a Pinterest mom with chaotic good energy. She pulls me in for a hug before I can even say hello.

"You brought flowers! Oh, Aurora, these are gorgeous. You didn't have to."

Before I could step inside, the door flew open wider, revealing my half-sister Indie, all gangly teenage limbs and shy giggles.

"You came!" She pulled me into a hug that surprised us both.

I squeeze the stems, trying not to sniffle from kindness overload.

"Wouldn't miss it," I assured her, following her inside.

What would my life have looked like if I had a mother like Kathleen?

"Well, it was the least I could do," I reply shyly as she hangs my jacket and ushers me inside.

Indie smiles and introduces me around, all smiles, behind her oversized glasses.

The house smelled amazing—and despite it being a dinner, people weren't in the dining room but milling about the kitchen. Laughter echoed from the kitchen, and I moved toward it like a moth to flame. This was what family sounded like. Real family.

The kitchen is a storm of activity—Grant stirring something on the stove, Kathleen back to chopping vegetables, my cousins Sam and Tyler arguing over music selections, and various aunts and uncles pouring drinks and setting the table.

"Hey." "Nice to meet you," I say as Indie takes me around the room. And with the information overload, I don't hear a single name but register everyone's smiles, warm hugs, and handshakes.

And just like that, I was absorbed into the Fairbanks family vortex, passed around for hugs, handed a soda, and simultaneously pulled into three different conversations.

Grant hugs me as I finish the kitchen and family tour. He's tourist-season-tanned, holding a spoon like he's mid-chef duties. "Hey, kiddo. Thought you might be late, and I'd have to bring you a dinner plate tomorrow at work, just so you didn't miss out."

I laugh. "I'll grab an extra plate for tomorrow. If it'd make you feel better."

"Please do. There's always plenty of food." He nods, all quiet pride and awkward warmth, and I feel this ridiculous swell of being wanted. I'm not too much or not enough—just a girl bringing flowers to her dad's pasta night.

Dinner is chaotic. I love the beautiful, cheesy, red-sauce-covered chaos.

Kathleen serves up huge bowls of homemade fettuccine. Indie plays music off her phone–a mix of indie bands and Taylor Swift, which I fully approve of– and promises to play her new song when it's polished. Grant pours everyone wine except for me and Indie, who he pours us orange soda in wine glasses.

I'm in the middle of twirling noodles around my fork when Kathleen pats my arm.

"We're really glad you're here, honey."

Something tightens in my throat.

"Me too," I croak, and Indie immediately dumps Parmesan on my plate like she sensed the emotion building.

Kathleen starts a story about Grant in college, which involves a canoe, a stuffed caribou, and a police warning. Everyone's laughing so hard that I half choke on garlic bread. I wipe my eyes, pretending it's the onion.

"So, Aurora," Aunt Maggie leans forward with the gleam of a woman about to deploy matchmaking tactics, "Grant tells us you're quite the rising star at your company. Any special someone we should know about?"

And there it was.

I take a too-large gulp of the bubbly soda. "Um, well—"

"Maggie, let her breathe," Grant chuckles. "She's only been a part of our lives for three weeks."

My eyes mist with the words, *a part of our lives.*

"Dad, Aurora totally has a girlfriend," Indie announces with teenage certainty. "She's, like, super pretty and important. I saw them at Ronnie's Sushi last weekend."

All eyes turned to me. *Well, shit.*

"I—uh—" I stammer, fork halfway to my mouth.

"Is it serious?" Kathleen asks gently.

"It's..." What was it? Alexis in the office: professional, remote, untouchable. Alexis in bed: passionate, commanding, intoxicating. Alexis everywhere else: a perfect mannequin of success who occasionally let me glimpse the woman beneath. "Complicated."

"The best ones are," Uncle Pete winks.

"She's my boss, actually," I blurt out, then immediately regret it when Grant's eyebrows shot up.

"Your boss? At the temp agency?" He sets his fork down slowly. "Alexis?"

"I thought she might have told you. But really we just made it official today," I explain, quickly.

"She didn't mention it." His expression is unreadable.

"She's very career focused," I offer lamely. "A great mentor too."

"She certainly is," Grant mutters.

An awkward silence descends, broken only by the clink of silverware.

"Well, I think it's romantic," Indie declares. "You guys could be the next lesbian power couple."

"She's like a boss and you're a university student so it's probably more like a hookup," Tyler snorted.

"Oh my god, Tyler, ew." Indie throws a bread roll at him.

Kathleen steps in with the social grace I desperately lack. "What about your friends, Aurora? Grant mentioned you are going to university. Are you doing summer classes and living at the dorm?"

Thank god for her maternal intervention.

I smile and exhale at the conversation change.

"I have an apartment with my friend, Lisa. She's great, works at a dating agency, actually. I've known her and her cousin Darius since middle school. She's like this blonde tornado of emotional support filled with terrible ideas." I relax on safer ground. "And then there's Darius, my best friend since forever. He actually works at the temp agency and got me the job."

"The fashionable one?" Grant asks. "He seemed very protective of you when I met him."

"That's Darius. He's basically appointed himself my personal stylist and life coach." I grin and do a little model pose with my green sweater. "He's dating Alexis's friend Richard now, so our social circles are getting weirdly tangled."

"That's Anchorage for you," Aunt Maggie laughs. "Six degrees of separation? Try two."

The conversation flows more easily after that, stories ping-ponging around the table. By dessert—homemade cheesecake with local berries—I feel something dangerous unfurling in my chest. It's an odd sense of belonging.

As people drift away from the table, I find myself helping Kathleen with dishes, and a comfortable silence falls between us.

"Your mom stopped by the office this morning," she says quietly, handing me a plate to dry.

My hands fumble. "What? Why?"

Kathleen sighs. "She wanted to tell us about your... medical situation."

The plate nearly slips from my grip. "She told you? About me being intersex?"

"I'm not quite sure why she felt we'd need to know, and if you need anyone to talk to or want someone to... I don't know... go to appointments with you or anything," she says warmly. Her eyes meet mine and melt any coolness remaining. "We are here for you and we love you, you know."

"I just found out from Dr. Winter," I say, setting the plate down carefully. "I'm still processing everything." The sound of laughing comes from the living room. "Does everyone know?"

"No. Not everyone," Kathleen says, touches my arm. "Grant and me. I know things are complicated with your mother. I'm sorry we learned through her."

"Complicated," I echo. The word of the night, apparently.

"I don't believe in keeping secrets, especially from my children. I thought she was stopping by to apologize for never letting us contact you," she continues.

My mother never apologizes for anything, so I'm unsure how to respond. I nod and whisper, " I wish I knew about you sooner or tried harder to find you guys."

She turns and squeezes me into a big hug. "We know each other now and let's make up for lost time, Aurora. You are welcome here, anytime."

I manage to nod back with her overwhelming love and acceptance, surprising me.

"We are happy you're at the family business. Also, we have your university savings account for you and your trust fund, of course. Next week at work I can give you all the details," she says, casually releasing the hug.

My head was spinning. "Trust fund?"

"Oh." Kathleen winces. "She didn't tell you about that either, did she?"

"There seems to be a theme developing, with my mom."

"Everything okay?" Grant quietly asks, concern lacing his voice as he looks in.

I smile at my father's concern. My *real* father. My *Dad.* The man who flaws and all, and still wants to know me.

"Yeah," I say. "Everything's good."

But for the first time in weeks, maybe even months, I wasn't just saying that. I *mean* it. *Everything is good.*

There's no rush to leave here. No pressing work assignments or meetings. No drama or reason to escape. Just... them. Just this messy, loud, beautiful dinner, where no one's pretending, and I'm not a third wheel.

I've always needed people—Lisa, Darius, Alexis—always clinging to whatever gave me a sense of being wanted. But here, in this room, surrounded by people who chose to include me, I feel like I belong. I am *seen*. I am not just a project or playing a role. I am a part of something.

The sounds of laughter, the clink of forks on plates, and the teasing between Grant and Kathleen fill the air. The extra sauce had spilled on my shirt in all the chaos. The family dinner is messy, imperfect, and precisely what I never knew I was missing.

And for the first time in a long while, I don't feel like I have to rush to the next thing, run away from my emotions.

I want to stay here forever with my family. I want to hold on to this moment, to this feeling of being *home.*

Chapter 22

Unjinxing My Life—One Muffin at a Time

My phone buzzes for the fifth time in an hour.

I wish it were Alexis, texting me to take me to the fancy dinner she mentioned. But since I agreed to give her time to consider meeting my family, she's been radio silent, even when I left the flowers for her at the office. I want to imagine that she's mulling over my feelings. Still, knowing her, she's simply taking the opportunity to work more hours.

Darius is blowing up my phone and has been for the last three days, demanding updates on my family dinner and how I'm coping with my diagnosis. Since researching Intersex and confronting my mom, I'm either subconsciously ignoring my emotions, or I'm leaning into what Dr. Winters said, that it doesn't change who I am. It's not something I need to treat or seek medical help for.

I'd promised to update him today after brushing him off this weekend.

Honestly? I'm not sure how I feel about my family dinner.

The dinner was a dream and too good to be true. I'm waiting for the other shoe to drop. I'm afraid I'll tell him how great it was and jinx it. Will my chaos magnet extend to my dad and new family?

I tuck my phone away and straighten my blazer—the fancy one I'd stolen from Alexis and call mine now. The blazer makes me look like I belonged in Alexis's world of polished business awards and executive decisions, instead of perpetually feeling like I'm faking being an adult and a career woman.

"You're going to face your problems head-on today: see Alexis and talk to Darius. No running away," I whisper to my reflection in the elevator's mirrored wall. My red hair cooperates for once, and I've even applied eyeliner without smearing it. I'm ready to slay today. *Progress.*

The elevator door opens to the executive floor of Alaska Temp Agency, and my stomach drops as my throat tightens. Alexis's office door is open, and I hear her rapid-fire conversation through the phone. Something about "quarterly projections" and "client acquisition strategies." CEO talk.

Darius's desk is empty.

I opened my phone to see what messages I missed from him.

"I must have got what Richard has." But the following text is a picture of him grinning in front of the Nordstrom off-the-rack sale.

I sent him a laughing face emoji. "I'll check on you later. I can't believe I'm the best employee out of us?!"

Alexis glances up, her impossibly deep brown eyes meeting mine. She gives me a quick smile before holding up one finger in the universal "just a minute" gesture.

I nod and try to look casual, like I'm not about to confront my gorgeous girlfriend to make dinner plans with the ulterior motive of discussing my medical diagnosis. And somehow weave into the conversation:

Oh, by the way, maybe I want to work at my dad's company permanently and leave

yours. Thank you for the opportunity, experience, and university scholarship. I still want to be your girlfriend and make out. I don't want to work for you anymore, okay? I'm choosing my family.

No pressure.

"Aurora, hey," Alexis says finally, setting down her phone. That's the most she's said to me in the last few days. She worked through the weekend, while I worked through a pint of Cherry Garcia ice cream and a new dating reality show. I'm hooked, and I totally think the lead contender for the bachelor's heart is actually a lesbian.*

Alexis looks exhausted but still somehow flawless and confident in her charcoal suit, yellow sneakers, and an expensive white t-shirt. I love her eccentric business-with-a-flair style. I'm totally adopting it when I'm successful and wealthy.

"Sorry about that. The board's breathing down my neck about my CEO transition. Apparently being a female and taking over the company your father built means twice the scrutiny and half the forgiveness." She smiles, but it looks strained.

"No worries," I say, aiming for understanding, but the fast delivery makes me sound more like a caffeinated squirrel. "Are you busy?"

"Always," she laughs, running a hand through her sleek black hair. "But never too busy for you, Trouble. What's up?"

This is it. The moment I'd rehearsed sixteen times in my shower this morning.

"I was wondering if maybe you'd want to have dinner tonight? Not like a work dinner, but dinner dinner. There's some stuff I want to talk to you about, and—" I'm rambling. I feel the hot flush creeping up my neck.

Alexis's expression shifts subtly, and my heart sinks before she even opens her mouth. I already know she will choose to work late rather than have dinner with me.

"Aurora..." she begins, and that one word contains her rejection. "I wish I could. We will talk more later. But the board sent over a hundred pages of documentation for tomorrow's meeting, and I haven't even started reviewing them."

"Right, of course," I say, quickly. "It was a last minute idea. No problem at all. That sounds important. You are the new CEO."

"It's not that I don't want—"

"Seriously, it's fine," I insist, forcing a smile. "We can do it another time."

"Definitely," she says, relief evident in her voice and already looking away at the stack of files on her desk. "Maybe next week when things settle down?"

We both know things wouldn't settle down. They never do. Our cozy coffee breaks and quick office makeout sessions have dwindled to nothing, and our late-night talks are replaced by short texts about work, if she even responds.

"Perfect," I lie, backing toward the door. "Good luck with your board stuff."

I'm almost out when her phone chimes with a text. She glances down at it, and a small, genuine smile crosses her face—the kind I haven't seen directed at me in a while.

"Aurora," she calls as I reach the door. "Could you close that on your way out? I need to take this."

I close the door, but not before hearing her answer her phone warmly, "Hey, Rachel..."

The hard click of the door closing matches the sound of something breaking in my chest.

I text Darius, "Do you know who Rachel is? Alexis is chatting with her but it sounded personal."

"Rachel is a pretty common name. It could be a new client?" Darius texts back a little too fast.

"But you know more. I can tell."

"She was dating someone named Rachel. I'm sure it's a coincidence. It's a super-common name," He sends back.

I shove half a chocolate chip muffin in my mouth and try to not worry. "I'm not worried, but tell me everything you know about Rachael, now!!!"

"Rachel is her ex from law school," Darius calls, and the shopping center is in the background as I take him to the bathroom with me to talk in private.

He continues, "I've met her and made restaurant reservations for them before. They didn't seem too into each other, but are from the same richy rich club. Rachel's got her daddy's hedge fund and a country club membership that is at the same club as Alexis."

"Do you think she's dating her, too?" I ask him point-blank.

"Alexis is too busy to date you! And there's nothing I have scheduled for them," he says. "I think you're over-thinking this."

I hear a cashier ask him for his membership card and if he wants Airmiles today.

"I gotta go, Girl," he says with a flash of a smile. "I'm sick, you know."

I swallow the rest of my tasteless muffin and chew on my lip, wondering what to do with this Rachael information.

My phone buzzes with a text from Zara, "You want to do some textbook shopping? I'm going to the bookstore after work."

Chapter 23

Campus Confessions and Platonic Book-Buying

Zara is easy to spot, leaning against a pillar outside the science building. Her dark hair is pulled into a messy bun, and she wears stylish black skinny jeans and a velvet jacket over a vintage band t-shirt. She looks deliberately styled rather than an outfit thrown together with whatever clean clothing she can find. She waves when she sees me, a warm smile lighting up her face.

"Hey, accounting genius, business major," she calls as I approach. "Ready to drop obscene amounts of money on textbooks?"

"As ready as I'll ever be," I reply, stepping beside her. "Though I might need a loan by the end of this."

"Nah, you've got a fancy scholarship," she bumped my shoulder with hers. "Some of us mere mortals have to ask their parents for money instead of relying on brains alone."

I laugh, grateful for her invitation to shop for university books and grab a coffee afterward. Zara isn't girlfriend material—at least, that's not how I see her—but she is definitely friend material. And honestly? I could use a study buddy and a fun campus partner-in-crime.

The campus bookstore is packed with students. We squeeze through the crowds, finding our way to the business section for my accounting textbooks and then to the science section for Zara's huge textbooks.

"I still can't believe your passion is science," I said, watching her load up with thick technical manuals. "That's seriously cool."

She shrugs, but looks pleased. "My sister thinks I'm crazy. Says I should go into business, like you."

"Ah yes, Jaime," I say, with a blush. "Of course, she says that, since she works in a government office. I love you, so I'll tell you the truth. Follow your passion... even if its fungi," I say, looking at her scary microbiology book's cover.

Her eyes are dancing, and she looks like I just accidentally revealed Jaime's secret, then I realize what I said. "I mean, I love you like a friend. Because we're Bucking good friends, right?" I joke, trying to redeem my wayward mouth. I'm trying so hard to protect Jaime's secret that I'm not even sure what I'm saying anymore.

Zara looks amused. "I know what you meant, Aurora. Though for the record, I love you, too. In a you-better-not-let-your-guard-down-or-I'll-buy-us-a-shared-poodle sorta way."

How can I throw out the word 'love' without blinking anymore? Maybe having my father in my life and my mom out of my life makes it less taboo and dangerous?

"Good to know," I laugh and bump into a display of highlighters. She grabs the rack before it falls.

After paying for our books—the total making my credit card weep silently—we wandered over to the student union building. It's modern and airy, with huge windows overlooking the mountains. Rainbow flags and inclusive signage decorated the walls, and students of all types mingled in the common areas.

"Want to check out the clubs?" Zara nods toward a row of tables where student organizations are recruiting new members.

We drift through the displays, collecting flyers and free pens. The LGBTQ+ Alliance table catches my eye with its colorful banner and friendly faces.

"You should sign up," Zara says, noticing my interest. "They do great events. I went to their winter formal last year."

"Maybe," I say, taking a flyer. "It's just... I don't know. I'm still figuring stuff out."

A sign for gender-neutral housing caught my eye, and my stomach does a funny flip, like maybe I need to actually see Dr. Winter and talk more about my diagnosis. Androgen Insensitivity Syndrome. The words are so matter-of-fact, like they don't completely upend my understanding of my body.

"Earth to Aurora," Zara waves a hand in front of my face. "Where'd you go?"

I blink, coming back to the present. "Sorry. Just thinking."

"About your ex?" she asked gently.

She's my girlfriend now, is what I should say. But I shrug. "Among other things." I sigh, not wanting to get into my drama in the middle of the student union. "It's complicated."

"Isn't it always?" She smiles sympathetically. "Look, do you want to get out of here? There's a nice quiet spot by the lake where we can talk. Or not talk. Whatever you need."

The genuine concern in her voice nearly broke me. "That sounds perfect, actually."

The lake is small but serene, tucked behind the science buildings. We find a bench under a pine tree and sit side by side, watching ducks glide across the dark water.

"So," Zara says after a comfortable silence. "Want to tell me what's really going on with you?"

I take a deep breath. "Have you ever had something you needed to tell someone, but you kept finding reasons not to?"

"Like coming out to my parents?" she asks wryly.

"Something like that," I admit. "There's something I need to tell my boss, but every time I try, either the moment isn't right, or she's too busy, or I chicken out."

"Must be pretty serious."

"It is." I pluck at the edge of my sleeve. "It's about me. Who I am. And I'm scared it might change how she sees me."

Zara is quiet for a moment. "Can I ask you something kind of direct?"

"Sure."

"Is it really your boss you're talking about?"

I shake my head, reddening at being caught. "It's my girlfriend who happens to be my boss, too."

"Okay. That's gotta be complicated," she says.

I stare out at the lake and decide I have nothing to lose. "What if I told you I was intersex? That I was born with male chromosomes but a female body? That I just found out?"

I hadn't planned to tell Zara—hadn't planned to tell anyone today. But something about her, the peaceful lake, and the feeling of being completely removed from my regular life made it possible.

"What would you think if I told you I was actually biologically a man?"

I turn to her, startled by the abrupt question. "Are you?"

She laughs. "No. But hypothetically. Would it change how you see me?"

I shrug and consider her. "No. I mean, you'd still be a mechanical moose riding biology major. I guess you'd look the same. I mean, I wouldn't care, Zara."

"Exactly," she says, nodding. "So, if that's how you feel about a friend, why wouldn't your partner feel the same way about you?"

"Because it's different when it's romantic," I say, quietly. "There are expectations. Complications. Fifteen year life plans that need to change."

"If she loves you for you, then those things are just details to work through together," Zara says, shrugging. "And if she doesn't... well, then you deserve someone who accepts you and can change plans for you."

I nod, tears pricking at my eyes. Hearing it from her, a friend I just made, and not Darius or Lisa saying these words, makes me believe them more.

Zara didn't miss a beat. "Biology is funny, right? Maybe you need to change your major."

I laugh, and then my emotions overwhelm me. I hiccup, and my eyes tear up. The tears spill over then, and Zara puts her arm around me. We sat like that for a while, watching the ducks and the sun setting while I pulled myself together.

"Thanks," I whisper eventually.

"For what? Being a decent human?"

"For making it seem so simple."

She squeezes my shoulder. "Sometimes it is simple. We're the ones who make it complicated."

My phone rang, interrupting the moment. It's Grant.

"Hey," I answer, wiping away the last traces of tears. "Everything okay?"

"Just checking in," Grant's warm voice came through the line. "Indie mentioned you posted a picture at the university bookstore. Do you need me to transfer you money before your funds come through?"

The concern in his voice is still new to me—this whole having-a-father-who-cares thing is weird, but kind of sweet, too.

"I'm okay," I say. "Just buying books and hanging out with a friend. I'll see you at work tomorrow or at family dinner if you're too busy to talk."

"I'm never too busy to talk, Aurora. Have a good night and be safe," he says, as I hang up.

My tears return, and I sit in stunned silence. Zara is waiting patiently.

"That was my dad," I say finally, the word 'dad' feeling foreign and strange. "He has a college fund for me. And a job, if I want it."

"Don't you work for your girlfriend? Would she be mad at you leaving?" Zara asks.

"I have a lot of things to talk with her about, She's just really busy, an important person."

My phone buzzes with a text. "The meeting ran long and I might have to cancel our morning check-in tomorrow. A"

"You know what's crazy?" I say, showing Zara the text. "I've told a practical stranger my biggest secret, but I can't even get five minutes with the woman I'm supposedly dating."

"First of all, *ouch.* 'Practical stranger'?" Zara fake punches my arm.

"You know what I mean," I laugh despite myself.

"And second," she continues, "maybe that tells you something important."

She's right. It does tell me something.

"If you just want to hang out anytime, I'm available." She stands and offers me a hand up from the bench. "In a non-dating, non-judgy capacity. No pressure."

I take her hand and stand, suddenly aware of how close we are and how warm I feel despite the chill.

"Just friends?" I clarify.

She smiles. "Just friends and platonic book-buying buddies. And maybe I can convince you to be my date to my brother's wedding."

I've told her all my secrets, but I can't spill this last secret, so I laugh instead. "Thank you. For everything today."

My phone buzzes again.

Darius. "EMERGENCY UPDATE REQUIRED. Did you confront the workaholic girlfriend? Are you drowning sorrows in ice cream? Do I need to bring tequila?"

I smile and type back, "No confrontation. No ice cream needed. But I think I finally know what I need to do."

Chapter 24

The Burger Blues

Okay. Breathe. I repeat this three times like it's a spell that might stop me from combusting into a ball of redhead rage or dissolving into tears.

She doesn't answer.

I don't wait. I walk to my car and scream into the steering wheel.

I can't do it. I can't be honest with Alexis if she doesn't communicate with me.

When I got home, Lisa was on the couch in a robe, with a face mask on, binging on the same dating show I had already started watching. I want to ask her if she can spot the lesbian, but I'll wait a few more episodes. I don't want to spoil it for her.

"How'd your date with Alexis go?" she asks, pausing the TV. "That was kinda quick?"

I plop beside her. "She never answered, so here I am."

"You okay, babe?" she asks gently, offering me a Poptart straight from the package.

"Do I look okay?"

"No," she says with a laugh, "You look like you tried to emotionally process through eyeliner and failed."

I groan. "I can't seem to corner Alexis to go on a date. Then, I told Zara about my diagnosis. I might quit the job. Also, I may need to invest in a reliable car and maybe a therapist."

She looks back at her show. "So the usual."

I laugh, and we both crack up watching dating episodes for the next hour.

My phone buzzes.

Alexis texts, "Sorry again. I'll make it up to you."

I type a message to Alexis. "I want to talk. For real. I need you to...idk.. Care?. Just pencil me in between conference calls. I'm dying here. You are being a bad girlfriend and a bad boss. Where are you?"

I don't send it. I slowly delete the message, letter by letter, and close my phone.

"We should see if Darius will stop by and bring us burgers."

"I might need more therapy than just burgers," I reply, wiping poptart crumbs from my chest.

She pulls out her phone. "Then let's add curly fries and chocolate malts to that order."

Chapter 25

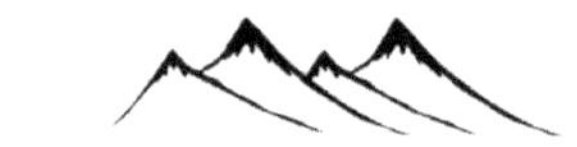

Quiche Me, Baby One More Time

Silence.

The kind that makes your heart drum in your ears, like maybe it's the background music for the awkwardness of being alive. I sink deeper into Donna's therapy couch, clutching an old birthday themed paper napkin that still holds the scent of a fresh blueberry muffin. Apparently, her brand of therapy here comes with freshly baked breakfast foods.

Despite the yummy muffin, my mouth stops, worn out from the marathon it just ran. I talked nonstop, nervously at first, and then everything came tumbling out. That's what it felt like—just an endless stream for twenty minutes, I unleashed every dramatic twist of my life like an Alaska avalanche—loud, unstoppable. This was way too much for a casual Tuesday therapy session.

And now, more silence.

Donna sits across from me, her classic thick black glasses perched stylishly on her nose—both sensible and elegant. Her eyes hold the knowing look of a wise grandmother, yet her youthful, middle-aged frame gives her an unexpected allure. She exudes a calm, collected presence that feels both grounded and effortlessly cool.

TILF. Therapist, I'd like to... well, you know. Is being attracted to my therapist going to be a problem?

I pause to collect my thoughts and admire her hair, clipped up in this messy bun. The flowy, blue-green jumpsuit with a ridiculously charming floral apron tied over it. Mom-ish, right? What does it say about me that I'm attracted to mom vibes? Only her thick, black-rimmed glasses screamed "therapist."

Does she even need glasses? Maybe they're purely aesthetic, a signal that she's a professional. A *very* attractive prop.

"Well." Donna leans back, tilting her glasses down to peer at me. "You've been holding that in."

"Ya think?" I squeak, then laugh.

She cocks her head and waits for me to continue.

I bite my lip, instantly regretting my sarcasm. "Sorry, nervous humor. My default setting."

I lick my lips. Okay, honesty time. "I know you can't tell me what to do, but maybe you can funnel me in the right direction?"

She leans forward and pushes her glasses up, her gaze unwavering. "My goal is to help you find your way. You have a lot to process, and a lot of changes are happening, but not all are bad."

Her words hang in the air, a verbal period at the end of my twenty-minute, caffeinated monologue. I'd just word vomited every last detail of my life since our last session—the discovery that I was intersex, the whirlwind of finding my biological dad, my terrible mom, and the overwhelming, terrifying, and exhilarating reality of working for him at the family business. My confession spilled out in a torrent, leaving me breathless and deflated.

I sink deeper into the plush armchair, its scent a comforting mix of old books and floral potpourri. Donna's home office is a sanctuary. Sunlight streams through a large window, melting the frost on the edges and illuminating the last mosquito of the season dancing through the air.

Glancing over at Donna, her gaze was gentle, unwavering, and utterly devoid of the shock I'd been bracing for. She nods slowly, encouraging me to continue. Unlike the therapists in movies, she isn't scribbling furiously in a notepad or, thankfully, chewing on a pipe. She's simply listening, her eyes imploring.

"You're breathing. You're here and facing these challenges head-on. And you're still alive with a sense of humor," she says, her voice calm and steady. "That's a good start."

I take a bite of the muffin and a sip of the tea. It's chamomile, and it smells like a hug feels. But then—*scalding lava*—I swallow a mouthful of molten disaster. My face scrunches in panic as I suddenly have to spit it back into the cup, awkwardly. Donna watches, half concerned, half trying not to laugh. "Well," I say, wiping my mouth, "guess it's... an extra hot mess like me today."

Donna remains motionless, watching me.

"I do feel better," I admit, a little shamefaced. "And also, I feel like I just confessed to a murder."

She chuckles, her eyes crinkling at the corners. "And what murder would that be?"

"The murder of my perfect life since I have a great job, a full ride to business school, found the dad I thought was dead, and I'm dating a woman totally out of my league," I explain, sighing dramatically. "Telling you the truth and everyone else, my diagnosis—My dad, my friends, even Zara. It's really liberating. But I've told everyone but the one person who matters most."

"And who would that be?"

"Alexis," I whisper. The name makes my gut clench. "I need to tell her everything. I just don't know how."

"Let's go back to what you said earlier," Donna suggests. "About telling everyone except the one who matters most. Why do you think that is?"

"Because it feels like a big deal," I say, the words coming out in a rush. "It's a big deal to *me*. And if I tell her, and she reacts badly... I don't know what I'll do. She's so... perfect. So poised. So together. I'm just this awkward mess."

"You're not a mess, Aurora," Donna says firmly. "You're a person who received massive information about your life. And you're processing it. And you're doing a damn good job of it. You found your biological family. You started a new job. You're building new relationships. You're telling people. That's really brave."

Tears prickle my eyes, and I blush for no reason. "But what if she doesn't want me? What if she thinks I'm a freak? What if all my secrets–my drama–are too much for her?"

"And what if it's not? What if she's exactly the person you think she is? What if she's so amazing that she loves you for exactly who you are, intersex. messy and all?"

"I don't know," I whisper, biting my lower lip and taking another warming sip. "It just feels so vulnerable. I've always been good at putting on a brave face. At pretending like everything is fine. Ever since I pretended to be her perfect employee, everything has been going fine. But when I show her the messy, emotional person, not the smiling perfect one... You know, that's what my mom taught me, to smile and suck it up."

"And what did your mother teach you about love?" Donna's voice cuts through the quiet, her gaze steady and intense, as if she's searching for something buried deep inside me.

"That it's a transaction," I say, the words tasting bitter even as they leave my mouth. "You give something, you get something. If you don't give enough, you don't get love."

She studies me for a long moment. "Do you believe that?"

I don't answer right away. Silence stretches between us, heavy and uncertain.

"Do you think you have to earn love?" Her voice softens. "Let me ask it another way. You told me about your neighbor's cat—the one you call Mr. Whiskers. Do you expect anything from him? Does he have to do something to deserve your love, or do you love him simply because he exists?"

I think about Mr. Whiskers—how I stroke his fur without demand, how his presence fills a quiet corner of my world. No conditions. No expectations.

Donna leans in, her eyes gentle but firm. "Babies, animals, old people, friends—they show us what unconditional love truly is. It isn't earned. It isn't given as a reward. It simply is. And you, Aurora, you are just as deserving of that love—without strings, without conditions. You don't have to prove yourself to be worthy."

Her words settle around me like a warm embrace, breaking down walls I didn't realize I'd built.

She waits, then asks softly, "And what do you want from love, Aurora?"

"I want a real relationship." I sniffle, my nose stuffy with emotion. "I want something serious. Something safe. Something where I can be myself, my dumpster fires and all."

"And what is Alexis offering you?"

"A casual arrangement," I say, a bitter laugh escaping my lips. "She's always busy working. She doesn't have time for me. She says she wants a relationship, but her actions say otherwise. I mean aside from our physical stuff–that's pretty intense."

"And what about this new friend, Zara?"

I smile, a genuine one this time. "She's... easy. She's fun. We have a lot in common. She's just a friend, though."

"Is she?" Donna asks, a hint of a smile on her own lips. "Or is she an escape? A way to feel safe without having to confront the difficult reality of your relationship with Alexis?"

I didn't answer. I just took another sip of my tea. She is right, of course. I held back the drama with my tryst with Zara's sister, since it seemed unrelated to my current stress. Plus, who'd believe my crazy coincidental story of sleeping with my blind dates sister.

"You're searching for safety and someone to love you, Aurora," she says, softly. "Because your mother didn't provide the unconditional love that children usually receive from their parents. She kept secrets from you. She made you feel like you had to earn her love, and you couldn't be you. And now you're looking for that safety in other people. In Alexis, in Zara, even in your new relationship with your father."

"But my dad is *different*," I explain, quickly. "He's so... accepting. He doesn't want anything from me. He just wants to know me. And my new family... They're seriously amazing. It's like the family I always dreamed of having."

Donna smiles. "And that's a beautiful thing. But don't let it blind you to what you need from your romantic relationships. You need to be able to communicate with the person you love who you are, without fear of judgment. You need to be able to ask for what you need."

"What if what I need is too much?" I ask, my voice cracking.

"Then they're not the right person for you," Donna asserts. "It doesn't matter what anyone else thinks about your diagnosis. It's a part of you. Just like your red hair. You're not responsible for their reactions or their emotions. You're only responsible for yourself."

A wave of relief washes over me. It's like she is giving me permission to be myself. To be selfish. To put myself first for once.

"You described your diagnosis, not as terrifying, but 'a relief,'" Donna says, her gaze holding mine. "Why?"

"Because it explains everything." The words tumbling out of me. "I've always felt different. The super tall, awkward girl in school. The outcast that didn't fit in with any groups. The one who bonded with the gay classmate, Darius. Because he was different too. And now I know why. I *am* different. Biologically. And it's not a bad thing. It's just... me."

"And what about your sexuality?" Donna prods. "You said you've been embracing your lesbian identity. Does this diagnosis change that?"

I shrug. "I don't know. I've never been sexually attracted to guys. I mean I've tried... So I kinda thought I was a lesbian. But if I'm not a real woman... Does that mean I'm also not a real lesbian?"

"Does it matter?" Donna asks. "Do you need a label?"

I think about it, and finish drinking my tea. "I guess not. But it's nice to have a word for it. It makes it feel more real."

"Then how about 'queer'?" Donna suggests. "It's a good catch-all. It's a word that says, 'I don't fit into a neat box, and I'm okay with that.'"

I grin and nod, unconsciously. "I like that. *Queer.*"

"So, what's next, Aurora? What are you going to do now?"

"I'm going to tell Alexis," I vow, lifting my chin. "I'm going to tell her everything. And if she can't handle it, then she's not the person for me."

Donna smiles, a genuine, motherly-proud smile. "That's a brave step, Aurora. A very brave step."

"And I'm going to choose me," I say, my voice steady and sure. "I'm putting myself first—for once. I'm going to start university and build the life I've always wanted. A life where I don't have to plan an escape route. In that life, I'll find a loving relationship that's safe, real, and true."

Donna smiles, a quiet warmth in her eyes. "You're already doing that. And you carry that love you're searching for—with your friends, within yourself, and in the connections you're beginning to trust."

The session ends, but I don't feel the usual weight pressing down on my chest.

Instead, I step out lighter, as if I've shed an old, heavy coat that no longer fits. The world outside feels sharper, more alive. The air bites crisp and clean. Even the Alaskan landscape, often dull and bleak this time of year, seems transformed—brighter, more welcoming, as if the trees and sky themselves are inviting me forward, daring me to meet whatever comes next with open arms.

Chapter 26

Telling Alexis

My car was a mess. A veritable graveyard of empty coffee cups, half-eaten protein bars, and crumpled-up napkins. I pushed aside a few of the more egregious offenders and started the engine. The drive from Donna's house to Alexis's office is a blur. The city of Anchorage is so spread out, and traffic slows as people test out the maybe-icy streets, but everything speeds up. The mountains in the distance shrink. Everything is muted, as if the world holds its breath, waiting for me to make my move.

I pull up to the sleek, glass building where we work. It's a cold place, all steel, polished glass, and expensive art. It perfectly reflects her: beautiful, intimidating, and hopelessly unattainable.

Taking a deep breath, and then another. I pep-talk myself. I'm a grown woman. I have a dad, job, and sense of self. I can handle this.

I enter the lobby, the air-conditioning a cold shock against my skin. Making my way to our floor and Alexis, I ran into Darius.

"I thought you were taking today off?" he asks.

"I'm here to see Alexis," I say, not wanting to get derailed.

He sees my intense focus, and he nods, stepping back for me to pass.

He adds, "She's in a meeting. It could be a while."

"I'll wait." And I sit down on her leather chairs, and text her that I'm outside.

I waited for thirty minutes. Then an hour. I'm about to give up when the doors to her office open and Alexis emerges, a sleek, black suit-wearing bad-ass boss. She is laughing, her head thrown back, and a beautiful, dazzling smile is on her face. Her clients, two men in equally expensive suits, are fawning over her.

She sees me, and her smile falters. Her eyes widened, and there was a flicker of something—surprise? Annoyance? Worry?—passing through them. She excuses herself from her clients and walks over to me, her movements graceful and fluid—a predator.

"Aurora," she says quietly, her voice dropping just enough to catch me off guard—like when my mother would quietly scold me in public, making me freeze for a second. "I wasn't expecting you. Is everything okay?"

"I need to talk to you," I whisper, then lick my lips and say louder, "It's important."

She hesitates for a split second, then nods. "Let's go into my office."

Opening the door for me, I feel like I always do inside her space, which is small and like I'm faking. I feel like I don't belong. Her office is a monument to her success. The glass windows overlook the ocean and city. Her walls are lined with awards and accolades, and her large mahogany desk makes me blush thinking about the last time I was sitting on it.

She gestures for me to sit on a plush chair, but I shake my head. I need to stand. I need to be on equal footing and don't want to get comfortable.

"What's going on?" she asks, her voice sharper now. "You look upset."

"I'm not upset," I declare. "I'm... relieved. I have something I need to tell you."

I take a deep breath. I tell her *everything*. About finding out I was intersex. About the doctors, the tests, and the diagnosis. Talking to my friend Zara but not being able to tell her. The relief, clarity, and how it finally made sense of my entire life. There's so much to tell her and so much I've been holding back. I study her face as I speak. The initial surprise gives way to a flicker of something hiding behind her business-like demeanor—discomfort? Confusion?—then her usual mask of neutrality. She doesn't interrupt me. She simply listens, her gaze fixed on her bookshelf.

When I'm finished, there is a long, heavy silence. The only sound is the faint ticking of the clock on her wall.

"I... I don't know what to say," she admits as her eyes finally meet mine. Her eyes have lost their warm, chocolatey color and are almost black.

"You don't have to say anything," I said, choking with the emotion of telling her everything. "I just needed to tell you. I couldn't... I couldn't not tell you. Not if we're going to be in a serious, long-term relationship. Not if I'm going to be your girlfriend and part of your long term plan."

"A long-term relationship?" she asks, a hint of a frown sketched across her angular face. "Aurora, we have an understanding. A girlfriend dating arrangement."

"But I don't want a work situationship arrangement," I respond with my voice cracking. "I want a real relationship. I want something serious. A relationship where we don't have secrets. Something safe. Something where I can be myself, flaws and all."

She sighs, running a hand through her hair. "Aurora, I don't need to know your secrets and I'm not sure how to respond to your health stuff. I don't have time for a relationship that's more than what we have. *You know that.* My career is my priority. I'm building an empire. I can't... I can't be tied down right now."

"What about the future?" I ask, a desperate plea in my voice. "What about five years from now? Ten years? What about the kids you always talk about?"

She hesitates, her gaze dropping to the floor. Outside the office, people leave for the day, and the lights are turned off. "I do have a plan, but this *drama*–all of *this*- doesn't fit into it. We work well, so let's just keep things as is."

My heart sinks. A cold, hard realization settles in my stomach. She's right. I know that. I've always known it. She wants something different from me and can't give me what I want. I can't believe she didn't even address my huge intersex diagnosis. But maybe it's better that she didn't, since I can't be her stay-at-home wife and carry her children.

"So you're saying... you don't want me if it involves more than a casual relationship?...nothing actually deep or complex that may disturb your perfectly curated life?" I ask, my voice barely a whisper. "Does my medical issue and not being able to have kids mean there's no future for us?"

"No!" she says, too loud. "Of course not. That's not what I'm saying. I'm not in a place to have a serious relationship right now. I'm not ready for everything you want."

"I gave you time, and I'm giving you me. What are you ready for, Alexis?" I ask her, unwilling to drop the issue and make peace, like usual, "What do you want from me? A casual arrangement filled with secrets? You can keep me in your back pocket until you're ready to move on to someone else?"

She doesn't answer. She looks at me, her face a mask of regret and... something else. Something I haven't seen before so I can't quite put my finger on. It makes me pause but only for a millisecond before I let my momentum carry me to the inevitable ending.

"You're not what I want," I say, the words a final nail in the coffin. "And I'm not settling for what you're offering."

"Aurora, don't be dramatic—"

"I'm not being dramatic. I'm being honest—with you and with myself. We want different things, and that's okay. But I deserve someone who wants the same things I do."

Alexis follows me to the door. "So that's it? You're ending things because I'm not going to get married to you?"

"I only ask for you to care about me and make me a priority," I say with tears already streaming. "I love you Alexis. I didn't know love until I met you." I turn to face her one last time, taking in her beautiful face, trying to memorize every detail.

She looks out her window at the dark ocean and the start of rain. "You don't have to end it."

"Then what?" I demand, unlike my usual quiet self.

"You are blindsiding me here. I'm giving you a better life and you're mad. I don't ask you enough how you're feeling or have time to see you everyday? You have friends for that. You see me at work and I'm doing everything to make sure you succeed."

I shake my head, as all she can think about is work, not my feelings or us.

"Aurora—"

I cut her off with a sad smile. "It's okay, *really*. Thank you for helping me figure out what I deserve."

"I'm sorry, Trouble," she says softly, using my pet name. "I really am."

"I know," I say, and another tear escapes, rolling down my cheek. "I know."

The door closes behind me with a soft click. I wait for the crushing sadness to overwhelm me, but instead I'm energized.

She doesn't follow me or try to stop me.

I turn and walk out of her cold office. I don't look back. I just keep walking, out of her business, out of her life, and back out into the world. The world that is still there, and warm enough that I don't need my coat. The world is still waiting for me.

I get into my car, and I drive. I don't know where I'm going. I just know I am going. I am going to be an adult. An independent woman. I am going to live on my own. I am going to find a life that I love. And I am going to find a love that is real. And as I drive, I look out the window at the sun setting in the endless Alaskan sky, and I finally understand what my therapist, Donna, meant. I am choosing myself. And it is the bravest, scariest thing I'd ever done.

Chapter 27

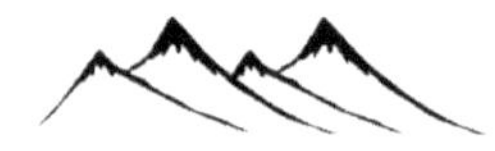

The Ex-Files

Lisa was already in pajamas when I got home, sprawling across our couch with a bowl of popcorn and watching a housewife murder show on the living room TV. She takes one look at my face and pauses the movie.

"Oh no. What happened? Did you 'quiche' your therapist again?"

Any remnants of guilt or uncertainty dissolve when I giggle at her guess. "No. The therapist was fine–great actually. It was afterwards when I was with Alexis."

"Wait. Did Alexis go psycho or do something? Do I need to slash her tires? Because *you know* I will."

I can't help but laugh as I collapse next to her, grabbing a handful of popcorn. "No tire-slashing necessary. I broke up with her, I think. Or more accurately, I realized we were never really together."

"Do I need to find Mr. Whiskers to comfort you?" Lisa's eyebrows shoot up as she starts to get up.

I hold her hand, "Nope. It's not dramatic enough to need my furry couch therapist."

She side-eyes me and grabs the popcorn. "Details. *Now*."

"She called our relationship an 'arrangement.' And referred to how much she's helping me professionally after I told her about my diagnosis. She didn't respond when I told her I wanted a serious relationship." I shovel popcorn into my mouth. "Turns out I'm a walking, talking business project and easy date to her this whole time."

"That cold-hearted bitch," Lisa hisses. "You were her side piece, a work booty call. I always knew there was something *off* about her. No one is *that* perfect, a hot lesbian CEO. She's seriously messed up."

"The weird thing is," I say, "I'm not as devastated as I thought I'd be. I mean, I'm sad and embarrassed that I misjudged things.. her... so badly. But, I'm also... relieved? Like I've been waiting for the relationship to implode, and now it finally has."

Lisa studies me curiously. "Your therapy session must have been epic."

"Oh, you have *no idea.*" I cover my face and whisper, "I'm choosing me and no more people pleasing."

"Yes! I love this for you," Lisa shrieks, popcorn flying everywhere as she bolts upright and reaches to pull me in a tight hug.

"Thank goodness I have you and Darius. I don't know what I'd do without you guys," I say, and grab for more popcorn.

"Aww, you are the best and super-entertaining," Lisa says, releasing me from the hug. "For what it's worth, I'm proud of you. Both for trying therapy and for standing up for yourself with Alexis. That takes mad guts."

My phone buzzes with a text. Darius.

"Richard says Alexis told him you guys are done. Cocktails and commiseration at our place in thirty. Non-negotiable. He's making his famous passion fruit margaritas, and I'm ordering takeout from that Thai place you love."

I show Lisa the message. "Wanna come? Apparently, Darius and Richard already heard. Richard's in our super-secret inter circle of trust, so it's all good."

She looks at her stained pajamas and laughs. "And miss the opportunity to trash-talk your boss while drinking Richard's legendary margaritas? Not a chance. Give me five minutes to change."

Lisa disappears into her bedroom, and I slump back against the couch, finally letting myself feel the relief, the hurt, and the strange sense of freedom.

My phone buzzes again.

"We have ice cream, too!"Darius texts and the pic of ice cream and an upside-down smiley face does cheer me up.

A smile tugs at my lips as I text back a thumbs-up.

"Ready!" Lisa announces, emerging in a ridiculous sequined top and leggings. "What's that smile about? Are you already plotting Alexis's downfall with Darius? Because I have some pretty diabolical ideas, too."

I shake my head, pocketing my phone. "Just thinking that maybe therapy was one of my better ideas. I learned quite a few things. I don't need a girlfriend, afterall. I just need friends like you guys!"

"Truth! And don't forget you did get a bonus makeout with your therapist," she laughs. "That'll warm your heart and make you forget all about Alexis is. Wait—" she pauses, slipping on her wedges. "What does your therapist look like, again? Is there a possibility of something starting there? I must meet her."

"No. It isn't—" I start to protest, then give up with a laugh. "Never mind. I'll tell you the story as we drive. Let's get drunk, eat too many calories, and make bad decisions."

"So our usual," she says with a wink.

Chapter 28

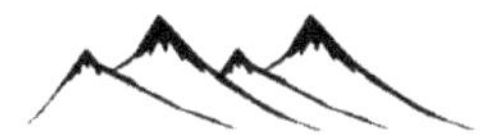

Mr. Whiskers' Purr-fect Distraction

"Don't let go!" I scream, my fingertips just inches from Mr. Whiskers' tail as he perches on the narrow ledge, looking infuriatingly unbothered by the whole situation.

Seconds after slipping on my shoes, I opened the door to Mr. Whiskers raced inside and instead of jumping on our couch, he leaped through the open window as if he was a bird and not a cat. I never thought I'd be in the middle of a cat emergency just after the most soul-crushing breakup of my life, especially since I don't even own a cat—but here I am—dangling halfway out my second-story apartment window.

Lisa's hands are clutching my ankles, both of us shrieking like we are going to be starring in the next murder documentary where the surprise ending is that the neighbor's cat killed us.

"Like I *would* drop you!" Lisa yells back, her voice strained. "But Aurora, I swear on my collection of eye palettes, if you get any taller, we're both going to die today! You are hanging out like seven feet."

"Are you calling me a giraffe in the middle of a crisis?" I stretch farther, my red hair hanging in a curtain around my face, and the cool September Anchorage air biting my cheeks. "And this is YOUR fault!"

"How was I supposed to know the cat would make a run for the open window?"

"Who opens windows in September, in Alaska?" I say, wiggling my fingers desperately toward Mr. Whiskers.

He simply licks his paw as if to say, "You amuse me, strange humans."

"The fresh air has good vibes. And I need to clear out the negative relationship vibes even since I let you stay here. I was clearing out that negative breakup energy that you've been carrying around. That's probably why Mr. Whiskers took a run for it, cats have a sense of these things" she huffs.

Through the blood rushing to my head, I can make out pedestrians below pointing up at us. *Great. Just what I need* after my surprise breakup with Alexis—now I'm becoming a viral sensation- *The Dangling Cat Girl of Anchorage.*

"Okay, new plan," Lisa says. "I'm going to pull you back in, and we'll call for help!"

"No! He'll run or jump if we leave!" I protest, watching Mr. Whiskers edge further away. "Our neighbor Liam will kill us if anything happens to his precious baby!"

"Liam will kill us if we splatter ourselves on the sidewalk too! I'm pulling you back NOW!"

With a mighty heave, Lisa yanks me backward. Unfortunately, her strength is more in her personality than her biceps. We tumble onto the hardwood floor in a tangle of limbs, knocking over the popcorn and coffee table.

"Text Liam!" I gasp, scrambling to my feet and racing back to the window. Mr. Whiskers has moved even further along the ledge, now sitting by the rusted old drainpipe.

Lisa fumbles for her phone, her blonde hair a wild halo around her flushed face. "What do I say? 'Hey, hot neighbor, your cat's about to become a pancake because we're idiots! '"

"Just tell him it's an emergency with Mr. Whiskers!" I keep my eyes locked on the tabby, trying to send telepathic stay-put vibes. "And mention that we may need a ladder. That'll make him come faster!"

Lisa's fingers fly over her phone as I catch my breath. "Sent! Oh, wait, I think I see him down there!"

I move my eyes from the stranded cat to down below.

"LIAM!" She starts waving frantically out the window and scares Mr. Whiskers further from us.

I peer down, spotting our firefighter neighbor looking up, confusion transforming into horror as he registers what is happening. Even from the second floor, I can see his face going from "concerned neighbor" to "professional rescuer."

"Don't move!" he shouts up. "I'm coming!"

"That's what she sai–" Lisa starts.

"That's our plan," I call back, before Lisa finishes. "But he's moving farther away!"

Lisa and I maintain our vigil at the window, watching Mr. Whiskers with the intensity of Alaskan caribou hunters waiting for their shot to line up.

"When did Liam give you his number anyway?" I asked, never taking my eyes off the cat.

"He didn't," Lisa says breezily. "I got it from your phone."

"You what?"

"After he helped me carry in groceries the other day, he mentioned he was waiting for you to call, per your conversation about getting together to discuss cat custody arrangements. He also referred to himself as your matchmaker, as if I'm not a professional matchmaker! Anywho, I grabbed your phone and stole his number off it. You should really change your passcode."

I would have been outraged at the invasion of privacy if I weren't so impressed by her foresight. "Remind me to be mad about *that* later."

"Will do. I'll pencil it in right after we save Mr. Whiskers and before I definitely-not-accidentally have a date with Liam."

Liam bursts in, his dark hair is slightly mussed, and breathing hard from sprinting up the stairs.

Lisa immediately blushes and is silent, for the first time in her life.

Liam crosses the room in three giant strides, his muscular frame filling the window space as he assesses the situation.

"He's behind the drainpipe," I explain, my voice reaching that special pitch reserved for emergencies and drunken karaoke nights. "And he's been inching further on the ledge for the past three minutes."

"Got it." Liam's expression softens when he looks at the cat, making me realize why those firemen with puppy calendars are so popular.

I wonder if he has any cute, single firewomen he works with? I immediately blush since I'd been single for less than an hour and I'm already ready to jump in the sack with a firewoman.

"Hey buddy, staying out of trouble I see?"

Mr. Whiskers meows in response, as if they are having an actual conversation.

"So what's the plan?" Lisa asks, batting her eyelashes "Heroic leap? Fire truck ladder? Elaborate pulley system? I can hold your shirt if that's getting in your way."

I swat her butt and shake my head at her blatant flirting.

"Nothing so dramatic," Liam says, focusing entirely on the cat. "I'm going to reach out and grab him." He makes it sound as simple as grabbing a box of cereal from a high grocery store shelf.

"We tried that," I protest. "I nearly fell out the window."

Liam flashes a grin. "No offense, Aurora, but I've got about six inches and fifty pounds of muscle on you. Plus," he adds, his expression serious, "I do this for a living."

"A professional," Lisa purrs and shimmies.

With a controlled movement that made my amateur dangling look like I was a flopping fish, Liam extends, flexing and stretching his muscles to reach out the window. His feet remain firmly planted inside, and one hand grips the window frame while the other reaches for Mr. Whiskers.

"Hey kitty," he coos in a voice so gentle it seems impossible it came from his broad-chested frame. "Come to Daddy."

Lisa makes a strangled noise beside me that I choose to ignore.

Mr. Whiskers, the traitor, immediately perks. The cat who ignored my desperate pleas now trots lightly over the windowsill ledge.

Liam scoops up the cat with impressive ease and speed and pulls himself back inside, cradling Mr. Whiskers against his chest. The entire rescue took less than twenty seconds.

"My hero," Lisa sighs dreamily.

I can't help laughing.

Liam gives Mr. Whiskers a once-over. "You're fine, aren't you, you dramatic little furball?" The cat purrs in response, rubbing his head against Liam's square, stubbled jaw.

"So," Liam says, finally looking up at us. "Anyone want to explain how my cat—who is supposed to be safe in my apartment—ended up on a ledge outside *your* window?"

Lisa and I exchange guilty glances and shrug.

"Well," I begin, "it's a funny story actually—"

"I borrowed him!" Lisa blurts out. "For emotional support. For Aurora. She's devastated. Broken heart. Very sad. Just awful. We need Mr. Whisker's good vibes."

I stare at her, mouth open. "And we haven't decided on the cat custody schedule yet."

"So you took my cat from my apartment," Liam infers and lifts a brow at me.

"Borrowed," Lisa corrects. "There is definitely an intention to return him. And technically, the cat escaped your apartment to come to ours."

"My door was not open."

"Ajar?"

"Locked."

"Huh." Lisa taps her chin thoughtfully. "Well, that's the mystery here. Do you want me to help you solve it?"

I start picking up popcorn and kick my shoes off. I have a feeling we are not leaving anytime soon.

Mr. Whiskers jumps down and settles onto our couch.

I sit next to him, suddenly exhausted by the adrenaline crash.

"Are you okay here alone while I make sure no one broke into Liam's apartment?" Lisa turns to ask me, taking Liam's arm.

"I do have my emotional support cat," I say, lifting my brows and wondering how she broke into Liam's apartment.

Liam shifts his weight, looking slightly uncomfortable at Lisa following him.

Lisa grabs his arm. "The least I can do is walk you back." She flashes him a brilliant smile.

I snort. Subtle as a freight train, Lisa is.

I pet Mr. Whiskers. "Should we leave them alone?" I whisper to him.

Liam laughs at something Lisa says as they walk out, and the cat curls up on me with his soft purrs vibrating and falls asleep.

"Maybe cat emergencies are therapeutic," I muse. "I'm not focused on my crummy night with all this cat drama."

The door flies open.

"I was tired of waiting, so I came to you, Girl!" Darius announces, sweeping in dramatically with a blender full of margaritas in one hand and a quart of ice cream in the other.

"Lisa said she was 'getting ready,' and I know that means at least an hour of contouring, lashes, and a heated debate about the different meanings in red lipstick shades."

"Ice cream, tacos, and drinks don't have time for all that." He kicks the door shut behind him like he owns the place. "So! I brought the essentials to you. Let's self-care and gossip."

Chapter 29

"Distraught" or Not

The Anchorage Daily News lands on our kitchen table with a thud that feels way too dramatic for this town. Lisa's already hovering over it, coffee mug steaming, eyes bright like she's about to announce she's won the lottery.

"Don't freak," she says, which is exactly what someone says right before they show you *why* you should freak. She slides the paper across the table like it's an offering.

Front page. Huge picture. Me. Hanging out our second-floor apartment window with Mr. Whiskers tucked out of sight, hair wild, sweatshirt slipping off my shoulder, face in mid-yell. The headline?

FIREMAN SAVES DISTRAUGHT WOMAN.

I blink. "Dist—excuse me?"

Lisa bites her lip, holding back a laugh that slips out in little snorts. "I mean, you *did* look like you were seconds away from swan-diving. That or auditioning for a fire safety commercial."

My phone buzzes on the counter. Then beeps. Then buzzes again like it's staging its own protest.

"Oh no," I groan, snatching it up. Notifications everywhere. Missed calls. Messages stacking like falling Tetris blocks.

Lisa cackles. "Anchorage is *so* boring that you rescuing our neighbor's cat is headline news. You're officially famous."

I drop my forehead to the table. "I thought maybe I'd get my name in the paper for making the dean's list or...I don't know...winning a fishing derby. Not because I'm the most unstable person in Alaska."

Lisa pats my back. "At least your hair looks amazing."

Before I can respond, my screen lights up again—this time with Darius's name. I swipe, already bracing.

"Girl!" His voice explodes through the speaker. "I cannot believe you didn't warn me. Do you know how many people from our group chat have texted me? Everyone's saying, *your friend's in the paper*—and I thought, finally, she's been discovered as Alaska's next top model–you know got the height for it. But nope. You're dangling like Rapunzel in a push-up bra. At least it was a flattering cleavage shot."

"Darius!" I bury my face in my elbow.

Lisa spits coffee back into her mug, laughing harder.

My phone buzzes again and again. Another call. Then the one name I don't want flashing across my screen: *Mom.*

Sandra.

I stab the red decline button, but the voicemail ding follows instantly. My gut twists.

"Guess I'll have to call her," I mutter, dragging out the words like they weigh a hundred pounds each.

Lisa snatches the phone. "Absolutely not. You, my love, are officially off duty. Doctor Lisa prescribes pajamas, trash TV, and a weekend of zero responsibilities. I'll be your personal assistant. I'll answer the phone. I'll tell people you're alive, stable, and eating your body weight in Pop-Tarts."

I squint at her. "You'll answer my mom?"

"I'll answer everyone," Lisa insists. "Your mom gets the same auto-reply as your ignorant ex. Which is: she's alive, thriving, and too busy moisturizing to deal with you."

My laugh escapes even through the dread swirling in my stomach.

Darius's voice cuts in from the phone speaker, still going: "Honestly though, I think it's iconic. You're like Anchorage's Paris Hilton but with flannel and a suicidal cat."

"Hey!" I protest. "Mr. Whiskers was in danger! I was saving him."

Right on cue, the orange menace strolls into the kitchen, tail high, jumps onto the counter, and promptly sits *on* the newspaper. Regal. Smug. Licking one paw like he orchestrated the whole scandal.

Lisa points. "Your accomplice has arrived."

"Traitor," I whisper, scratching under his chin. He purrs like a chainsaw.

Darius laughs so hard I imagine him clutching his designer throw pillow. "At least people think you were rescued from being locked outside. Which, babe, between us, makes you sound way more tragic and mysterious than chasing a cat. *Distressed window girl.* Hot firefighters lining up to save you."

"Ugh." I flop back against the chair. "I'm going back to bed before the memes start."

Lisa jumps up and snatches my phone completely. "Go. I've got this." She scrolls furiously, already typing replies. "See? I'll tell everyone you're fine, tell your coworkers you're fine, tell your mom you're..." She pauses. "Well, maybe not fine, but alive."

"Thank you," I sigh, hauling myself up. Outside, rain slaps the windows, sheets of water sliding down like the sky's trying to wash Anchorage off the map. September is gloomy. Perfect weather for hiding.

By noon, I'd fully migrated into Lisa's room like a feral raccoon claiming new territory. Her bed is bigger than the sad couch, and her ridiculous, fluffy duvet swallows me whole. I pull it over my head while the storm drums outside.

On the nightstand, a stack of murder documentaries glares from her Netflix queue. Perfect. Nothing says *mental stability* like binging serial killers who look like your uncle's fishing buddies.

Mr. Whiskers crawls onto my stomach, purring, rumbling like he's in on the joke.

My phone buzzes on the dresser, but Lisa barges in, snatches it, and holds up her hand like a bouncer. "Nope. I told you—you're off the grid. I'm handling your PR crisis."

"Lisa—"

She flops down dramatically beside me. "Aurora Thompson, you are under my protection. You've survived a breakup, a weird diagnosis, a newspaper scandal, and your mom's passive-aggressive voicemails. This weekend, your only job is eating Doritos and not crying into my pillow."

I peek out from the blanket cave. "What about Monday? I'm starting a new assignment for Alexis."

Lisa rolls onto her stomach, chin in her hands, eyes gleaming. "Right, your VIP silver fox client who happens to be your bio-dad. Exciting!"

I groan. "Try terrifying." I pull the blanket tighter.

Lisa's eyes soften, but then she smirks. "You're telling me you rescued a cat, broke up with Alaska's most eligible lesbian, and now you met your long-lost father and was asked to be a part of the family business in the span of a week? Babe, you're a soap opera. You have got to start a social media account labeled Alaska's Distraught Drama Diva."

"I'm staying right here in bed. You're taking care of everything, remember?"

And by Saturday night, I've fully committed to hermit life. My murder documentary marathon has taught me three things: 1) never trust a guy who collects antique knives, 2) lie detectors are fake, and 3) serial killers have unnerving levels of confidence.

Somewhere between episodes, I dig out my old rainbow gecko diary from high school, the one with a lock so flimsy even Mr. Whiskers could pick it. Pages crinkle with embarrassing poetry and crush confessions. But near the back, there's a list I forgot about.

Things I'd ask Dad if I ever met him:

- Do you know my favorite color?
- Did you picture what I'd look like as I grew up?
- Were you proud of me—even from far away?
- Why wasn't I good enough for you to stay

My stomach knots. Too much for a first day on the job. I flip the page, but the questions linger like ghosts.

On-screen, a killer stares down a polygraph machine, calm as ice. I laugh bitterly. "If he can do that, I can do this."

Mr. Whiskers stretches across my chest, paw smacking my chin like he's seconding the motion.

"Okay, okay," I whisper. "I saved you, I dumped Alexis, I scored a scholarship, and I'm medically...special." The word stumbles out, but instead of dread, there's a weird flicker of pride. Not broken. Just different.

I scratch under his chin. "If a clueless kitty can trust me with his life, I can handle meeting my father."

The rain pounds harder, wind rattling the windows. My heart hammers with it, but this time, not from dread.

"Tomorrow," I whisper into the dark. "Tomorrow, I will stop hiding."

Mr. Whiskers yawns like he's unimpressed, then curls tighter against me. His warmth presses into my ribs, and for once, I almost believe my life is getting back on track despite the continuous speed bumps to my perfect life.

The storm finally chills out by Sunday morning, and my perfect life is back on track. The steady drum of rain on Lisa's window is downgraded to occasional drips sliding off the gutters, which thankfully means Mr. Whiskers doesn't even think about sneaking outside. Anchorage air smells like wet spruce and exhaust—the kind of crisp, soggy fall Sunday where the whole city hibernates with soup.

I burrow deeper into her duvet until Mr. Whiskers decides he's my alarm clock. He stretches, digs claws into the blanket, and launches off my stomach like I'm his personal trampoline.

"Ow—thanks, buddy. Really considerate," I mutter, rolling over. My hair's a bird's nest, my sweatshirt smells faintly like Cheetos, and my brain finally feels...less like a shaken snow globe.

Lisa barges in with two mugs of coffee. "Sleeping Beauty lives. How's the mental stability report today?"

I sit up, rubbing my eyes. "Improved. Still a little murder-documentary-cursed, but trending upward."

"Excellent." She plops down beside me, handing over coffee like it's communion. "Any plans for today?"

I shrug. "I thought I'd, you know, ignore tomorrow's work stress in silence."

She flicks my forehead. "Nope. Tomorrow you're showing up like—" She waves dramatically. "—Aurora career-focused, style-slaying employee of the month in spirit, even if never in actual title."

I laugh into my mug. "What does that even mean?"

"Means we're practicing your pep talk. Stand up."

Before I can protest, Lisa yanks me out of bed and positions me in front of her closet mirror. My reflection looks like a hungover scarecrow. She ignores it.

"Okay," she commands, "say: *I am not a tragic cat lady. I am a strong independent woman who can confront her estranged dad and nail this job.*"

I groan. "Lisa—"

"Say it!"

I roll my eyes but repeat, "I am not a tragic cat lady. I am a strong independent woman who can confront her estranged dad and nail this job."

She claps. "Yes, Girly! You are almost ready for me to set you up on a date with your soulmate."

I shudder and grimace.

She only winks. "And smile like you don't have any crippling anxiety. Perfect."

I giggle despite myself. Somewhere between her ridiculous coaching, matchmaking threats, and the caffeine, a weird fizz of energy sparks in my chest. For the first time all week, the idea of Monday doesn't feel like an avalanche waiting to crush me.

###

By evening, I've showered, tamed my hair, and swapped Lisa's sweatshirt for actual jeans. Darius FaceTimes to check in, his face framed by an aggressively patterned scarf.

"Well, well, if it isn't Anchorage's headline queen," he teases. "How's celebrity rehab?"

"Over," I grin. "I'm rejoining society tomorrow."

He claps theatrically. "Good. Show up looking hotter than Alexis, and your victory arc writes itself. I think you'll impress the VIP client, aka *your dad*, so much he'll buy out your employment contract. I mean you'll miss seeing Darius and flirting with your hot boss and your work drama but Grant is your family. And I bet you get free cruise tickets so we could all do a party cruise for Christmas!"

I blush so hard I hide behind Mr. Whiskers, who claws my shoulder in protest. "Ow—traitor!"

Lisa yells from the kitchen, "Ignore him! You're not changing your career, or competing with Alexis, you're outgrowing her!"

Darius smirks. "True. But still—serve an outfit. Shock and awe. You want her drooling and him"—he wiggles his brows—"to regret walking out eighteen years ago."

I groan but laugh. "I don't even know what to wear."

"Something with power," Lisa yells again. "Something that says, 'I'm your daughter, but I don't need you.'"

I sip my coffee, shaking my head. "You two are trouble, not me. Besides he was really nice last week and maybe I'm the one with issues, not him."

"You can have issues, *and* he can be the problem. Just confront him already and live your childhood dream of telling him off," Darius corrects.

He's right. I do need to talk to my dad more and tell him how I feel. By the time I hang up, my heart beats steadier.

Spreading my old diary on the bed again, the cringey neon gecko cover stares up at me. I skim my messy handwriting, those sharp questions scrawled across the page.

Why wasn't I good enough?

My chest tightens, but there's this tiny ember of courage instead of dread. I trace the ink with my fingertip, then flip to a blank page in my old journal.

New list:

– Tell him I'm ready for him and it's up to him.

– Tell him I'm building my own life.

– Tell him that I'd love to stay at his business, the family business, permanently.

–Accept his money, because I deserve it.

Mr. Whiskers noses at the page like he's editing. I laugh and scratch his ears. "Fine, add: thank you for nothing, but also thanks for my statuesque height and auburn hair."

Rain taps the window one last time before clearing, moonlight breaking through. Tomorrow's going to be messy. Maybe humiliating. Probably dramatic.

But I'm ready to confront all the drama in my life and start living on my own terms.

I close the diary, shove it under the pillow, and curl up with Mr. Whiskers tucked against my ribs.

Reading these questions, I realize that I'm assuming he'll be full of more excuses and selfishness like my mom. What if he's different? What if he is the father I've dreamed of that rescues me? He is showing me that he's not like my mom.

"Okay," I whisper into the dark. "Let's do this. I'm ready!"

And since the breakup, the newspaper fiasco, and everything that happened this weekend, I actually believe it. I'm ready to find out who my dad is in my life today and in the future.

Chapter 30

No More Moose-stakes: Alexis Gets the Boot

The September sun slices through the front windows of Alaska Tours & Cruises, drenching the office in a warm, golden glow straight out of a tourism brochure. It beams off polished desks and laminated trail maps, making the whole place shine like it's flirting with me. Two weeks in, and every morning still hugs me hello—unlike the icebox that was Alexis's temp agency.

"Aurora, honey, can you check these numbers for the glacier tour package?" Kathleen calls from her desk, voice smooth with that steady, mom-who-always-has-extra-hot-cocoa kind of kindness that still catches me off guard.

After I reassured them that the news article was an overdramatization of me trying to save a cat, the workplace mood returned to normal. Kathleen slides a printout across her desk. "Grant thinks we can increase capacity, but I want a second opinion."

I squint at my screen, elbow-deep in vendor payments and cruise deposits. For once, the numbers line up in a way that doesn't make me want to chew through a pen. Alexis's corporate spreadsheets always felt like cold punishment. Here? The numbers almost sing.

"Sure thing," I say, typing the last cell before swiveling toward her. "Let me wrap up these deposits."

"No rush," Grant chimes, strolling out of his office with his signature mug. The thing reads *World's Most Adequate Dad*, a Father's Day gift from Indie. He carries it like it's a trophy from the Dad Olympics.

He leans against Kathleen's desk, casual as usual. "How's the transition? Temp agency treating you alright?"

My fingers freeze above the keyboard. "About that..."

The office phone rings. Of course it does.

Kathleen answers with her practiced customer-service lilt. "Alaska Tours and Cruises, this is Kathleen... Oh! Hello, Alexis. Yes, hold on."

My stomach swan dives straight into my hiking boots. Kathleen's lips thin as she covers the receiver and turns toward me. But then she nods at Grant.

"I'll talk to her in my office," he says.

Alexis isn't calling to talk to me? I shake my head, and Kathleen puts her hand on my arm. "Grant wanted to tell you after he had it all worked out."

He's standing in his office, gesturing firmly and typing furiously on the phone with Alexis.

Are they replacing me? I thought they liked having me here, and I was doing a good job.

I bite my lip and frown, but Kathleen tightens her grip. "I don't want you to worry. We are trying to buy out your employment contract so you can work here. I mean, if you want to work here."

"Oh," is all that comes from my lips. *It's not bad news.*

"She wants to speak with you," Grant says, standing at his door and gesturing to me to come in. His tone was soft but laced with something steelier. Kathleen follows, wringing her hands.

I take the phone with fingers that totally aren't shaking. "Hey, Alexis."

"Aurora." Her voice cuts across the line—crisp, clipped, businesslike. There was not even a hint of the woman who kissed me lightly and was ready to rescue me at any moment. She slips back into professional mode, as if I were never anything but another employee file on her desk. "We need to discuss your contract situation."

I straighten in my chair. "I thought we already did. I requested the transfer to Alaska Tours, and—"

"And I'm denying it."

The words slap harder than a glacial wind to the face. Around me, the office air stops moving. Even the space heater seems offended.

Grant's expression darkens. Kathleen freezes mid-paper shuffle.

"You're *denying* it?" I repeat, my voice climbing. "On what grounds?"

"Your skill set's too valuable to lose. Especially mid-contract." Alexis's voice slides through the phone like it's printed in fine legalese. "You signed an employment agreement, Aurora. We are funding your business classes."

I shut my eyes. That old familiar weight settles fast—like a lead blanket of someone else's control pressing on my shoulders again. Same pressure, different scenery.

"Alexis, this is ridiculous. You don't get to *force* me to work somewhere I don't want to be."

"I'm not forcing anything," she answers, her tone dipping into that cool, condescending softness that *pretends* to be kindness. "I'm honoring our contract. And let's be honest—you're not ready for the kind of responsibility Grant's offering. You're better suited to temporary placement work."

The sting's instant, sharp. The words land like she's plucking my worst fears from my spine and laying them on the desk for everyone to see. Too scattered. Too unqualified. Too *temporary*.

Before I can say anything stupid—or cry—Grant steps forward, calm as a glacier but twice as strong.

"Let me speak to her," he says, voice low but solid.

I hand him the phone like it's burning.

"Alexis? Grant Fairbanks." His voice shifts into executive mode, every syllable soaked in authority—the kind earned, not inherited. "I understand your concern about releasing Aurora from her contract. I'm prepared to buy out her remaining time at triple the standard rate."

Even across the room, I catch Alexis's breath hitching over the phone, and I realize he's hit the speaker so we can all hear the conversation.

"That's... generous," she manages. "But this isn't about money, Grant. She's a company asset I've invested heavily in. She needs stability. Jumping jobs won't help her—"

"What Aurora needs," Grant cuts in, polite steel in his voice, "is a workplace that values her for who she is—not for what she provides. Frankly, I'm questioning the ethics of keeping an employee who's *explicitly* asked to transfer."

"This is business, not personal—"

"Everything about this is personal. And we both know it." Grant's gaze locks with mine. His tone softens without losing strength. "Aurora is family, Alexis. *My* family. And I protect my family."

Silence falls—thick, charged, and heavy enough to crack the air. Even the copier in the back corner shuts up.

Then Alexis returns, clipped and barely holding her edge.

"Put Aurora back on."

Grant passes the phone to me with a steady hand and a reassuring squeeze on my shoulder.

"I'm here," I say.

"Aurora," Alexis sounds less like a CEO and more like someone holding a cracked glass in her hand. "You haven't returned my texts or calls all weekend. I understand you wanting radio silence after our talk but this is business. Is this *really* what you want? To throw away everything you're building toward—a stable, upward path—for the fantasy of playing office with your biological father—a guy you just met?"

My grip tightens on the receiver.

She never called me this weekend.

Then, suddenly, I understand—Lisa must have blocked or screened out all her calls.

Alexis is mad that I was ignoring her, instead of her ignoring me. This contract negotiation is strategic, emotional warfare. Designed to detonate every landmine to get me back and win at all costs. She wants the past version of me. Alexis doesn't actually want my contract or me to work with her. She doesn't like the version of me I'm finally starting to *be*.

Three months ago, I'd have caved and been delighted that playing hard to get had finally gotten Alexis wanting me, seeing me. I'd even have apologized to her for asking to quit.

But three months ago, I didn't know my dad or myself, or what I really wanted. I want to be *seen*. I'm not a business prize to negotiate– I'm a person and I deserve to choose what I want.

I didn't know what it felt like to belong to a family and then to work somewhere where we all work as a team. I didn't know my father's name. I didn't know that he'd clear his schedule to help me troubleshoot a broken Excel formula or offer to buyout a contract with no hesitation. I didn't even know I was intersex. Didn't know how much I'd been twisting myself into a shape I didn't fit.

When summer started, I thought success meant high heels, client folders, and pretending I wasn't unraveling under fluorescent lighting.

Now? I've tasted something different. Something real.

And no contract can stuff me back into that old version of myself, no matter how thick or binding.

"You owe me, and I'm doing what's best for your career," Alexis states in the silence, which feels yuck. Suddenly, I knew that I did not want to ever go back to Alexis' office.

"I owe you?" I echo, my voice dry as moose jerky and about as forgiving. "Alexis, you paid me for working but that doesn't mean I owe you. You barely even noticed me except when you needed me. You built a system that worked for *you*. I was a convenience. You don't value you as an employee and you didn't value me when we were in a relationship."

"That's not—"

"It is," I cut in, holding my anger and not apologizing. I don't care if my family hears this. They are on my side, after all.

I glance toward Grant by the windows, and Kathleen is near the printer, who gives me a small smile and nods.

"Working with my family is what I want. Here, I'm part of a team building something together. People want me here because I *am* good at my job, not because I'm cute, or a work project to fix."

The line goes so still, I wonder if she hung up or if we're both drowning in the same thick silence.

"Fine," Alexis bites out. "But don't expect me to make this easy."

Click.

I hold the phone for a beat, like it might apologize for being a part of that conversation. Then I passed it to Kathleen. She sets it down, but not before pulling me into the hug that says *you're safe* without any contracts or conditions attached. Vanilla lotion and coffee beans fill my nose.

"Oh, honey," she murmurs against my hair. "That woman is a disaster with too much power."

"Boundary issues," Grant mutters. He's standing like he wants to throw the phone across the office, but his eyes soften and he places a reassuring hand on my shoulder.

"She's hurting," I say, automatic and dumb, like my empathy reflex forgot to shut off.

Indie sneaks into the office. "I'm not going to lie. I was listening in, *and* you are hurting too," she points out, all soft eyes and blunt delivery. "But you're not calling people during business hours to sabotage their entire career."

I blink at her. "When did you get *this* wise?"

She lifts her chin and confidently announces, "I read romance novels. I know toxic alpha behavior when I see it."

A laugh bubbles up before I can stop it. "Romance novels as life skill prep. Bold choice. I thought I needed therapy. Maybe I should borrow some books from you."

"Speaking of therapy," Grant says, slowly sitting. "How are *you* doing with... the other stuff? Your mom? The medical stuff?"

The air shifts. Tightens. "I'm processing," I say, but the word tastes like cardboard. "It wasn't such a surprise learning why I'm different or my mom's reaction. But it still hurts."

Kathleen leans against my desk like she's ready to catch me, if needed. "Sweetheart, you don't have to carry this alone. Whatever you're holding, we can help."

I blink too fast. Her voice softens all the parts of me that used to live in full defense mode. I spent years walking on eggshells around my mom, then months molding myself into Alexis's perfect employee. I never figured out how to *be*—not please, not perform. Just *be*.

"I'm still learning how to talk about it. I'm intersex." The word lands like a confession, like a freight truck full of new definitions backed into my identity without asking. "And I don't hate it. It's not even... bad. But it's different, and it's weird to figure out how much of *me* is me, and how much I never knew."

"Do you want to talk about it?" Indie asks, folding one leg under herself. "Or do you want us to act weird and pretend we don't know?"

"Option B has been my entire coping plan," I murmur. "And I think it sucks."

"We're your family and we will love you no matter what. Even if you tell us you want to work for Alexis. Hiding from your truth won't make you happy," Grant says, his smile full of warmth instead of pity.

"We do want you to be happy," Kathleen adds.

I snort, then cry. "This has been a wild ride. Sorry, I'm not sure how to feel about anything. I'm so happy you want me to work here and anxious about Alexis. I've been just surviving for so long, it's hard to know what I feel and what... to do."

Kathleen shakes her head. "There's no right way to feel about this. Whatever you're feeling is right."

"You *are* who you are," Grant says, squeezing my hand. "Diagnosis or not, you're still my kid. My funny, top of her class, accident-prone, excel-sheet-wizard daughter."

"And you know what?" Kathleen leans in, all kindness and mischief. "Anyone who thinks differently gets homemade cookies. With raisins."

I burst into full-blown ugly laughter. "You monster."

Indie gasps. "Not the raisin betrayal!"

Kathleen smiles smugly. "Passive aggression, baked fresh daily."

My breath comes easier. My hands stop shaking. The storm inside me quiets—not gone, but held. "I love you guys," I blurt, the words escaping before I can second-guess the truth in them.

"We love you too," Grant says, like it's always been obvious, like the ground's always been this steady. "Which means you don't ever need to go back to Alexis's circus of work manipulation. Her contract? We'll handle it."

My chest tightens, but not in a scary way. In the way a balloon tightens before it gains momentum and flies.

Chapter 31

Special Delivery

A knock at the door interrupts my teary mascara smudge-fest in the workplace.

Indie tilts her head. "Expecting someone?"

Grant glances at his phone. "Did we order lunch and forget again?"

"Plot twist," Indie mutters. "It's Alexis in a trench coat with a boombox and emotionally weaponized new work contracts."

Kathleen's already crossing the office, humming like it's any ol' Tuesday, and when she swings open the door, in steps a delivery guy wearing shorts, despite it being cold enough outside to freeze moose nostrils.

"Delivery for... uh, Aurora Thompson?" he says, holding out an obnoxiously large bouquet like it might bite him. It's not subtle either—hot pink lilies, sunflowers, eucalyptus, and big weird curly willow twigs sticking out like jazz hands.

My heart does a funny little hiccup and tightens.

"I didn't order these," I murmur, blinking like the flowers might explain themselves.

He shrugs and hands over the little card. "Already paid for. Have a nice day!"

Grant raises one eyebrow. "Secret admirer?"

It's Alexis, pops into my mind. If she can't have me working for her, she wants me for her backup girlfriend. Or, maybe she's apologizing and offering to let me out of my contract. *This would be the fastest apology and flower delivery ever!*

I flip the envelope open with the grace of someone unraveling a tabloid scandal. Inside, in huge purple handwriting that screams chaotic energy, "WE LOVE YOU AND YOU'RE MAGIC. DINNER THIS WEEK OR WE RIOT. – D + L"

"Darius and Lisa," I whisper, and then I snort-laugh. "Of course. Who else threatens to riot with glitter emojis?"

Indie perks up. "Are they the ones who karaoke with you to Britney Spears in full sequin jumpsuits?"

"Every single Tuesday," I say, clutching the flowers like a life raft of rainbow petals and love. "But we don't always wear the jumpsuits, though."

Kathleen claps her hands together, eyes twinkling like she's about to drop the coziest bombshell. "Well then, let's invite them over!"

"Huh?"

Grant nods. "You talk about them so much, I feel like I already know them. Sounds like they're the kind of people who show up for you, and those are the people I want at my family table."

"You want... Darius and Lisa at family dinner?" I blink at them. "I mean, that's ambitious. Lisa might bring an entire boy band with her. Darius might judge your cheese selection and bring his boyfriend."

Kathleen grins. "We've survived teenage Indie and moose rutting season. I think we can handle your chaos crew. They will fit right into the family."

Indie raises her mug in silent cheers. "I'll clear space on the group chat and invite them asap."

I'm still holding the bouquet like it's sacred. It kinda is. This isn't the fragile, tiptoe-around-it love I grew up with. This is messy, loud, bright-as-sunflowers love. The kind that pulls up a chair, texts you inappropriate memes during your workday, and buys you flowers for existing.

I press the card to my chest and smile—a real, not-for-anyone-else smile. "Okay. But only if Grant makes those ridiculous bacon-wrapped scallops he promised last time. And you have to serve your chocolate chip cookies and give him the raisin surprise cookie."

"The only surprise you'll get is gaining ten pounds from one dinner!" Kathleen says, laughing.

"You drive a hard bargain," Grant says, already reaching for his planner like this is a high-level business meeting. "But I'll allow it."

Indie pulls out her phone. "I'll message Lisa and Darius now. Text me their numbers."

"Are you ready for chaos?" I ask.

"We are genetically predisposed to it," Story retorts.

"That explains a lot," I say with a laugh.

The office fills with laughter again—warm, ridiculous, alive.

And for the first time in forever, I don't feel like I'm standing outside the window of a perfect life, nose pressed to the glass. I'm inside. I belong.

Messy, complicated, completely me.

And absolutely all my family is invited to the family dinner.

I bite back another smile as I apply my lipgloss.

Chapter 32

Bribes & Office Maneuvers

The office looks closed—lights dimmed, parking lot bare, not even the scent of over-brewed coffee lingering. I parked two blocks down like a criminal, hood up, glasses on, moving like a raccoon with a secret. Because even though I told myself I was done with working at Alaska Temp Agency, the endless games of 'Am I your girlfriend or your employee?', and the ache that hits when Alexis doesn't text and cancels our dates—here I am.

I quietly enter, clutching my timesheet like a lifejacket in this perilous situation.

"I'm not seeing her. I'm just dropping this and bouncing." I whisper my plan aloud to remind myself of the plan. "Get in, desk-clean, get out."

My shoes squeak across the tile. The familiar hum of the heater kicks on—comforting, nostalgic, and cursed. I duck past the kitchenette like she might leap from behind the coffee pot. Nothing. Just a half-eaten box of maple donuts someone clearly left and forgot.

Almost to my desk.

Then I hear it. The sharp clack of expensive heels on laminate flooring.

Shit.

My stomach nosedives. I freeze mid-step, half-hidden behind a filing cabinet. The loud click of the shoes are Alexis's. Power-stride. Boss-level echo. She's the only person here who enters a room like the beginning of a climax in a movie. The air shifts. My pulse forgets how to regulate.

Reaching for the drawer to retrieve my belongings, a voice cuts through the stillness.

"Aurora?" Her voice, smooth and sharp, slices through the silence.

I debate running. Like, a literal sprint. Maybe launching myself through the side door, leaving behind my hoodie and pride.

But I step out. "Hey. Uh, hi."

She's leaning against the doorway to her office. Hair shining in a sleek twist, with her power outfit of a midnight blue blazer over a silk blouse. She doesn't look surprised to see me. She looks like she expected this. Worse—like she planned this.

"You're here late." She folds her arms, unreadable. Classic CEO poker face.

"So are you," I say, defensive and breathy like a child caught stealing cookies.

"I live here." She gestures around. "I had a feeling you'd come back."

I bite my lip as she gestures for me to enter her office. Quickly, I shut the drawer. I might as well get this over with.

Alexis is standing in the doorway of her office, her silhouette framed by the warm glow of her desk lamp. She's dressed impeccably, as always, her presence commanding yet softened by the vulnerability in her eyes.

"Didn't expect anyone to be here after hours," I say, attempting a casual tone.

"I can't say the same. I was waiting to see you."

She steps back, revealing a garment bag draped over her arm and a sleek leather briefcase in her hand.

"Aurora." Her voice lowers. I hate how much it still makes my chest flutter. "I feel terrible about this morning."

I wave her off, looking for the nearest exit.

"Wait, I have something for you. *Please.*"

Alexis lets the word hang in the air, and I'm not sure how she wants to finish it as she turns to hand me a massive garment bag in one hand and holds a sleek leather briefcase in the other.

I should leave. I tell myself to leave. But my shoes root me there like a spruce weathering a blizzard. "What's this?" I ask.

"A gift." She unzips the bag and reveals the most gorgeous suit I've ever seen—rich charcoal gray with deep green silk lining. Tailored to my measurements. Which means she must have planned this weeks ago.

My breath stutters. "You got me a suit?"

"A *bespoke* designer suit. For your business situations. At university, you'll need to present and network. I thought you deserved to show up like the boss you are." She opens the briefcase. There's a brand new laptop inside. An engraved leather folder with my initials. Matching shoes. The whole thing screams elegance, success, and 'future CEO.' It's a business person's dream kit.

It's also...a lot–*too much.*

"I—I don't know what to say." I touch the deep emerald lining. "This is my favorite color. It's beautiful."

She smiles like it cost her nothing. "You're beautiful."

I flinch.

Because this suit? It's not what I need from her.

"I had these made for you." She hands me the briefcase, our fingers brushing as I add it to my bags. Her fingers cause chills to rush, and I'm electrified and frozen. Our chemistry has never been the problem.

"Thank you," I whisper, running my fingers over the soft fabric.

"I thought they'd be perfect for your new chapter of starting your business degree and as you venture into the business world. Everyone needs the basics. Also with your father paying for your university, you won't need a scholarship, but everyone needs a good power suit."

My eyes tear up. I blink back the emotion. Alexis isn't asking me to stay. This is her apology.

She smiles, a hint of pride in her eyes.

"I also wanted to discuss us."

I brace myself, sensing the weight of the conversation to come.

"I've been thinking about our relationship, about you falling off that window ledge, and I'm willing to make changes."

"Changes?"

"Yes." She takes a deep breath. "I'm ready to be exclusive, to prioritize us... our relationship. And if you stay at the Alaska Temp Agency, we can build something together."

I pause, the words hanging in the air.

"Alexis, I appreciate the gesture, but I told you what I want. It feels like you're offering conditions."

"No conditions, just possibilities," she says in a clipped voice.

"But what about what I want?"

She looks taken aback. "This is what you want. I know from experience, as a young woman breaking into the business world--"

"NO," I say more forcefully than I intended, or maybe the echo in the empty office makes it sound harsh. "I want to be seen, to be heard, to be loved for who I am, not for what I can do *for you*." I'm not even sure where the words came from because they sound so confident and final, unlike my usual stuttering and word salad that I say when I'm in stressful situations.

She steps closer, her expression earnest.

"I don't care about your *diagnosis*," the last word slips from her mouth harshly and loaded.

Time stops. I freeze.

She smiles and tilts her head. "I want you to know that it doesn't change how I feel about you."

I'm offended despite her soft words. I shake my head. "It's not about how *you* feel, Alexis. It's about how *I* feel."

She nods slowly, the realization not sinking in as I see the wheels spinning for her following argument to keep me here.

"I want you to stay," she says simply, looking into my eyes. "Stay working here. Stay with me."

My throat tightens.

She nods, slowly, like she's rehearsed this. "I can make it work. I'll restructure your hours, delegate some projects. We will work closer together and I'll mentor you. You don't need to go to university and get a degree. And we can make our relationship exclusive. Fully committed. You and me."

My breath hitches.

"She's showing you her priorities with her actions," my therapist's voice whispers in my head.

And her actions don't make my life easier. What she's doing makes her life easier. Her words aren't for me.

They're still her. Her terms. Her business. Her schedule.

She's not *asking*. She's offering and negotiating. Like I'm a candidate for promotion, not a girl with a battered heart trying to choose herself. She's not giving me a gift. This is a bribe.

I take a deep breath. "No, the fact—"

"It's all worked out. Don't worry," she says with a dismissive wave.

She didn't let me finish. I wanted to talk about my family. She didn't give me a chance and certainly didn't wait to ask me how I felt about our relationship.

The pit deepens, the stone in my stomach heavier.

My voice barely breaks through the lump in my throat. I look at the suit and the briefcase. "Is this gift...an apology or is it a bribe to stay and work here?"

She shrugs, like the answer doesn't matter. "It's yours. No strings. I *also* want you to stay."

I don't answer.

I can't.

Because her gift is wrapped in silk and money and everything I'm supposed to want—but not love. Not understanding. Not the kind of future where someone waits to hear how *I* feel first.

And that silence between us, growing louder by the second, tells me what I already know.

This isn't the beginning.

"Thank you," I whisper. I want to say more, but I'm afraid of what might come out of my mouth, with Alexis so close to me, and my mind is reeling as her familiar scent overwhelms me.

Then I turn, leaving with my arms full, saying nothing.

Chapter 33

The Break-Up Kiss

The brisk Alaskan air bites at my cheeks, but the heat of my anger—and maybe a little lingering heartbreak—keeps me warm. I fumble for my car keys, the little metal object a beacon of freedom. My Subaru, with its dents and chipped paint, looks more appealing than a Michelin-star dinner. I'll be free of this building with one door, one push. This company. This woman.

I have my hand on the handle when a voice, smooth as an ice rink and just as cold, cuts through the quiet of the parking lot.

"Going somewhere?" A voice comes from behind me. "You aren't going to stop and say anything else to me?"

I flinch, my heart leaping into my throat. Even without turning, I know who it is. The scent of her expensive perfume, the subtle coolness in her words, is already in the air.

I take a deep breath, turning to face her. Alexis is a vision, even in the fading light. She is a perfect storm of elegance and power, her hair still in that flawless, gravity-defying chignon. She looks like she owns the world, and she probably believes she does.

"I'm fighting for you! Please, Aurora, stay," she says again, her voice low and persuasive. "With me. Here. At the agency."

The words hang in the air like the last breath of summer, beautiful but fleeting. I square my shoulders, stuffing my hands into the pockets of my hoodie. "Are you really ignoring everything I said to you? Are you asking me to choose between you and my family?"

"I'm asking you to choose what's best for your future."

"Right, but what's best according to who? You?"

Her jaw tightens, just barely. A survival skill I've picked up. You learn to read the micro-expressions of a woman who could buy and sell your entire existence before lunch.

"I'm offering you something better than what you'd get there."

"Which is?"

"Partnership track. Your own office. A real career, not just playing tour guide for cruise ship passengers."

I blink. And then I blink again. "Please stop. Let me go. I think you are trying to buy me but you don't actually want the real me."

"No. I'm trying to give you opportunities," she says, stepping closer.

"With strings attached."

"With career benefits and me attached."

This is the part where I should probably feel flattered. Alexis Anders, CEO of the most successful temp agency in Alaska, and the business-woman I most looked up to, wants me to stay. She's offering me things I didn't even know I wanted. But instead of feeling chosen, I feel like she only wants what she can't have.

"What about me?" I ask because apparently, I like poking sleeping bears.

"What about you?"

"Are you… I mean, are we getting back together? Or is this just a professional offer with professional benefits and professional boundaries?"

She steps closer, and I catch a whiff of her perfume. It smells like winter mornings and possibilities. "I want us together."

"Because you love me, or because it's convenient to have a casual work relationship? You enjoy having me at your beck and call."

"Aurora."

"No, seriously. Because there's a difference between wanting me around and wanting me."

"I want you." Her brown eyes contain a fire and intensity I've never seen.

The way she says it should make my knees weak, should make me forget every doubt I've had about us. Instead, it just makes me tired.

"Do you, though? You always chose work over me. You don't return my texts. I think you want the version of me that doesn't complicate your life."

"You're overthinking this," she says with a shrug.

"Maybe. Or maybe I'm finally thinking clearly for the first time in months."

She crosses her arms, and I know I've hit something. "What's that supposed to mean?"

"It means that when we were together, I felt like I was constantly trying to be the best date so I could earn being your girlfriend. I was faking that I was a polished businessperson. I was never myself with you. And now you're offering me a job and a relationship like they're a package deal, and I can't tell where the personal ends and the professional begins."

"That's not—"

"Isn't it?" I interrupt, cutting through the careful words to get to the truth. "You want me to stay at your company, be your girlfriend, fit into your world on your terms. What about what I want?"

"What do you want?"

The question catches me off guard. Maybe she's ready to listen to me now.

"I want to matter," I say, the words feeling strange in my mouth. "Not just as an employee or a girlfriend, but as a person with my own life and my own choices. I want to accept myself for me. I want to explore my new family."

"You matter to me."

"Do I? Because when I told you about meeting my dad and my diagnosis, you didn't ask how I felt about it. You asked how it would affect my work schedule."

She flinches. I feel a pang of guilt, but also vindication.

"You are only thinking about yourself, though. Maybe not intentionally, but you are. You're saying you'll be with me if I stay, and you're offering me all these professional benefits, but you're not asking what I actually need from you as a person."

"What do you need?"

Another good question. I'm two for two on catching her off guard today, which would be more satisfying if I felt like I was winning instead of just... revealing how broken we both are.

"I need you to want me to be happy," I say. "Even if my happiness doesn't fit into your plans."

"I do want that."

"Then why does your offer feel like a cage?"

She doesn't answer right away, which is answer enough. The space heater cycles off, and the silence gets even heavier.

"I'm scared," she finally admits.

"Of what?"

"Of losing you. Of failing. Of not being enough," She trails off, then starts again. "I've never cared about someone the way I care about you. I want to help you and take care of you. And I don't know how to do it without trying to control the outcome."

It's such an Alexis thing to say—framing love like a business problem with variables to manage and risks to mitigate. But it's also heartbreakingly honest, and I can feel myself softening despite everything.

"You can't control whether people stay and what they choose," I tell her gently. "You can only control whether you give them reasons to want to choose you."

"Is that what I'm doing wrong? Not giving you reasons?"

"You're giving me your reasons. But you're not asking about mine."

She nods slowly, like she's processing new information. "What are your reasons for wanting to work with your father instead of staying here?"

Finally, the right question.

"Because when I'm with them—my dad, Kathleen, and Indie—I don't feel like I have to prove I deserve to be there. I don't feel like I'm auditioning or faking a role, like when I'm here faking like I'm an accounting expert or the perfect casual girlfriend. I am just working and part of the business and their family without putting on any masks."

"And you don't feel that way here? You have to wear a mask for me."

"I do. I feel like I'm constantly trying to earn my place. In the job, in the relationship, in your life. And I'm tired of feeling like I'm not quite enough as I am."

"You are enough."

"And you are too. You never asked me to wear a mask or not be myself, but here, I feel like I have to fit in and to fit into your life."

She nods and waits for me to finish.

"Why are you trying to change my mind instead of supporting my choice? Only when I played games and said I was leaving did you want me. So why can't you just let me choose for myself?"

The question hits home. I can see it in how she flinches and her hands clench her planner.

"Because I'm selfish," she says quietly. "Because I want you here with me, and I'm trying to make that happen instead of trying to understand what you need. I have a life plan and I know I can find a way to fit you into it."

"And what if for my life plan, what I need is to take the job with my dad?"

"Then I guess I need to figure out how to want that for you too." She sighs. "I support your relationship with your newfound family," she says carefully.

"But not enough to let me out of my contract so I can work with them."

"That's different."

"Is it? From where I'm standing, it looks like you support the parts of my life that don't inconvenience you."

The quiet settles in, thick with unspoken things.

"I saved you," she says finally, her voice raw. "When we first met, you were a mess. No job, no place to stay, no plan. I gave you all of that."

"You did," I admit. "And I'm grateful. But gratitude isn't the same as love, Alexis."

"I never asked you to be grateful."

"No, but you sure like to remind me that I should be. You've always made me feel like your voice is the only one that counts."

The words hit their mark. I can see it in the way her shoulders set.

"That's not fair," she says.

My mouth falls open. "You're right. It's not fair that I have to feel like your project, a business asset you gave a better life, and now you can't figure out how to be in a relationship with me because you think you're better than me and I don't fit into your carefully constructed world."

She recoils as if I've struck her. The crushing feeling is identical to the way my mom made me feel, and I don't like it.

"So what are you saying? That you don't love me?"

It would be so easy to say yes and make this clean. But the truth is messier than that. The truth is, I do love her, or at least I have. I'm just tired of fighting for a place in her life.

"I'm saying that I don't know if what we had was love or just convenience."

Her face goes still, which is somehow worse than anger.

"What about therapy?" she asks. "What about working on us?"

My cheeks flush as I remember kissing my therapist, and my therapist's thoughts about Alexis..

She takes the pause as her cue to continue. "We were making progress."

"Therapy was illuminating and made me realize I need to love myself first, which is what I am doing."

She sits down heavily in her chair, and she looks small for the first time since I've known her. Alexis never looks small.

"I don't know how to do this," she admits.

"Do what?"

"Be someone's girlfriend. Be in love. I know how to run a business. I know how to make deals and manage people and solve problems. But I don't know how to just... be with someone without trying to fix everything."

It's the most honest thing she's ever said, breaking something loose in my chest. "You don't have to fix everything," I tell her gently. "You just have to show up. And I'm fixing myself."

She looks at me, trying to figure out what I mean. It would be funny if it weren't so sad.

"I'll tear up your contract," she says, her voice uncertain. "I'm sorry. I know you deserve to choose your own path."

"Apology accepted. And I'm sorry, too. I know you want what's best for me, but I need you to trust me to decide on my own."

She walks through the parking lot, closing the distance between us. When she reaches out to touch my face, her hand is shaking. That tiny sign of nervousness makes her seem more real, more human. The wall I was building starts to crumble, and I lick my lips, feeling the heat between us.

"Can I kiss you?" she asks, her voice barely a whisper.

"That depends. Are you kissing me because you think it'll convince me to stay, or because you want to?" I whisper, looking at her hungry vulnerability.

"I want to. Because I've missed you. Because I want to say goodbye."

I nod. Not trusting my mouth to say the right thing.

When she kisses me, it isn't the confident, controlled kiss I'm used to. It's desperate and uncertain and sincere. And maybe that's the difference between the old us and whatever this new thing might be. Less perfect, more real.

I kiss her back, my hands finding their way into her perfect hair, pulling it loose from that chignon. She makes a soft sound that goes straight through me.

"I'll miss this, Trouble," she murmurs against my mouth.

"Just this?"

"All of it. You. Your weird finger guns. How you find trouble. Us. The way you taste like coffee and optimism."

"That's weirdly specific."

"I'm a detail-oriented person."

I laugh and hug her tight, knowing this is our last kiss. We are both breathing hard, and I can feel that familiar pull—the chemistry that was never our problem. It would be so easy to let this turn into more, to let physical connection stand in for all the emotional work we still need.

"We should probably talk more," she says, stepping away.

"Probably."

Instead of dismissing me, she pulls me hard against her and kisses me again, harder this time. I forget about job offers, family obligations, and the careful balance between personal and professional. Right now there's just this—the taste of her mouth, the sound she makes when I bite her bottom lip, the way her hands grip my waist like she's afraid I'll disappear.

"Goodbye, Trouble," she murmurs, hot against my neck in the cold parking lot.

Chapter 34

Aurora's Powersuit Breaking Point

The voicemail is waiting like a landmine. Red dot blinking on my cracked screen. I don't even need to press play. I already know who it is.

Mom.

I should have left her blocked!

I tap the screen, and the sound of her voice claws through the car speakers.

"Hey. I can't get money out of *our* bank account. Call me back."

Our account. Sure, Sandra.

I stare out the windshield, Anchorage skies so heavy they could punch a glacier. Sleety rain smears across the glass, and my breath fogs up the inside. I'm parked behind Lucky Wishbone, boxed between a tour bus and someone's jacked-up truck with moose antlers zip-tied to the grill. My fries are cold. My fingers smell like chicken grease and betrayal.

The voicemail plays again.

"Call me back."

A laugh claws out of my throat. Not the cute giggly kind that Alexis liked... *used to like, that is.* The unhinged, too-loud laugh that might get me put on a mental health wellness checklist.

This is it. Rock bottom. Soggy fries, sleepless nights, breakup heartbreak, secret diagnoses, and now my financially unhinged queen mom dialing me to create more drama while I'm the lowest ever.

I called her back.

Ring. Ring.

"Aurora, honey, it's Mom." Her voice dripped with that fake sweetness that always made my skin crawl. "I went to the bank today and they said I can't access *our* account. I don't know what happened, but I really need access. It's important, sweetheart."

Our account. Right. The checking account that I'd stupidly left my mom on, because why would a mom steal money from her daughter?

"Hi, Mom," I say, trying to act normal. My hands shake as I respond, "You want access to *my* account? You have been ignoring me these last few weeks. How's the weather up on your self-delusion mountaintop?"

"Don't sass me. I had to put groceries back at Safeway like a broke-ass hippy tourist. People *recognized* me. Do you have any idea how embarrassing that was?"

"Oh no, not a school secretary, having to live off a school secretary income! Is it hard without using my university savings or the monthly child support you never told me about? Gosh, how embarrassing. Someone alert Oprah or maybe Taylor Swift for a new song inspo."

"You think you're so grown. So independent now that you're playing house with your perfect father and rich girlfriend and her business galas. Well, let me tell you something, Miss High and Mighty, you wouldn't have had any *normal* life if I hadn't raised you and protected you. Your dad wanted nothing to do with you. I protected you!"

My stomach rolls. I pick at a soggy old fry from my car cup holder, my fingers shaking.

"Protected me from what? From the truth? From my father? From my own health information and family?"

"Don't take that tone with me, young lady. I raised you better than that." Her voice shifts from saccharine to sharp in record time. "Oh, here we go again with the dramatics."

I can hear her lighting a cigarette, the click of her lighter sharp through the phone. "You want to talk about your little health... situation? Fine. Let's talk."

My stomach drops. She never brought up my intersex condition until I told her, and now she's acknowledging it to try to win an argument or make me feel guilty.

"I did you a favor, Aurora. Do you understand that? A favor." Her voice turns vicious now, all pretense of maternal love evaporating. "When the doctors told us about your... abnormality... I couldn't tell anyone. You know, I could've let you grow up knowing you were a freak. But I didn't."

The words hit me like a physical blow. I grip the steering wheel so hard my knuckles are white.

"I gave you a normal childhood," she says, each word calculated to cause maximum damage. "I let you play with dolls, wear pretty dresses, and enjoy school. I let you pretend to be normal even though we both knew you weren't. And this is how you repay me? By cutting me off?"

"Stop," I whisper.

"You owe me, Aurora. You owe me for giving you a life where people didn't point and stare and whisper about what was wrong with you. You owe me for keeping your embarrassing little flaw a secret all these years."

"STOP!" I scream into the phone, my voice echoing in the small car. "Just stop! You didn't do me any favors. You stole my identity from me. You kept my father away from me. You made me hate myself and feel like I was different with no explanation *For years.* I knew something was different but I didn't know what, and you hid my true self from me."

"Don't you dare blame me for your problems. I did the best I could with what I was given. Do you have any idea how hard it is to raise a child like you?"

A child like you. The words settle into my chest like lead weights.

"I'm done," I say, surprised by how steady my voice sounded. "I'm done with your guilt trips and your manipulation and your conditional love. I'm done pretending that what you did was okay just because you're my mother."

"You ungrateful little bitch," she growls. Her mask is completely off now. "You'll come crawling back. And when you do, don't expect me to be waiting with open arms. I could have been a better mother if you would have been a better daughter."

I hang up before she can say anything else, my hands shaking so violently I almost drop the phone. The tears are fast and hard, ugly sobs making my whole body convulse. Outside, the sleet is falling harder now, blanketing the world in grey slimy wetness.

Then I throw my phone into the passenger seat and lean my forehead against the steering wheel.

My heart's thumping too loud. My chest hurts. Everything hurts.

This was the final thread.

She's done this my whole life. Guilt. Shame. Manipulation dressed up as motherly concern. And for what? So she could stay the victim? I would thank her for the crumbs of affection she's given me. So I could keep being the good little peacemaker?

No more.

Bzzzz.

Text from Lisa, "Indie says we are invited to come for your family dinner. Grant's roasting a whole pig. Hawaiian theme. Also... Did u know they get free vacation cruise tickets? WHEN R WE GOING TO FLORIDA PARTY CRUISE??"

I laugh so hard that I explicitly start to cry.

Lisa is already scheming. I'm more than fine with the distraction. *Pig. Hawaiian dinner.* Indie, being her quiet, goth, adorable self, invited my friends into her family—my family. It is a family I barely know, but who makes more room for me than the woman who raised me.

And then, surprisingly, one from Indie herself, "Hope it's alright. I'm at your place with Lisa. We are doing an impromptu dinner for you since Lisa said you've had a rough day. Also, I brought my guitar in case you want to hear the new song I wrote."

I wipe my face on my sleeve, shake the cold off my fingers, and drive to my home at Lisa's apartment.

Twenty minutes later, I stood outside my apartment door, fishing for my keys with hands that had finally stopped shaking. I could hear laughter through the thin walls, and something that sounded suspiciously like Darius attempting to sing along to what was definitely not a song I recognized.

The door swung open before I could even get my key in the lock.

"There she is!" Lisa practically tackled me in the doorway, her blonde curls bouncing enthusiastically. "We've been waiting forever! Well, okay, like twenty minutes, but in Lisa time that's basically forever."

"I brought the food and reinforcements," Darius called from the couch, holding up a bottle of wine like a trophy. "And by reinforcements, I mean Lucky Wishbone family chicken dinner with chocolate peanut butter shakes and our emotional support. Also, your sister is cool."

Indie was perched cross-legged on my floor, looking perfectly at home in her black jeans and band t-shirt, my guitar balanced on her lap. She looked up with a shy smile that was so much like Grant's it made my chest tight in a good way.

"Hey," she said simply. "I think your friends are cool, too."

I nodded, not trusting my voice yet.

"Speaking of cool," Lisa said, bouncing on her toes with barely contained energy, "is that a new suit and briefcase you got?"

"Alexis got these for me to bribe me to be her work girlfriend and maybe a partner in her business someday," I explain and toss them on the couch.

"Wait, we called you first," Indie says. "You can't leave the family business when we just found you."

I laugh at her protectiveness.

Darius grins, "You took the gift and said no right."

"Absolutely," I said immediately. "But I'm returning that. I can't keep it."

"That's fitted for you and engraved, so non-returnable," he says, adding, "Fashion show time, Girl!"

Lisa clapped her hands together. "Exactly! And we want to see you in it."

Indie and Lisa chant 'fashion show,' and I reluctantly go to put on the power suit.

"Come on, Aurora," Darius said, his voice gentler now. "When's the last time you did something just because it made you feel good? Not because it was practical or responsible or what someone else wanted. Just because it made *you* happy?"

I laugh. "Fine. But someone better queue a runway song. I want my debut to be to a moody 90s song or maybe Lady Gaga– you decide!."

Minutes later, I emerge from my room in the sleekest, most ridiculous power suit ever. Charcoal gray with tiny pinstripes, wide lapels, and pants that hug my legs like they were personally blessed by Queer Eye.

Lisa gasps. "She's giving lesbian CEO. She's giving bisexual tax accountant."

Darius fans himself. "Girrrlllly! She's giving *you can't afford me but I might interview you out of pity*."

Indie, whispering, goes, "It looks good. You should keep it. Even if Alexis is the worst."

I spin once, arms out, tears poking at the corners of my eyes.

I looked around at the three of them – my chosen family and my actual family, all crammed into my tiny living room, all looking at me with expressions of such genuine love and support that it made my throat tight.

"Fine," I said, grabbing the garment bag. "But if I really look ridiculous and you aren't telling me, I'm not sharing the food."

"Deal!" Lisa called after me as I headed toward my bedroom. "But spoiler alert – you look incredible!"

The suit feels even more beautiful than it looks. I'm wrapped in a cloud of confidence and sassiness. Looking in the mirror, I saw someone I barely recognized – confident, professional, put-together. Someone who belonged in boardrooms and corner offices.

Someone who isn't broken or wrong or freakish.

Three hours ago, I'd been sitting in my car, listening to my mother tell me I was a freak who should be grateful for her lies. Now I was sitting in my living room, wearing a power suit, surrounded by people who loved me exactly as I was.

"To my people," I say, raising my glass. "To my family, the family that I choose."

Chapter 35

From Power Suits to Lesbian Flannel Fabulous

"Oh my God, look at that tourist trying to take a selfie, riding the funky moose statue," I snort, nearly spilling my iced coffee all over the sidewalk. "Does he not realize it's literally made of glass, fiberglass?"

Darius adjusts his perfectly coordinated scarf—because even in Anchorage, he insists on accessories—and follows my gaze. "Honey, that man is wearing cargo shorts and tube socks with sandals. Critical thinking is clearly not his strong suit."

I can't help but giggle at his deadpan delivery. This is precisely what I needed today—mindless people-watching with my best friend. "At least he's committed to the look."

"Committed to crimes against fashion, maybe." Darius sips his oat milk matcha latte and makes a face. "Why did I let you talk me into trying the tourists' hipster coffee cart? This tastes like grass clippings."

"Because all the places downtown are tourist traps, and soon the tourist season is over, you'll miss all the overpriced Alaskan weirdness?" I bat my eyelashes at him, making him roll his eyes harder. "And you love me!"

"Love you, yes. Trust your coffee choices? Absolutely not." Darius makes an exaggerated gagging sound and dramatically tosses the rest of his latte into the trash. "Ugh. Let's get some retail therapy before I actually start to consider cargo shorts as an option. You have university move-in day and you need an outfit to slay! My plan is for you to look so hot, you have to beat the guys and girls off of you!"

"Darius!" I can't help but hear Lisa in my mind. *That's what she said.*

"I don't beat anyone off," I say, almost choking on my coffee. "And I'm sticking to girls. Or maybe no one, because I'm a serious student."

He sideeyes me, "Right... seriously hot and you probably know small business accounting better than your professors. You should major in dating and chilling. Don't make me force you to have fun."

I clutch my drink to my chest. "And this is why we're best friends. You use fashion as a solution, I enable, and we both wind up with glittery shoes and regrets."

"You mean *you* end up with glittery shoes. I end up looking iconic."

We weave through the downtown sidewalk crowd, dodging slow-walking cruise people and aggressively polite sign-holding end-of-season tour guides offering glacier walks and souvenir maps like they pass backstage passes to Benson Boone. My boot scuffs the curb, and I almost lose my coffee for real this time.

Darius catches me by the elbow. "Graceful as ever, my sweet gangly giraffe."

"I am *statuesque*, thank you."

"You are a hot mess."

I snort and whack his arm with the back of my hand, then we cross over to 4th Avenue. The August air smells peppery for reindeer sausage from the street cart and faintly like salmon from the nearby river. *Ah, Anchorage.*

"So," Darius says, in that syrupy tone he uses when he's about to say something deeply judgmental disguised as care, "are you seriously planning to wear that *executive realness* power suit Alexis gave you to move into university?"

I glance down at my outfit. I decided to wear the suit because I look professional and hot. Plus, it fits me like a soft calf leather glove. The crisp grey blazer, subtly cropped slacks, and a lacey white tank top that might be too low-cut if I have to meet any professors. "She tailored it for me. It fits *perfectly*. And it screams *organized lesbian with a five-year plan.*"

"It screams, *please ask me to join the student council* and *never invite me to a student rave.*" Darius steers me by the shoulders into a boutique called Salmonberry Chic, which is part consignment, part high-key gay-owned chaos. "No offense, but it's giving 'tax accountant at her niece's piano recital.' It fits, but not for university move in day and you have to wear a lesbian thirst trap outfit. I want to see you breaking hearts. We need vibes. We need charm. We need..."

He makes a sweeping gesture at a rack of floral jumpsuits.

I groan. "We do *not* need a floral jumpsuit. I'd rather wear the moose statue."

"You're going to meet new people, possibly your next girlfriend. You don't want to show up dressed like you're there to negotiate a lease."

"Okay, but it's not like I'm going there to get *laid.*"

Darius raises one sculpted brow. "Oh, honey. You're eighteen. Everyone's going there to get laid."

My cheeks burn. "Can we please just find me a pair of jeans that don't make me look like I time-traveled from a 2009 Hot Topic clearance bin?"

"See, now *that* I can work with." He claps. "You're lucky Ricard's sick today and you get me for the whole day. Let's go gay up your wardrobe."

I trail after him, sidestepping a mannequin wearing a pink fishnet shrug and a sticker that says *SHE/HER, BUT MAKE IT FASHION.* He hands me outfits faster than I can protest. A vintage bomber jacket. A mustard-colored crop top. Denim overalls that *might* be ironically cute. At one point, I catch my reflection in the mirror and think *I could be someone new. I could be someone fun.*

"So," he whispers, while I shimmy into a high-waisted plaid skirt in the changing room, "how's the heartbreak stuff now? You mooning over Miss Boss when you look like a hot dyke in this?"

I tug the curtain back and step out. "Mooning is strong. Maybe like... casual disappointment that my dream girlfriend wasn't actually my dream."

Darius folds his arms. "Are you still watching *Bridget Jones' diary* on repeat?"

"Only because I like romances—*ugh!*" I press both palms to my cheeks. "Shut up, I'm disgusting."

"You're *rebounding*," he corrects gently, then flicks the price tag on the skirt. "But that doesn't mean you should let her live rent-free in your life. I mean Richard and I would love to do some double dates with you and your new soon-to-be discovered hot girlfriend."

My stomach clenches. "Yeah. About that..."

Darius squints at me. "Wait. What?"

I tug the curtain closed again, heart pounding like I'm about to perform a striptease for someone's mom.

"I don't know if I should hang out with you and Richard. I mean, he's Alexis' workout partner so I don't want him to have to choose sides."

Dead silence.

I peek through the curtain. Darius's expression isn't dramatic anymore. It's stormy.

"He doesn't need to choose a side. He's on my side, which is your side, Girl," Darius asserts.

"Well, he does see Alexis everyday. Heck, he saw Alexis more than me and I was her almost-girlfriend and employee," I shrug.

"He's choosing you, and that's final," he says with passion. He looks at a sequin-embellished floral jumper.

I yank off the flannel crop shirt with pearl buttons and pull on faded jeans with rips in the knees. The fabric's soft, worn like it's already lived through some heartbreak. Perfect.

Darius looks over the outfit. "So what now, Miss Thing? Are you heading into your university era in a full butch look or are we embracing your hot girl renaissance with an elevated 'fit?"

I step out in the jeans and the mustard crop top. I turn once. "This hot girl educational renaissance say 'Hey, I got trauma *and* a cute belly button.'"

Darius fake-wipes a tear. "My baby's all grown up. You do look comfy and confident."

We pay, Darius slapping down a rewards punch card and winking at the cashier like he owns the place, and I sling my old outfit into a paper bag. The blazer feels heavier now, and I'm ready to hang it up in the closet and slip on my comfiest hoodie.

We walk back toward the parking garage, sunlight glinting off the hood of my scuffed-up Subaru and my new confidence. I hop in and buckle up.

"Want to hit the thrift store or go eat loaded fries until we hate ourselves?"

"I need food," I declare. "But let's go out since I'm feeling fabulous and you're looking fabulous, as always."

He winks. "Guilty! I could use a good creme brulee."

I put my hand on my lapel and trace the fitted suit, thinking about Alexis picking it out, giving the person my measurements, and imagining me becoming her partner as she bought this for me.

"Love's a bastard," Darius murmurs. "But you're Aurora, amazing-pants Thompson. You survived growing up with a nightmare mom, worked your butt off, and got into college *on your own*. You're chaos, glitter, and a caffeine addiction in a business suit. That's who you are."

I grin. "You forgot the statuesque giraffe."

He smirks. "You're *statuesque hotness*. You are going to slay dorm move-in day!"

"Yes! I'll keep it simple. Jeans. Crop top. Hot girl attitude."

"Don't forget your glittery shoes."

"Oh, I'm wearing my kickass boots. Those babies say 'I will kiss your girlfriend and out-hike all the guys.'"

Darius laughs. "That's the Aurora I know!"

I tap the table. "You think I'll find anyone *worth* kissing?"

He winks. "Oh, honey. It's a university. You're about to meet girls from *everywhere*. Someone's bound to fall in love with your goofy laugh and tragic backstory."

I roll my eyes. "I don't have a tragic backstory."

"You *absolutely* do. And you've got lesbian sweet vibes with that Alaskan grit. You'll be more popular than Nordstrom's annual sale."

I grin, wide and real, like the air's finally letting me breathe again. He's right. Maybe I don't have to have it all figured out to start fresh. I just needed a new outfit.

New boots. New school. New chapter. New me.

And maybe, *eventually*...

A new girl.

I smile at Darius and lean forward. "Do you think that boutique would take this suit on consignment? I don't think I'll need it, afterall."

"Ummm, maybe not *this* suit," he says, looking at me up and down. "But, you do have an expensive blazer you don't need." He winks and laughs.

"Food time, Girl," he says, pulling me downtown.

Chapter 36

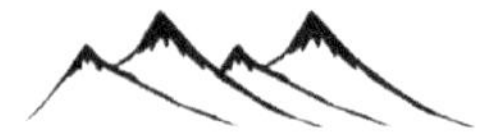

Dinner with a Side of Drama

The evening air bites with that familiar Alaskan warning—summer's over, and winter's coming whether you're ready or not. The sun's hanging low over Cook Inlet, painting everything gold and amber. Still, a nippiness makes me pull my new bomber jacket tighter as Darius and I walk toward the restaurant district.

"I still can't believe you let me buy a yellow crop top," I say, nudging his shoulder with mine.

"It's mustard. You are the sunshine we will all need in a few months," Darius replies, adjusting his outfit—a vintage burgundy velvet blazer. "That's exactly the energy you need–sunshine and disco, girl!"

With the tourist season winding down, the streets are clear except for a few locals enjoying what might be one of the last warm evenings before hibernation. I can smell the salt air mixing with the scent of grilled halibut from the restaurants ahead.

"Let's talk about fashion, university, and desserts. No more comments about my love life," I say, linking my arm through his as we walk toward the restaurant district.

"Aurora, darling, I make no such promises. Your romantic ineptitude is one of my greatest sources of entertainment."

"You're the worst best friend ever," I say with a giggle as we meander through our little city.

"And yet you keep me around. What does that say about you?"

I laugh-snort, the sound carrying on the sharp breeze. "That I have terrible judgment and a weakness for dramatic queers who steal french fries."

"I prefer to think of it as quality control. You deserve the best and your last fries deserved better seasoning, Girl."

The Glacier Brewhouse is one of those quintessentially Alaskan places that tourists love and locals actually enjoy—all polished wood and ocean views, with the kind of atmosphere that screams "authentic Alaskan" while still being posh enough for a low-key dinner. They make decent salmon and chips with homemade tangy tartar sauce, and it's close enough to downtown that we can walk back to my apartment afterward if we have too much to drink.

Outside, the windows are catching the last of the golden hour light, reflecting off frothy waves. "I'm thinking we start with those loaded nachos and work our way up to emotional eating," Darius says as we approach the entrance. "Then maybe some of that chocolate lava cake with the salmonberry ice cream."

"Are we celebrating or mourning?" I ask.

"Both. It's called multitasking, sweetie."

The hostess, a college-aged girl with perfectly winged eyeliner, greets us with the kind of practiced enthusiasm from working downtown during tourist season. "Hiya! Table for two? There's a cozy table by the fireplace."

I nod, following her toward the back, already mentally calculating how many beers it'll take to make me forget my nerves about starting university in a week, with precisely zero idea what my life will look like a month from now.

That's when I see them.

Richard is sitting at a large table near the windows, his dark hair perfectly styled in that effortless way that takes him twenty minutes and three different products. He's laughing at something someone said, that easy, confident smile that made Darius fall for him in the first place, spreading across his face. But he's not alone—another guy is sitting next to him, someone I don't recognize with sandy hair and a fitted Hawaiian shirt that's too flamboyant to be straight but not quite gay enough to be intentional.

And sitting across from them, looking absolutely stunning in her lucky yellow shoes and her grey blazer that brings out her eyes, is Alexis.

My heart drops into my stomach and keeps falling until it hits the restaurant floor with an audible thud. The golden hour light streaming through the windows catches her hair, and I forget how to breathe for a second.

"Oh, hell no," Darius mutters beside me, and I realize he's seeing the same thing I am. "What's it been three seconds since you broke up?"

There's a woman next to Alexis, too—blonde, polished, the kind of effortlessly put-together that I'll never be, even if I practiced for the rest of my life. She's way too comfortable, leaning toward Alexis and saying something that makes Alexis throw her head back and laugh. I want to disappear into the floor.

Alexis is laughing. The rare laugh. God, I used to live for *that laugh.*

"Is that—" I start to ask, but Darius is already moving.

"We should all try the saL-mon fish and chips. They are the best," Alexis says, no one correcting her egregious mispronunciation.

"It's salmon, with a silent l," I say, interrupting her and making the entire table look up from their calamari starters.

"Richard!" Darius announces, his voice carrying that particular tone that means someone is about to be murdered with kindness. "Fancy seeing you here!"

The entire table turns toward him, and I consider making a run for it. Richard's face goes through about seventeen expressions in two seconds—surprise, guilt, panic, and something that might be relief. Alexis remains calm and collected, with no flicker of guilt, which infuriates me more than if she'd looked caught.

"Darius," Richard says, standing up slowly like he's trying not to spook a wild animal. "Hey, babe. I didn't expect to see you here."

"Clearly." Darius's smile could cut glass. "Aren't you going to introduce us to your friends?"

Alexis looks between Darius and Richard, then her gaze lands on me. Here she is on a double date with a perfect blonde woman, so much for her promises of making me her partner in business and life.

"This is Marcus," Richard says, gesturing to the Hawaiian shirt guy, "and Rachel." He nods toward the blonde. "This is Darius, my—"

"Boyfriend," Darius finishes, with a frosty edge. "You know, the one who tucked you earlier? The one you texted two hours ago saying you were still in bed, under the weather?"

He turns his eyes to Marcus. "Wait, is your name weather? Maybe I misunderstood."

The silence that follows is the kind that makes other diners start looking over, sensing drama. I can practically touch the couple at the next table leaning in to listen.

"Darius," Richard says, quietly, "can we talk about this outside?"

"Oh, we're absolutely going to talk about this," Darius replies, but his attention shifts to Alexis like a predator switching targets. "And you—I thought you were better than this."

Alexis stands up, her jaw tight. "Excuse me?"

"You proclaimed your undying love to Aurora and you're dating the day after you guys break up—"

"Whoa, dude. Hold on," Marcus interrupts, looking confused and like he wishes he were anywhere else. "What's going on here?"

I finally found my voice, though it comes out smaller than I'd like. "Alexis, I didn't know you were... I mean, we just..." I gesture helplessly between us, then at the table. "What is this?"

She looks at me with an expression I can't read, something between defiance and something that might be guilt if I squint hard enough. "Aurora, what are you doing here?"

"Having dinner with my best friend," I say, gesturing toward Darius, who looks like he's about two seconds away from causing a scene that will get us banned from every restaurant in Anchorage. "What are you doing here?"

"Having dinner with friends," she says, but something defensive in her voice makes my chest tighten.

Rachel clears her throat delicately and shifts in her seat. "I think maybe we should—"

"No," I interrupt, surprising myself with the firmness in my voice. "I think I deserve to know what's going on. I mean, yesterday Alexis was offering to marry me and talking about partnerships, and now..."

I trail off, gesturing at the cozy little double date scene in front of me.

Richard runs a hand through his hair, messing up all that perfect styling. "It's.. We are just having a business dinner."

"Really?" Darius crosses his arms, and I can practically see the frost forming around him. "Because it looks like you're on a double date while your boyfriend is picking you up a new sweater and soup. Because he cares about you."

"Join us and you'll see, it isn't like that," Alexis says, but she won't meet my eyes.

"Then what was it like?" I demand. "Because from where I'm standing, it looks like you never cared about me... moved on. Found someone new to have dinner with while I've been—"

I stop myself before I can say "crying over you" or "wearing your blazer" or any of the other pathetic things I've done since our breakup.

Marcus shifts uncomfortably. "Should we—"

"Stay," Darius says firmly. "You're part of this now. You'll want to know who you're dating."

The restaurant quiets around us, or that's the blood rushing in my ears.

"Aurora," Alexis starts, but I hold up a hand.

"No. You know what? I'm done." I take a shaky breath. "I'm done pretending this meant something to you when it clearly didn't. I'm done hoping you'll realize how awesome I am. I'm done making excuses for why you can't commit to anything real."

My voice is getting louder, and I can see other diners openly staring now, but I can't seem to stop.

"I gave you everything," I continued. "I rearranged my entire life around you. I turned down job opportunities because I wanted to work with you. I planned my future around the possibility of us. And you... you replaced me in forty-eight hours."

"It's not about replacing you," Alexis says, finally showing some emotion. "It's about moving forward."

"By dating someone else before the sheets are even cold?" Darius interjects. "Very professional, Alexis. Really mature."

Rachel speaks up. "I think there's been a misunderstanding. This isn't—"

"A date?" I finished. "Because it sure looks like one. And even if it's not, even if you're just friends, the fact that Alexis is here with you, making time for you, shows me everything I need to know."

I turn to Richard. "And you. I trusted you. Darius deserves better."

"Aurora, I'm sorry," Richard says, and he sounds like he means it. "I really am. I messed up."

Darius's expression goes from anger to hurt in about three seconds. "You're right." He glares at Richard. "We're done. Don't call me, don't text me, don't show up at my apartment. We're done."

"Darius, wait—" Richard starts, but Darius is already shaking his head.

"No. I'm not waiting anymore. I'm not making excuses for you anymore. I'm not pretending this didn't happen." He looks at Marcus. "Enjoy your date. I hope you know now what you're getting into."

A rush of pride swells within me for my best friend, even as my heart is breaking again.

"And you," I say to Alexis, surprised by how steady my voice sounds. "Thank you for showing me who you really are. Thank you for making it clear that I was right to end things between us. Thank you for proving that I deserve better."

"Trouble—" she starts again.

"No," I say firmly. "You don't get to trouble me anymore. You don't get to make me feel crazy for wanting something real. You don't get to act like I'm the problem when you're the one who can't commit."

I take a deep breath, feeling something like clarity washing over me.

"I'm eighteen years old," I say, loud enough for the whole restaurant to hear. "I'm about to start university. I have my whole life ahead of me. And I'm not wasting another second of it on people who don't value me enough to choose me."

"Alexis, you screwed up," Darius summarizes, then adds, "And you sound like a clueless idiot tourist. It's salmon. *Samm-On*."

I link my arm under Darius's. "Come on. I don't like the vibes here."

As we turn to leave, I hear Alexis call my name one more time, but I don't look back.

The cool September air hits my face as we walk out of the restaurant, and I realize I'm shaking—not from the cold, but from adrenaline and relief.

"Holy shit," Darius says as we get a block away. "Did we really just slay a double breakup?"

"We really did," I confirm, then start laughing. "Oh my god, we really caused a scene at the Glacier Brewhouse."

"The most satisfying scene in history," Darius says, throwing his arm around my shoulders. "I'm so proud of us."

"Are you okay?" I ask. "About Richard, I mean?"

He's quiet. "I will be. It hurts, but... I'm not surprised. I dove in too fast."

"Yeah," I say softly. "I know that feeling."

We walk in comfortable silence for a few minutes, the lights of downtown Anchorage twinkling around us as the sun finally disappears behind the mountains.

"So," Darius says eventually. "Grab a reindeer sausage and chill at home?"

"Lead the way," I say. "Lisa's going to love to hear this tea."

"Can we wait a few days? I'm not sure if I'm ready for her next round of matchmaking," he says, shaking his head.

"Darius?"

"Yeah?"

"Thank you. For having my back in there. For... everything."

He squeezes my shoulder. "That's what best friends are for, sunshine. That's what family is for."

Chapter 37

Dorm Life

I clutch my dorm keycard, heart fluttering as I step into the building for the first time. The walls smell like fresh paint and new beginnings—sterile, but full of promise. I'm here to pick up my room keys before moving in later today.

I scan the lobby, searching for Zara—the only person I actually know on campus. I should've called her, maybe asked to meet for coffee. But no. Time to stop hiding behind familiar faces and start meeting new people. Time to dive into college life headfirst, even if it's scary.

Fresh start. New chapter. *I can do this.*

That's when I see her.

A beefy girl with a messy ponytail and a flannel shirt rolled up at the sleeves, gripping the railing like it might snap. Her oversized hoodie hides her face, but her eyes—dark with flecks of gold—catch mine, steady and curious.

"Oh," she says softly.

"Hey," I say, trying to sound casual though my heart's doing flips. "You new here too?"

She nods, glancing at the keycard in my hand. "Picking up your keys?"

"Yeah. First time here. I'm Aurora."

"Mary," she says, a shy smile tugging at her lips.

We fall into step, wandering through the hallways like we own the place—which, honestly, we don't. I make small talk about how weird it is to move into a place that's supposed to be "home," how huge and kind of intimidating campus feels, and how neither of us really knows what we're doing.

We step into the elevator together. She stiffens, fingers curling tighter on the railing.

"Hey, you okay?" I ask.

She bites her lip, eyes darting around. "First elevator ride."

"Wait, first... ever?" I blink.

"From Portlock," she says quietly. "Tiny village. No buildings tall enough to need one."

I grin. "That's actually amazing. I would love to live in a village. I'm from Anchorage. How about I show you around Anchorage sometime—I'll be your personal tour guide."

Her lips twitch into a smile. "Deal."

I glance at her chin, noticing the dark, bold lines tattooed there—sharp and soft at the same time. "That's a seriously cool tattoo. What's the story?"

She shrugs, cheeks flushing. "Just a tradition back home. It reminds me who I am."

I nod, captivated. "I get that. So, what do you do when you get nervous in elevators? Besides gripping the rail like a boss."

She laughs—a warm, genuine sound that wraps around me like sunlight. "I fix things. Engines. Planes."

"Whoa. You fix planes? That's ridiculously cool."

I shrug. "My nervous habit? Rambling. Way too many questions. And stress-eating late-night ice cream. Like, dangerous amounts."

Her eyes sparkle. "Maybe I'll try the ice cream next time... y'know, if we make it out of this elevator alive."

I laugh. "Elevators are basically boring theme park rides. All the noises? Just the robot doing its thing."

She bites her lip but looks a little less tense.

"So... do you know Zara? She's pretty much my only campus friend right now."

Mary shakes her head, but she seems more at ease.

I shake my head. “Honestly, I’m pretty nervous about starting university. But I think most people are, they are just hiding it.”

She smiles, a little overwhelmed. “There are so many people here... It’s kinda wild. Totally not like Portlock.”

I grin, nudging her gently with my elbow. “Well, welcome to the wild city. We’ve got ice cream, terrifying elevators, and zero idea what we’re doing.”

She smiles back, eyes bright. “Coffee later? Maybe we check out that ice cream place? I’ve never been to an ice cream shop.”

I hesitate, then nod. “Yeah. I’d like that.”

The elevator dings, and Mary jumps.

“That’s the polite elevator robot telling us we’re almost there,” I say.

The doors slide open, and a pack of students floods inside—laughing, carrying boxes and suitcases, pressing buttons, and joking. Mary’s shoulder brushes mine, warm and steady. Suddenly, electric butterflies flutter in my chest and tingle down my fingertips.

Before I can say anything, she slips out on the second floor, swallowed by the chaos.

“Ma—” I called, but she disappeared.

The doors slide shut, leaving me standing there, breathless, and grinning like an idiot.

I came here hoping I’d find myself and my confidence—and somehow, I’ve found someone who is more nervous than I am.

For the first time since stepping on the campus, it isn’t foreign or scary. It feels like the beginning of something good.

Chapter 38

Move-In Day

You know when your life does that sudden pivot thing? One week you're googling "how to remove mascara stains from pillowcases," and the next you're standing in a parking lot with a brand-new dad, two best friends, and a support crew large enough to storm a small castle?

Yeah. That's me.

"You know, when I imagined my biological father helping me move into college, I definitely didn't picture him driving a truck the size of an Alaskan village," I say, shading my eyes to squint at Grant's Ford F-350. The thing looks like it could tow an actual glacier and still have room for a family of moose in the back.

Grant grins, patting the hood like it's his favorite sled dog. "Honey, in Alaska, this is a compact car. Besides, you've got enough stuff for three students. Good thing you have a small village to help unload."

And what a village.

Darius is standing in an immaculate scarf-and-blazer combo that screams Paris runway instead of the Anchorage dorm parking lot. Lisa is bouncing on her toes, vibrating like a chihuahua who just downed three Red Bulls. Zara's there to meet us and point me to the right dorm as she's scrolling her phone like moving-day logistics are her jam. Kathleen, clipboard in hand, was orchestrating the chaos like a four-star general. And Indie—quiet, observant, probably memorizing our neuroses for her future best selling album.

I take it all in, and my chest does this ridiculous swelling thing. Six months ago, I thought I'd never survive moving out and pretending to be an adult. I thought I'd be alone forever. Now I have... this. People. My people.

"I still can't believe starting university with my family helping isn't a dream," I murmur, hugging a box to my chest.

"Dreams are boring," Lisa announces, wobbling under the weight of my ridiculously overstuffed duffel. "Reality is way better. Dreams don't have cute college girls."

I choke. "Lisa!"

"What? Just setting expectations. You're at a university now. Fish in the sapphic sea, babe."

Darius groans dramatically and swoops in like the fashion police incarnate. "Aurora, darling, please tell me you're not planning to wear that tragic hoodie when meeting your new roommates." He gestures at my sweatshirt—navy blue, peeling University of Alaska logo. "This entire ensemble screams, 'I've given up on life and embraced the void.'"

"It's comfortable!" I protest, tucking my messy bun tighter. "It's not tragic, it's... casual."

"Effortlessly tragic," he corrects, pushing oversized sunglasses up his nose with Broadway-worthy flair. "You're nineteen, gorgeous, and finally free of certain emotional baggage." He side-eyes me so hard I almost trip. "This is your red-carpet moment, girl. Debut into the sexy social scene of higher education."

"Can we please not call it that?"

"Too late," Darius sings.

Grant chuckles, arms full of boxes. "You two crack me up. Now listen, Aurora—I meant what I said about jobs for you and Darius. I talked to Alexis, and she's agreed to let me buy out your temp contract so you can come on full-time with us. And if Darius is interested, I'd like to offer him a spot too. You two make a hell of a team, and Alaska Tours and Cruises would be lucky to have you both."

My stomach flips. Alexis. Her name still makes my chest tight and not in a fun, romantic way. More like a root-canal-by-angry-wolverine way.

"Grant, you don't have to—"

"I want to," he says, firm but kind. "You're family now. That's what family does. I want to see you succeed in school and in business."

Darius arches an eyebrow, clearly pleased but keeping it cool. "Grant, you cannot just throw job offers and emotions at me at eight in the morning. My under-eye concealer has boundaries."

"Nothing could ruin that face," I tease.

"Obviously." He gives me a dazzling smile, then flips his phone around to check his reflection before slipping it back into his pocket. "Now, important follow-up questions... Is there an espresso machine in the office? And which holidays do you actually observe—because I require time off for both Beyoncé's birthday and the solstice."

He hooks his arm through mine, chin held high. "This face? It's ready for impact..." Then he turns to me, gently lifting my chin with one perfectly manicured finger. "...and this face," he says, locking eyes with me, "is ready to take on the world—and finally control her own damn destiny."

I laugh, but there's heat behind my eyes. Not from sadness—from power. From finally knowing I'm not walking into this next chapter alone.

We move forward together—Grant balancing another box like he's auditioning for World's Strongest Dad, Darius dramatically flinging doors open as if he's my personal concierge, and me, marching in with all my worldly belongings packed into three duffel bags and a suitcase that's seen better days. My friends and family trail behind us in a chaotic parade of bags, boxes, and unsolicited advice. A mismatched group, no doubt—but a family all the same.

The University of Alaska Anchorage stretches out before us like a promise wrapped in snow-capped mountains and crisp morning light. Postcards don't do it justice. They don't capture the way the Chugach Mountains rise like guardians behind the campus, making everything feel bold, wild, and a little bit magical. Cook Inlet shimmers beyond the city, and even the steel-and-glass dorm buildings seem to glow against the arctic backdrop, like they're daring me to believe in possibility.

Grant catches the look on my face. "Nervous?"

"Terrified," I admit, adjusting the strap digging into my shoulder. "Good terrified, though. Like bungee-jumping terrified—but the kind where I might discover my true calling on the way down… and maybe even survive calculus."

Darius snorts. "Girl, if you survive math, I'm making you a crown."

"I'll hold you to that," I grin, and we cross the threshold into whatever comes next.

The actual moving-in part? Total chaos.

It feels like running a marathon I didn't train for—equal parts sweat, regret, and existential dread. Grant carries box after box like it's nothing. Lisa muscles a trunk up two flights of stairs and snaps, "I've got it, don't touch me!" at anyone who gets too close. Darius floats between all of us like an over-caffeinated spirit guide, tossing out commentary on everything from my bedding to the dorm's "questionable lighting," all while sipping an iced latte he refuses to set down.

"Please tell me you didn't bring this polka-dot comforter on purpose," he says, holding it like it's a biohazard.

"Polka-dots are cheerful," I reply, grabbing it from him and making the bed anyway.

He shrugs. "Cheerful or tragic. Time will tell."

Despite the chaos, the room starts to take shape—flannel folded, books shelved, socks stuffed into drawers. Grant walks in just in time to see me trying to discreetly shove my underwear out of sight.

He raises an eyebrow but doesn't say a word. Thank God. Dads and lucky underwear should never coexist in the same sentence.

Finally, everything's in place. The room looks lived-in. Mine. I take a breath, and for the first time all day, it actually feels real.

And it feels good.

Grant reappears with the last box just in time to see me hurriedly shove my underwear into a drawer. He bites back a laugh that makes him tear up, but, mercifully, says nothing. Some things should remain a mystery to dads. Lucky underwear definitely qualifies.

When everything's finally in its place, I surprise myself by throwing my arms around him. "Thank you. For all of this. For being here. I know it's... weird."

He hugs me back, warm and steady—like the solid anchor I didn't know I needed. "Not weird," he says, his voice thick with something deeper. "Unexpected, sure. But never weird. You're my daughter. Stepping into your life... it's the best surprise I've ever had."

Cue waterworks.

Darius places a hand over his heart, while watching from across the small dorm room.

Before the tears fully take hold, Grant clears his throat. "Okay, before I get weepy too, let me plant a seed about Christmas. A working Christmas."

Darius makes a dramatic grimace. "Ugh, cancel my acceptance. I don't do labor over the holidays."

"Stop, Dad!" Indie calls out from the hallway. "He doesn't mean *real* work. He means a holiday cruise. The company gets free tickets from vendors."

Wait. What?

I've never even *been* on a cruise. I don't have a passport. I barely have a suitcase.

Grant smiles at me. "It's a trip for after your first semester. It's part vacation, part work—you'd get to see how the cruise side of the business operates. You and Darius could share a room, and I'd cover everything. I'd like you both to see what we're building and be an active part of the business."

Darius straightens his scarf like he's just been offered a starring role on Broadway. "She says yes too. This is basically career development. Maybe even *college credit.*"

I shake my head, laughing. "I've never been on vacation. I'd like that. Thank you, Grant."

Darius gasps. "Tropical Christmas? Swimwear? Evening wear? Aurora, we're going shopping *immediately.*"

I roll my eyes. "We have months. And I need luggage first. You'll probably need a full trunk and sink the ship."

"If we sink, darling, we paddle to the nearest swim-up bar and order piña coladas. Problem solved."

Grant winks. "I'll send you the details tonight—about the job I want to offer you and the cruise."

Kathleen steps into the room, pulling both of us into a warm hug. "Aurora, it's just a few hours a week during school, then full-time in the summer. We don't want your studies getting interrupted."

"Thank you. Really—thank you for including me in your family."

Kathleen smiles softly. "Aurora, you *are* family." She hugs me again before she, Indie, and Grant wave goodbye and head out the door.

Then it's just me and Darius, standing in the center of my newly decorated, questionably stylish dorm room.

He holds up one of my flannels. "This says—approachable, lesbian lumberjack. Perfect for mingling."

"Why do you care so much about my love life?" I ask.

"Because you're hopeless at it," he says sweetly. "And because you deserve *everything.* Messy kisses. Bad decisions. The kind of heartbreak that turns into hilarious stories later. All of it."

My throat tightens. "You're ridiculous."

"Ridiculously supportive." He pulls me into a hug, squeezing the air out of my lungs. "Call me for *anything.* Emergency chocolate. Fashion rescues. Pep talks. I've got you."

When he finally leaves, the silence that follows doesn't feel empty—it feels full. Like space. Like potential. Like the door to my new life has swung wide open.

I glance out the window toward the parking lot, where the truck waits with Kathleen and Indie. Grant's standing just outside, looking up at my window. When our eyes meet, he lifts a hand—and something in his expression changes.

He mouths, *"There's one more thing."*

I blink, confused.

One more thing?

What could possibly be left?

And that's when my phone buzzes.

It's from my dad, one sentence, "But I haven't told you the real reason I want you on that cruise."

Aurora's Wilderness Love:

Christmas Cruise Mistake

Escaping an Alaskan winter?

Check.

Accidentally fake-honeymooning on a Christmas cruise?

Unfortunately... also check.

When a last-minute tropical cruise pulls university student Aurora out of a brutal breakup and an even colder Alaskan holiday, she knows exactly what to do. Pack bikinis. Pack sarcasm and sass. Relax. Flirt irresponsibly. Forget her ex ever existed.

Thanks to a cruise-line booking disaster, Aurora finds herself trapped on a couples-only cruise, pretending to be the bride of her gay best friend.

Oops!

Now Aurora is fielding newlywed questions, stumbling through love workshops, and faking marital bliss for the sake of free activities and unlimited desserts. She's barely surviving when sparks ignite with the older, dangerously sexy cruise ship captain—and suddenly the lie feels a lot more complicated.

The plan? Fake it 'til they dock.

But between tequila, tangled lies, and tension not even a conga line can fix, Aurora's story is falling apart—and her dream vacation might be the real disaster.

The odds are still good.

The drama?

It's a full-blown shipwreck.

Other Titles by MELODY BEST & HARMONY NOBLE
For the most up-to-date list visit Harmony's website at
www.HarmonyNoble.com

Aurora's Wilderness Love:

Hot Girl Summer Love
Just a Little Fall Crush
Christmas Cruise Mistake

Wilderness Rescue Sapphic Romance Series:

Crashing Into Love
Unthaw My Heart
Winning Love
Stormy Hearts
Scoring Love
Flooded Hearts
Healing Hearts
Tides of Love
Iditarod Love
Tangled Love

Coffeehouse Romance Series:

Love, Joy & Lattes (Joy's Story)
Test Driving a Millionaire (Tara's Story)
Shattering Crystal a Bully Romance (Crystal's Story)
Choosing Love, Namaste (Meaghan's Story)
The Wrong Bride for Christmas (Monica's Story)

Coffeehouse Romance Short Stories:

Joy's 4th of July Holidate
Tara's Valentine Holidate
Crystal's Easter Holidate
Meaghan's New Year Holidate
Monica's Halloween Holidate
My Accidental Christmas Fiancé
Joy's Coffeehouse Romance

Snag the latest swoon-worthy reads and stay tuned for upcoming stories at www.HarmonyNoble.com.

About Author –
Melody Best & Harmony Noble

Meet the unstoppable twins from the rugged wilds of Alaska, the writing duo, Harmony & Melody. Fueled by endless lattes, their character-driven stories brim with authenticity, humor, and heart—featuring Alaskan grit, journeys of self-discovery, and swoon-worthy happily-ever-afters.

When they're not crafting adventure romances, these twins can be found hiking trails with breathtaking views, enjoying charming coffee shops, or exploring new worldwide destinations together.

Join the e-newsletter for exclusive content and giveaways at website:
https://harmonynoble.com

Email: TrueLoveWriters@gmail.com
Instagram/Facebook/TikTok: @truelovewriters

www.ingramcontent.com/pod-product-compliance
Lightning Source LLC
LaVergne TN
LVHW010649110826
845149LV00014B/3003

* 9 7 8 1 9 6 3 0 7 4 4 2 0 *